MW01616082

A TENDER HEART

A Sweet Romance

Hearts of Aspen Valley
Book 4

CAROLYNE AARSEN

Misty Ruby Publishing

Copyright © 2023 by Carolyne Aarsen

All rights reserved.

No portion of this book may be reproduced in any form or by electronic or mechanical means including information storage and retrieval systems, except for brief quotations in critical articles or reviews, without the express written permission of the author, except where permitted by law. Further, this work may not be used in any manner for the training of Artificial Intelligence (AI) technologies without the express written consent of both the author and publisher.

Chapter 1

This was a waste of time.

Drew Rozak gave the woman lounging in the chair across from him a polite smile as she twirled her hair around her fingers. Even from across the desk, the musky scent of her perfume overwhelmed him. He then looked over her one-page resume, going through the motions of the interview.

"Any medical experience at all, Megan?" He had to ask, even though none was stated on the resume.

"Does binge-watching *Grey's Anatomy* count?" She added a grin, which did nothing to help his grumpiness.

He internalized a heavy sigh and placed the résumé in a folder he had mentally marked "Absolutely Not."

"I'll let you know when I've decided." His smile was forced, but considering she was the fourth unsuitable woman he interviewed, he was at the top of his game. Friendly wise.

Megan pushed her bleached-blonde hair out of her face. "I'm guessing that's a hard pass."

What could he say? May as well go with the truth. He dragged his hand over his face, tired of hedging. "I'm sorry, but you're right."

"I got it. I didn't really want the job but figured, hey, worth a try. Besides, I got to get a good look at you."

Who knew what she meant? He sure wasn't following through on her comment. He'd spent enough valuable time already on this so-far futile project.

"Thanks for coming." He pushed back from his large wooden desk, his chair creaking as he stood.

"It was all my pleasure." After another appraising look, she grinned. Then she pushed herself up and left the office.

He pursed his lips, blowing out a frustrated breath. Four interviews today, three yesterday, and he was no further ahead than when the doctor told him and his mother that she would need help around the clock when she was discharged.

On Monday, which was only two days away.

He grabbed his suit jacket, shrugged it on, then entered the hallway. "I'm heading out to get some coffee." He paused in the doorway of his partner, Aria's, office.

She looked up at him from the pad of paper in front of her, pushing her reading glasses further up her nose, her hair swept up in a fashionable sloppy topknot. Somehow, she still made it elegant. She flashed her winning smile, twirling her pen. "I'll take a flat white."

Once, that smile would have created a flicker of connection. But dating hadn't worked out for either of them. Adjusting to being good friends, then partners in this law firm suited them both better.

And now she was engaged and getting married next week.

"If you're taking orders, I'll have a black, two sugars." Freya, their paralegal joined them, her arms full of file folders.

"We need another guy in here." Drew shot her a frown. "I'm tired of doing the coffee runs."

"I thought you had some more interviews to do?"

"Done for the day."

"I'm guessing from your grumpiness you haven't found

2

anyone yet." Freya shifted the folders, scrunching up her paisley blouse beneath them.

"Not even close."

"When does your mom move into your place?" Aria rocked back in her plush leather chair, twirling her pen.

"Too soon." He exhaled his frustration. "Monday."

"Something tells me this might be a bad time to ask a favor?" Her rocking stilled, and her smile shifted from winning to forced.

"You can try." Arching a brow, he let a wry note slip into his voice.

"I need someone to plan our party when Lucas and I come back from our honeymoon."

"I thought that was the point of eloping. To get away from all the wedding stuff." He crossed his arms over his chest and hitched his hip against the doorframe. "And why are you asking me anyway?"

"Because Courtney is eyeball deep in diapers and I don't dare ask her. Brooke is probably spending half her time on Pinterest looking for wedding plans and there's no one else I trust with this."

"What about Freya?" Drew nodded to their paralegal.

"Busy, busy." She smirked. "Cole wants me to go with him to a bull sale, and his father hasn't been feeling well either. So I've been helping with the chores where I can."

"I drew up a few ideas to get you started." Aria brandished a folder. "Lucas's sisters are helping as well, so you're not completely on your own. I just need someone to supervise them. Because, well, we are talking about Roxie and RayAnn."

Drew shrugged, then held out his hand for the file Aria was already waggling at him. "I'll check it out."

"It's straightforward. Nothing fancy, but it would be nice for the party to have some structure. Something you're good at."

"Perfect line for my dating profile. Is good at structure."

"Whoa." Freya's eyes grew twice the size. "You have a dating profile?"

"No. I don't."

"I could help you with that."

"Hard pass." He quoted the young woman he'd just interviewed.

"Getting back to me." Aria drummed her deep-purple fingernails on her walnut desk. "If you could take care of it, that would be awesome. Because you know, me and Lucas…"

"Are getting married in Cabo San Lucas." Drew finished her sentence as he paged through the file. "We are all aware of that. Though is it called eloping if everyone knows about it?"

Aria waved off his snarky comment, her wide smile proving nothing could get her down. Then she folded her arms on her desk. "I know you cleared your desk to help your mother, but I'm hoping you can take care of this as well."

"You're taking advantage of the fact that I have no social life." He tapped the folder against his leg.

"Not for lack of many single girls in Aspen Valley trying," Freya returned. "You don't even need a dating app, to be honest."

"Don't you women have anything to do?" He leveled her a hard look. "Aren't you supposed to be filing motions and closing off on land deals?"

"This is more fun." She wrinkled her nose at him. "Just bring my coffee to my office when you come back."

"Seriously. This equal rights thing doesn't seem so equal to me." He rolled his eyes as he brought the file folder back to his office. He dropped it on his desk and scowled at it. Perhaps he should stay and go over it.

No. He needed to get out. Not think about planning his partner and ex-girlfriend's wedding party.

So sad.

"Be back in a few minutes." He didn't look back in case the girls decided they wanted to add to their order. Louisa, their receptionist, was out running errands, or he was sure he'd have had to pick up her coffee as well.

Aubrey's restaurant was empty when the humid cinnamon-and-coffee-scented air welcomed him inside. As a blender whirred, laughter drew his gaze to a booth on the left where Shelby, Brooke, and Karissa sat.

Shelby waved him over, grinning. "Aria lets you out of the office once in a while?"

"Aria's not the boss of me. I'm the boss of my own self." He added his own grin to show her he was kidding.

"Well, she sure has our brother Lucas dancing to her tune." Shelby chuckled. "I hear she's got him convinced to wear a white shirt and pants at their wedding."

"Why did they have to make their wedding private?" Drew raised a hand in supplication. "I'd pay for everyone's return trip just to see Lucas Prins out of his plaid shirt and blue jeans for once."

"How much do you want to bet he'll pack his cowboy hat?" Brooke asked from her corner, brushing her hair back in an exaggerated gesture. Shelby and Karissa studied him as well.

"Why do I feel I'm supposed to say something?" He glanced from one woman to the other, confusion flowing through him.

Brooke stroked her hair again. Prisms of light flashed from a diamond on her ring finger.

"Oh brother." He groaned. "Another bachelor bites the dust. It's like an epidemic."

"That's all you have to say?" She mock-pouted.

"My deep apologies." He gave her a warm smile. "Congratulations to you. Grady is a good guy, and you two will be very happy." Then he gulped. Surely, he hadn't put his foot in it. "It is Grady, isn't it?"

For years, Brooke had a not-so-secret crush on George Bamford, the owner of the Grill and Chill down the street. But since Drew had come back to town, Grady and Brooke had been dating. Supposedly.

"Of course, it is," she snapped.

"Sorry." He loosened his taut shoulders and widened his stance, preparing to make up for lost ground, then nodded to Shelby. "Can I ask when the baby is due, or is that going to drop me in hot water as well?"

Shelby gave him a patronizing smile. "That's okay. We make allowances for silly men."

Somehow, the way the three women looked at him brought back pathetic memories of junior high and high school. When he was the awkward brother of Arlen Rozak. The guy most young girls in Aspen Valley yearned to date. The guy whose initials were doodled in the margins of countless notebooks.

Whereas Drew, Arlen's tongue-tied younger brother, couldn't string two coherent sentences together or make more than fleeting eye-contact with girls. He stifled a shudder over the jokes and cold shoulders he'd endured in the purgatory of junior high and high school.

"To answer your question," Shelby continued, "the baby is due in a month. Although I'm hoping it's sooner. This heat is torture."

"I bet you're jealous of Courtney right now." Brooke fiddled with her engagement ring as if still getting used to it.

"Not really. Their baby is fussing all the time. Fenna was grumbling about it in church on Sunday."

This was his cue to leave. Despite bringing up Shelby's due date, the baby talk was way outside his comfort zone. As were babies and young children. He ended up treating them like young adults. Which often netted him an eye roll from their mothers.

He was about to say his goodbyes, put his order in, and scuttle back to the office when the door opened again. A slim young woman stood in the entrance, looking around as if trying to get her bearings.

Her blonde hair flowed over her shoulders and down her back. Green eyes enhanced by dark eyebrows gave her a mysterious air. Yellow words—*sarcastic comments loading*—arched over the bright-orange T-shirt she'd tucked into khaki shorts.

Other than the row of earrings marching up one ear and the dove tattoo stamping her forearm, Nadia Prins had changed little since she left Aspen Valley.

With his brother.

———

NADIA'S EYES rested on the tall slim man standing by her sister, Shelby, his eyes narrowed, his features grim. What was his problem?

She was about to dismiss his reaction to her when her steps toward the group of girls faltered and recognition dawned.

Drew Rozak.

Her ex-husband's younger brother.

The man she had once tried to date. The man who turned her down so fast she was surprised there weren't skid marks on her psyche.

For a flash, she saw the similarities between the two men. Both had thick hair that refused to be tamed. Both had those heavily lashed eyes that always made her jealous. At one time Arlen was taller than Drew, but she suspected now they would have been the same height.

If Arlen were still alive.

But the similarity collided with past reality as she took in the suit that hugged Drew's broad shoulders and emphasized his narrow waist, the tie cinching the neck of his pristine white shirt. Drew was always the quieter, more reserved one. Nadia had always been drawn to him, but he kept his distance.

Arlen, however, was all swagger and confidence. Blue jeans, country music, and fun.

He would have sneered at the lawyer Drew had become.

Memories of Arlen muddled her thoughts and resurrected memories that twisted her heart, sliding over her initial reaction to the boy who had become a stunningly attractive man.

Nadia swallowed unwelcome reactions and emotions, lifted her chin, and strode toward the gathered group, fighting to keep her self-control intact. Ignoring Shelby's concerned look, she gave Drew a tight nod as she sat down beside her sister-in-law, Karissa.

"We couldn't wait for you forever, so we started without you," Shelby chided.

"Always a bossy older sister." Nadia slanted her a smile, hoping she sounded more good-natured than she felt.

She squeezed her trembling fingers together, disappointed at her reaction to seeing Arlen's brother.

Another quick breath and she felt like she was together enough to look up at Drew and give him a quick smile. "Hey Drew, good to see you."

Drew's eyes held hers; as if he was delving into her soul, trying to unearth her secrets.

"Hey yourself. Been awhile," was all he said. "Missed you at Arlen's funeral."

Was that condemnation in his voice?

And what could she say that wouldn't sound like she was making excuses? Or rationalizing.

"I had my reasons," was her vague response, disappointed at the breathlessness in her voice. Hoping her sister, Karissa and Brooke would put it down to rushing to get here. "And

I'm not surprised you became a lawyer." She went on a defensive to mask her reactions, compensating with an arch smile. "You always were the bookish type."

"Thanks, I guess?" He slipped his hand in the pocket of his pants. This only enhanced the broadness of his shoulders and the leanness of his hips. "I'm sure Aria would be happy to hear that."

"Oh, that's right. I heard you two are partners now. Which works out well for her now that she and my brother are taking off to elope."

She looked at Shelby, wrinkling her nose, shifting to an easier topic, going for a breezy and joking tone. "I still can't believe we didn't get an invite. I mean, who's going to witness this monumental event?"

Shelby leaned forward, her eyes wide. "And even bigger news. I just heard Aria convinced Lucas to wear a white shirt and linen pants and go barefoot."

Nadia's mouth fell open in shock. "No! What I wouldn't give to see that."

"That's exactly what Drew said."

Why did her heart jump at the mention of his name?

Nadia's eyes flashed up to him again, then away, disappointed at how just a simple glance could create this welter of unwelcome emotions.

"Before you go," Shelby said to Drew, "and I can see you're eager to get going as the female-to-male proportion grows. I also hear your mom's coming home from the hospital. Did you find anyone to help you out with her?"

"Still looking."

When Shelby looked over at her, Nadia saw the question in her eyes and was about to stop her when Shelby plowed on, still holding her gaze.

"Nadia, you have time, don't you?" Shelby asked, giving her a wide grin. "Celeste said you're getting tired of hanging around the trailer, and Liam said your job at the hospital won't start for at least another six weeks."

Nadia gave her sister a nudge under the table, adding a glare, but Shelby just ignored it.

She had no intention of working with Drew, nor did she need the money. She had just enough money to tide her over until she started at the hospital.

Hard not to think of where her bank account should have been...

She pushed that aside, shame burying those thoughts.

But Drew didn't need to know how close she was cutting things.

Drew with his organization, his self-control, and the savings account she knew he had started when he got his first weekly allowance. Drew was the kind of guy who was born clutching a five-year plan.

"I doubt Drew needs to know the details of my life." Her sister's comment about her hanging around the trailer made her feel like a loser.

"You're right." Drew took a step away. "I'll leave you all right now. I need to get coffee."

Shelby was quiet as she watched him leave, then turned back to Nadia, leaning closer, lowering her voice. "Why don't you take Drew's job? It would be perfect for you and keep you here longer before you take off again."

"I'm thinking of making a trip to Vancouver Island. You know that."

"Well, yeah, but you can do that after you cover that maternity leave."

"That takes me to November, and I'm going to much warmer places then."

"Right. You were talking about Vietnam." Shelby shook her head, disappointment wreathing her features. "Have you ever thought of settling down and reconnecting with your family?" Shelby's aim at the guilt zone was always spot on.

And deep down she knew the time she'd spent away from her family was wearing on her.

"Besides," Shelby continued, leaning forward. "I always thought you and Drew's mom got along great."

"We did." Joined by their affection for Arlen, she and Lily always had lots to talk about.

"Past tense?" Brooke pressed.

"I haven't seen her for a while. So, I wouldn't know if she's changed."

"She's gotten more reclusive since Arlen died. No secret, it gutted her." Brooke glanced at Drew, now pulling out his wallet to pay. "Drew struggled as well, but he's doing better now."

Nadia watched Drew joke with Stephanie. The young girl was positively glowing, batting her eyelashes at him. Nadia didn't blame her for flirting.

When she first saw Drew, shock was hardly the word to describe the change time and education had achieved. He looked confident. Self-assured. Were Arlen still alive, Drew would have no trouble stepping out of the shadow of his favored older brother right now. In fact, Arlen would be the one who would suffer by comparison.

"And how about you? How are you doing? I mean, it's only been a year since Arlen died," Brooke asked, concern edging her voice. "I have heard little other than the bits I've gotten from Shelby and Celeste, and even that was pretty thin."

"It was thin because Miss Nadia here has an aversion to texting." Shelby leveled Nadia a wry look.

"It seems impersonal."

"Calling isn't."

Nadia shrugged, then eased out a cautious smile. There was no way she was letting Shelby corner her into even more guilt. She'd struggled enough with that the last year.

"Arlen's death was hard." She fiddled with the napkin in

front of her. "But we were divorced for a couple of years, so that gave me some emotional distance."

She was pleased with how casual she sounded, but couldn't stop a quick glance Drew's way, wondering if he heard them.

Thankfully, Drew had his coffees and left without another look their way.

As the door sighed closed behind him, Nadia's breath came easier.

"I still think you should take the job instead of going to the Island." Shelby was like a dog with an especially delicious bone.

Nadia ignored her, pretending to be engrossed with the menu. "Aubrey has some really good choices," she said.

Prices were within her budget as well.

"Why won't you work for Drew?" Brooke continued, fiddling with her ring.

Nadia didn't want to get into all the details. That meant mining memories she preferred to keep buried.

Despite dating Arlen, she had always been drawn to his brother. But she knew Drew was not her type. Too good. Too even-keeled.

She couldn't come up with a way to explain it, so she opted for what her sister, sister-in-law, and friend would recognize as the most obvious.

"I don't think I want to be reminded of Arlen all the time."

Brooke's gaze shifted to sympathetic, and Karissa rubbed her shoulder in commiseration. Nadia was appreciative of the support, yet a chill of self-reproach crept in.

"I can see that," Shelby admitted with a gentle sigh. "Oh well. You know best what you need."

Her words said one thing, but her tone was pure passive-aggressive older sister.

Which made Nadia even more determined to turn the job down. Though she doubted Drew would offer it.

While their mother had always cared for her, Drew seemed to prefer to keep Nadia at a distance.

No need to put herself through that.

Again.

Chapter 2

"You're making a joke, right?" Nadia stared at the mechanic tugging a rag out of the back pocket of his coveralls and wiping his hands.

Alan Petrusko looked from her to the engine and shook his head as if looking at a corpse. "I wish I was, but this car needs major engine work."

"And the cost of said major engine work?" Nadia cringed as she waited for the verdict. She had owned her vehicle long enough to know that anytime a mechanic used the word "major," the zeros increased exponentially.

"Ballpark estimate, you're looking at about $4000.00, which ain't too bad considering how ancient this car is."

"Don't insult old Murdoch here," Nadia said, forcing a grin. She'd bought the car in Toronto years ago, and it had never let her down. "But if I don't get the work done? What then?"

"I give this vehicle maybe 80 kilometres at best."

"That won't take me far." Nadia grimaced.

"Give you a couple of grocery runs," Alan said with a wide grin. "If you ration yourself…"

"Already been doing enough of that," Nadia muttered.

"I wish I could give you better news."

"And it was just supposed to be an oil change." She plunged her fingers through her hair, grasping the back of her neck. "What would I get if I sold it?"

Alan chuckled. "Right now, I doubt you'd get much for it."

"Maybe."

Nadia massaged her neck, rolled her head, then blew out a breath, trying to sort out her options.

She had the money for the trip she wanted to take, but she needed the car for that. And fixing the car would take away all her trip money.

The never-ending circle of being broke.

"Honestly, Nadia, I don't recommend driving this thing at all," Alan told her, reality dropping into her thoughts. "Despite the 80 K lifespan I gave, you just never know. And if you cause further damage, this car is a total write-off."

"Can I leave it here for now? While I think about this?"

"Sure, no problem. I can get Preston to move it to the back, and we'll take care of it when you give us the go-ahead."

"How much time will you need if I say okay?"

"Probably take about a week or two to get the parts, depending on supply and delivery, which has been erratic lately. We'd only need a day to put it together, but we'll have to squeeze it in. So best guesstimate, two weeks?"

Each word cut one more week off her trip. Guess she wasn't going to Vancouver Island soon.

"Okay. Guess I need to hitchhike."

"If you stick around till closing time, I could give you a ride."

"Thanks for the offer, but I'll see if someone in the fam can come and get me." It would have to be one of the brothers. Shelby was due any day. Karissa was working today, as was Aubrey, her brother Liam's fiancée. Beth said she was working on some new orders for the craft shop she had purchased.

She was the only one in the family, other than the teenage twins and young Jacob, not gainfully employed.

Not a good feeling.

"Okay. So just let me know when you want this done, and we'll go ahead on it," Alan said, closing the hood of the car with a definitive clank.

Nadia thanked him, slung her purse over her shoulder, and trudged out of the mechanic shop.

She pulled her phone out of her purse, biting her lip as she stared down at it. Who to call? Who in her family would give her the least amount of aggravation?

She knew the answer to that. None of them. They had been hassling her about her old beater the last time they got together for a family dinner, surprised it was still going strong.

Not so strong anymore.

Sucking in a deep breath, she sent up a prayer for strength. Not that she was so sure God would take care of that, but it was instinctive. Something woven into the fabric of her childhood. You prayed when you needed help. But you also prayed just to talk with God.

Something she also had done little of lately.

In fact, yesterday, Celeste had asked Nadia if she wanted a ride to church. Nadia had said no. Made some vague comments about being tired.

So, she stayed home, fighting her guilt.

And there her brain went again, circling the drain.

She punched in a number, then waited.

"Hey girl, what can I do for you this beautiful Monday morning?" Lucas' deep voice reverberated in her ear.

She hesitated, biting her lip. Lucas would give her mountains of grief about her car, but at least it wouldn't come with that inflection of superiority and frustration that Burke had perfected.

May as well get to the point. "My car is at the mechanic,

and they don't want me to drive it home. So, I need a ride from town to home."

"To our home or the trailer?"

"The trailer. My home," she said. Guess the word "home" to her family would always and forever mean the rambling farmhouse they were all raised in.

"Give me about half an hour, and I'll be there."

Her shoulders released their tension at Lucas' easy-going reply.

Not that he wouldn't tease her once he picked her up, but she had time to prepare for that.

"I'll start walking," she offered. "I can use the exercise. I'll meet you on the highway somewhere."

"Sure enough. Don't take rides from strangers."

Nadia ended the call and wrinkled her nose, wondering how far she could get in the half hour it would take Lucas to arrive.

She could hang out at Karissa's fabric shop or Beth's Craft store or have some coffee at Aubrey's.

Then she nixed those thoughts.

Somehow, being around her busy and successful sisters-in-law would be too vivid a reminder of her own rootless and financially stressed life.

Besides, she was already antsy and wanted to get moving. That always made her more comfortable.

An apt metaphor for my life lately, she thought with a wry grin.

She dropped her phone into her purse's side pocket, slipped her bag over her shoulders, and started the journey.

But despite wearing her trekking sandals, twenty minutes later, she was regretting her choice. The sun pounded on her bare head, and she was building up a very discreet sweat. The trucks roaring past her on the highway, spitting out the occasional rock in her direction, only enhanced the negative ambiance.

A far cry from the crisp mountain air of the Scandes

mountains in Finland. She allowed herself a smile at the memory. It had been a glorious trip. One she had planned out as she worked in the hospital ward of Sunnybrook in Toronto.

Her phone dinged, and she pulled it out.

> Running late. Be another half hour. Min.

Lucas' text said.

Seriously?

But she couldn't risk venting on her rescuer, so all she sent back was a terse,

> No problem.

> While you wait, you can plan the party you'll be throwing for Aria and me when we get back from our honeymoon.

he texted back to her.

> Wait? What party?

> Tell you later.

> Tell me now.

But nothing back.

She blew out a sigh, then dropped her phone back into the pocket of her crossbody purse. That purse had accompanied her on many an adventure after she bought it at a market in Bali. Adventures and many of the jobs she had undertaken to pay for said adventures.

Now she had to pay for car repairs that would eat into her meagre bank account and take a huge bite out of her income from her upcoming job.

Shoving her hands into the pockets of her linen skirt, she

stepped up her pace, as if trying to out-walk the concerns that crowded her head. She had come back to Aspen Valley to recalibrate, reconnect with family, and build up her bank account. Work for Liam for a year max, then off to her next adventure. But being home underlined the chasm between her life and her siblings' lives. They were settled, having babies, and getting married.

Making regular money.

This was the reason she left Aspen Valley to start with. To escape the plodding repetitiveness of life. The boring sameness of life in a town where everyone knew each other. Where people remembered exactly how she behaved at the Christmas concert when she was four. The snubs she had meted out and had received from classmates. The long drip, drip of history that slowly wore away whoever she thought she wanted to be, molding her into yet another Prins girl. Unable to change her genetics, or her story, and, therefore, re-identify herself.

As she walked, she let herself imagine her next trip to Jordan and all she had planned to do there. A perfect distraction. Petra, Madaba, open-air markets, from there to Jerusalem and so much more.

And when that's over, what then?

This wasn't the first time her father's insidious voice slipped into her thoughts as she made her life's plan.

It was a question he had often asked her whenever she daydreamed aloud with him as they were hauling hay, working in the shop, or driving to town to get groceries. Anytime her father had the opportunity, he tried to spend one-on-one time with each of his children.

No small feat with nine other kids vying for his attention.

While he never talked down her plans like her mother did, he often asked questions about her future. Gently challenged her assumption that leaving Aspen Valley was her only option.

She would tease him that he just wanted her around, and he would laugh and agree.

Nadia walked a little faster, but the words stayed with her. What did it matter? Why not travel? Why not experience as much as possible before she had to settle down? Before she might – and it was a big *might* – get married again?

A car pulling up beside her broke off her thoughts, and she spun around, clutching her purse, taking a step back, and looking around to see if anyone else was close.

Then she saw who was behind the wheel of the silver Mercedes, and her heart dropped to the soles of her sandals, thinking a menacing stranger might have been preferable.

"Do you need a ride?" Drew asked through the rolled-down passenger window.

Her first thought was "What was he doing here?" Her second was, "Why did it have to be him?"

Her ego made her want to turn down his offer, but she knew Lucas was at least an hour out yet, and her feet were sore.

Despite her predicament, she still bit her lip, hesitating.

"I'm sticking my neck out here. I'm guessing you're not doing this for exercise." Drew gave her a wry grin, which only enhanced his appeal, but also increased her resistance.

"How do you know that?" she challenged, unable to let go of her pride completely.

"Although sandals are made for walking, I'm guessing you didn't plan this as the event of the day."

Nadia considered her circumstances, then swallowed her pride, shelved her memories, walked over to the car, and climbed in.

"Much as I hate to admit it to you, you're right. I hadn't intended on hiking my way home when I left this morning." The car was blessedly cool when she closed the door, and she settled into the comfortable leather seat.

Of course, it was leather. Drew did nothing by halves. If he couldn't get what he wanted on his terms, he would do without.

Was that why he turned her down all those years ago?

"Back to the farm or back to the trailer?" Drew asked as he pulled into traffic.

She wanted to question how he knew where she was staying but figured that was futile. This was Aspen Valley. Everybody knew everything about each other. One of the reasons she was happy to leave.

"No. Just back to the trailer. I've got a bunch of things to do."

She was getting great at this lying thing. She had nothing to do except fold the laundry, still hanging on the makeshift line she had strung up between two trees.

"So, you've been keeping busy?" Drew asked, glancing over at her, then back at the road.

That was the biggest problem with lying. You had to have an excellent memory and a good imagination. The imagination was no problem for Nadia; it was her faulty memory that always tripped her up.

"Yes. This, that, and the next thing."

"Sounds important," Drew countered. "Or very secretive."

"I may be a spy, for all you know."

"Then very secretive."

"Yes. Loose lips sink ships and all that."

"Okay." His voice held no inflection, and she sensed he was tiring of her banter. Drew was never one to indulge her silliness for very long. Not like Arlen. The two of them could go on all day. But she didn't want to think about Arlen right now, so she figured she should just come clean, in case he started delving deeper, his questions growing more incisive, like the lawyer he was.

"Actually, I really don't have that much to do," she finally admitted.

His only acknowledgment of her comment was a polite nod.

They drove in silence for a moment, which grew more uncomfortable with every mile.

"So did you ever find anybody to take care of your mom?" she asked, needing to fill the silence. "I thought she was coming home today?"

"Thankfully, the doctor put off her discharge till tomorrow. And despite two more interviews this morning, I still haven't found anyone."

The comment hung between them as if inviting a reply.

Nadia swallowed a knot of apprehension, feeling like she was about to step into a minefield that could potentially blow up in her face.

But what choice did she have? Maxing out her credit card, spending most of her time working to pay it off, and then unable to make the trip she had so hoped to do?

"Would you be interested?" Drew asked, taking the decision out of her hands.

Nadia hesitated a moment as if she needed some time to consider it. She knew it was a childish power move. Her reality was that she needed the job, but something about Drew made her want to feel at least a bit in control.

"I think I would be," Nadia finally responded, feigning a note of laid-back indifference, as if she could take it or leave it. The reality was, she really needed to take it, despite the potential hazards.

"How long will the job be?"

"About four weeks, if all goes according to what the doctor says," Drew told her.

Which would be perfect. Nadia would start her job at the hospital in eight weeks.

"I think I could manage that," Nadia said. Then she caught herself. How was she supposed to get back and forth to this job?

"I also need to tell you," Drew continued, "I would need you to stay overnight at the house for the duration. My mother will need help to go to the bathroom, and we don't want her falling again."

Well, that neatly solved everything in one fell swoop.

"That's not a problem," Nadia agreed. "As you can see, I'm walking because I don't have a vehicle. So that could work out well."

Another few beats of silence, and then she heard Drew sigh gently.

"Not gonna lie, Nadia, but this is an actual answer to prayer. I was wondering how this was all going to work out. I can take some time off work, but not enough, what with Aria leaving and all the stuff I have hanging over me."

"Nice that we can solve each other's problems," Nadia returned with a quick wave of her hand. "When did you want me to start?"

"I'm picking my mom up from the hospital tomorrow afternoon. If you want, I can pick you up first, and we can arrive together. I know she'll be happy to see you."

"No, no, don't worry about that," Nadia protested. "I'll get Celeste to bring me to town. In the meantime, I should tell Lucas I don't need a ride."

She hesitated a moment, then glanced sidelong at Drew. She was disconcerted to see him looking at her, his thick-lashed eyes narrowed. Then when he noticed her looking, his head snapped back to face the road, his expression grim.

As if judging her.

Second thoughts about taking the job raged through her. But she would probably have minimal interaction with him if she was staying at his mother's place.

She dialled Lucas' number, and he was tickled that she got a ride and thankfully didn't ask her who had picked her up.

She tucked her phone back into her purse and laid her head back against the seat, closing her eyes, as if shutting off any further conversation. Drew complied with her wish for silence, and twenty minutes later, he dropped her off at the trailer where she'd been living.

"Thanks for the ride," she offered. "I guess I'll see you tomorrow. What time?"

"About 4:00 at the hospital."

"I'll see you then."

Drew just nodded, and Nadia got out, closing the door behind her. He reversed, and as he pulled away, unease niggled her brain at working for him. But then Alan's words plowed out from where she had suppressed them for the past few minutes, $4000.00. It would empty her travel fund, leaving her nothing.

She couldn't help feeling a flicker of shame at her situation.

It's not your fault, she told herself. *Circumstances are out of your control.*

With those words of affirmation ringing through her head, she walked up to the trailer and stepped inside. *It will all work out,* she told herself.

Even if, at times, it didn't.

* * *

Drew stood in the doorway of the spare bedroom, watching as Nadia eased his mother onto the hospital bed, which he had ordered specifically for her.

"This bed doesn't feel very comfortable," his mother complained, shooting a frown at Drew.

"You can't sleep in a regular bed," Drew told her. "It's too low, and we need the bars to make sure you don't fall off."

"I don't need the bars up," his mother argued. "I'm not a baby."

"You are taking pain medication which can cause disorientation," Nadia assured her, lifting her legs up onto the bed. "Once everything settles down, we can lower the bars."

"I guess," his mother acquiesced, smiling up at Nadia.

24

Then she patted Nadia's hand. "I'm so glad you're here helping me. You'll be such a comfort to me."

Drew resisted the urge to roll his eyes. His mother had always loved Nadia, even after she and Arlen had separated and divorced.

"I'm glad I could help," Nadia told her. "Now I hope you can get some sleep. This afternoon, the physiotherapist, Patrice, will be coming to go over your exercises."

"Why do I have to have her in the house?" Again, his mother looked past Nadia to him, as if expecting him to fix it. "I don't want strangers in the house."

Drew pushed away from the doorway and stepped closer to the bed. He gave his mother an encouraging smile. "Patrice is not a stranger. You've met her at the hospital. She is very helpful and very kind."

"I can vouch for that," Nadia told his mother. "She has worked with my sister Roxie for almost a year now."

His mother frowned as if thinking. "Roxie? Is that the girl that got into that car accident? Doesn't she have a twin sister?"

Nadia nodded. "RayAnn and Roxie are twins, yes. And Roxie enjoyed working with Patrice. I'm sure you'll be just fine with her."

His mother made a face that Drew knew all too well. That wrinkled nose, the slight curl to the lip. The narrowing of the eyes.

Not convinced. Not happy.

"Did you arrange this?"

Drew fought down his frustration at the accusatory tone in her voice and forced a smile. "I don't have that much power. The doctor made that call. And it's a requirement."

"Once we've got a routine set up for your exercises," Nadia said, "I can talk to her about taking over for her."

"You're such an angel. Thank you for thinking of my needs."

As if Drew never did.

He brushed the grumble off, realizing how petty it was. Though it was the story of his life. Arlen couldn't do anything wrong, and he couldn't do anything right.

"How nice that Drew got you this bed and that special recliner in the living room," Nadia added.

His mother shifted, as if still unsure what to think about what Drew had done for her.

"I suppose." She yawned, and Nadia patted her shoulder.

"You should sleep now. If you need anything, just ring," Nadia told her, pointing to the silver bell on the bedside table.

Nadia, it seemed, had thought of everything. When they picked up his mother from the hospital, Nadia had packed a couple of magazines for Lily to read, a pillow for her head, her favorite chocolate bar (Drew was amazed that Nadia even remembered), and a few other things stashed in the large bag she wore over her shoulder. One of which was this bell. Like an old-time school bell that teachers would have on their desks.

His mother nodded, then turned her head away from them, her hands folded over her chest.

Nadia fussed with the sheets a bit more, then turned and walked past Drew. He caught the faintest scent of oranges. She still used the same shampoo, the smell conjuring up memories he preferred to stay buried.

He followed, closing the door behind him.

"Okay. So, she's settled. Now, where can I put my stuff?" Nadia gave him a quick look, then away.

"I thought you could stay in my room."

Nadia's gaze flew to his, eyes wide. "No. No, I can't do that."

Drew shrugged. He wasn't crazy about the idea either, but they had little choice.

"There are only two rooms on the main floor, and I thought it would be best if you stayed as close to my mom as possible."

"I understand, but still…" She let the sentence trail off, as if trying to find another objection to the situation. "Where will you stay? Upstairs?"

The faint hope in her voice made him smile. As if he might not be staying in the house after all.

"I'll have my pick, so I won't be uncomfortable."

"How many bedrooms are in this house?" she asked, as if surprised that a single guy like him needed so much space.

"Two down and two up. One I use as my office."

"Of course. I wasn't trying to, you know, judge you or anything." She fiddled with the strap of her purse, as if embarrassed.

He wanted to reply with a joke or a light-hearted comment, but to his dismay, she stood too close for him to act as unconcerned as he wanted to feel. To joke his way out of the awkwardness.

Something Arlen had always excelled at.

"I bought the house and acreage from a family with four kids," was all he could come up with. "I love the location just outside of town. Private enough and with a large yard."

Drew inwardly groaned at his sudden verbosity.

Suddenly, the idea of staying in town had an enormous appeal.

"It's a nice place, for sure," Nadia added, with a careful smile. As if patronizing him.

"Anyhow, this is where you'll be staying," he said, adopting the brisk tone he often used with his clients. He opened the door beside them, and Nadia looked the room over, a gentle smile teasing her lips.

"You got a bay window," she observed. "Just like you always wanted."

The casual reference to their shared memories created a prod of regret. A sense of melancholy.

You had a chance, he reminded himself.

Then behind that came the reality of how quickly she had gone running to his brother after he turned her down.

Not only gone running to him, but married him.

No, though Nadia would stay with him and his mother, he had to keep her at arm's length. Stay detached.

Because he knew for a fact that once she was done working for Liam, she would leave again.

⸺

"I WOULD LOVE it if you could tell me more about Arlen," Drew's mother requested, her expression expectant, hopeful. "I missed out on so much of his life. What was he doing when he first moved to Toronto? He never said. Just that he hated his first job."

They sat in the living room, Lily in her recliner and Nadia on the couch. Drew sat at the dining room table working on his laptop. Keeping his distance, yet available if Lily wanted to say something to him. He'd picked up takeout for dinner, and she and Lily had eaten together, but Drew had gone back to the office. He returned a couple of hours later with his laptop and had been working since.

Nadia turned her attention back to Lily, scrambling through her memories, trying to find the right way to tell Lily what she wanted to know.

"You know he worked at that consulting firm," Nadia said. "But like he told you, he didn't love it."

Lily pursed her lips and shook her head, a sad smile curving her lips as she cradled the mug of tea Nadia had made for her. "I'm not surprised. Arlen was always so creative. I could never imagine him working a stilted office job like that."

"Arlen definitely had a gift," Nadia agreed, choosing her words carefully. "I remember how alive he would come when he was painting."

"His father discouraged him from taking the art degree he wanted, but I think it could have been good for him," Lily shared, a yearning note in her voice. "So I'm glad he taught himself."

"He worked hard at it." Which was a bit of a stretch. When Arlen did paint, he was focused. It was just getting the muse to speak to him, he often said, that got him in front of the easel.

It was one of the things they had fought about. Nadia counseled him against quitting his job, but he said he had options.

Turned out those options were his mother's bank account.

"Such a gift he had," Lily said, stifling a yawn.

"He did," Nadia agreed, grabbing an old receipt to mark her page. "It has been a busy first day home for you, so you should get ready for bed."

"Is that Patrice girl coming again tomorrow?" Lily grumbled as she set aside the blanket covering her legs.

"Yes, she is."

"Can't you do the exercises with me?"

The entire time Patrice was taking Lily through her exercises, Drew's mother had complained and fussed about having strangers in the house. Which was interesting, considering Lily wasn't even in her own home. Patrice paid little attention to her.

After they were done, Nadia followed Patrice outside and apologized for Lily's behavior. Patrice just laughed and brushed it off.

"Patrice suggested that," Nadia returned. She put down the book she hadn't been reading, but before she got up, she snuck a glance at Drew. He seemed lost in what he was doing, frowning at the screen.

She suspected that had his mother not been home, Drew would have still been working at the office. He was that dedicated. Different from his older brother.

She struggled not to draw comparisons between the two.

Once Arlen had quit his job, he let his hair grow out, adopting the very artiste persona his mother said was part of his character. He wore paint-stained tunic shirts and cotton pants and wore sandals until the snow made it impractical to do so.

A far cry from the structured suits and starched, collared shirts that Drew favored.

As if sensing her scrutiny, he looked up, frowning. "Do you need some help?"

"No…no, I was just…thinking."

He nodded and looked down again.

She disliked this awkwardness between them. Despite her dating Arlen, she and Drew used to joke together. They would share a laugh, favorite books, and television shows. In fact, Arlen was jealous of her connection with his younger brother. He would often tease Drew about his 'crush' on his brother's girlfriend.

Nadia knew Drew had been attracted to her. Many times, she had caught him looking at her, a puzzled expression on his face, as if wondering why she was with his brother. There were times she wondered herself. Until Arlen broke up with her after a fight about that very thing. Her and Drew's friendship.

After the breakup, she had started spending more time with Drew. Talked to him more. Then, one day, she asked if he wanted to go out with her.

And he turned her down.

Humiliated and hurt more than she wanted to admit, she left Aspen Valley as she had always vowed she would. However, she didn't envision this scenario all those years ago when she packed her bags, leaving town, family, and friends, promising herself she wouldn't come back.

Here now, back in Aspen Valley, taking care of Drew's mother in Drew's house.

Only temporarily, she reminded herself, turning her attention to Drew's mother.

"I think it's time for bed," she told her with a smile.

"Oh my. That's exactly what I used to say to the boys," Lily chuckled. "Didn't I Drew? Say exactly that?"

"You did," he murmured, shooting his mother a quick glance over the top of his computer screen, adding a faint smile.

Then the frown returned as he turned his attention back to his laptop.

Nadia wondered what he was working on that put that concerned look on his forehead. Not that he would tell her, of course. Drew was the epitome of discreet.

In fact, when she left Aspen Valley, she thought everyone would know that he had turned her down. The girl who snagged Arlen Rozak, one of the more eligible guys in town. Her brothers, apparently, had rated as well, but they didn't have the Rozak dollars and prestige.

But...nothing came out of Aspen Valley. Not even a hint of a rumor.

Discreet. Considerate.

Nadia picked up the remote of Lily's recliner, pushing the button to make it lift so Lily easily came to a standing position without having to push herself up. She wasn't surprised that Drew had bought this for his mother. He was methodical about doing things the right way.

"This chair is so handy," Nadia commented, bringing the wheeled walker close for Lily. "It was nice that Drew got it for you."

Lily didn't even acknowledge that, focusing instead on trying to grab the handles of the walker.

Nadia wanted to put her lack of appreciation down to the pain she was probably feeling right now. Lily was due for her medication. And yet, Nadia wished Lily would show a little more gratitude for these unspoken things Drew had done for her.

Drew's mother grasped the handles of her walker and released the brakes, then walked carefully across the hardwood floor of the living room.

"You could use a nice cheerful rug in here," she informed Drew.

Drew looked up from his laptop, giving his mother a lopsided smile. "I had one, but I put it away for now."

"Why would you do that?" his mother asked.

"Tripping hazard."

"I wouldn't have tripped, you know."

Nadia felt a glimmer of sympathy for Drew. She knew Arlen had always been his mother's favorite. But she didn't realize the negativity that Drew might've had to live with as a result.

She followed Lily to the bathroom, where she helped her get ready for bed.

She leaned one hip against the counter, her arms crossed, as Drew's mother brushed her teeth. Nadia patiently waited while Lily went through her fifteen-minute skin routine, wondering how many potions and lotions a person needed. Judging from the variety of bottles lining the counter, a lot.

"A rug in the living room would have been a problem," she observed, feeling the need to defend Drew's decision. "And I'm sure he took it away on the advice of the physiotherapist."

"Well, what does she know?" Lily snapped, her features tight.

"Patrice knows what she's spent eight years learning and another eight years applying. She's very good at what she does. In fact, do you know Rebecca? Whose sister lives just down the road from you?" *In that fancy, expensive subdivision,* she wanted to add. "She moved here specifically so Patrice could help her."

Lily just tapped her toothbrush against the side of the sink and dropped it into a cup. "I need a pain pill."

Nadia frowned, pointing to the bottle beside the cup holding the toothbrush. "It's right there. If you want it."

"I can't open that bottle."

Nadia stifled a sigh, then reached over, grabbed the bottle, pressed down the top, gave it a twist, and opened it up. She tipped out a couple of pills and handed them to Lily.

A few moments later, she had Lily in her bed and was about to leave, knowing the poor woman had to be tired, when Lily caught her by the arm.

"I'm not that sleepy yet. Could you sit and talk to me? Tell me more about Arlen?"

Nadia shot a quick glance at the clock. It was already half an hour past the time that Drew's mother usually went to bed. And truth to tell, Nadia was hoping for some time to herself. She wanted to tuck herself in that massive bed just across the hallway, with a book she had downloaded just a few days ago.

But when she saw the tears glistening in Drew's mother's eyes, she felt a burst of sympathy, followed by a twist of her own complicated emotions connected to Arlen.

So, she pulled up a chair and sat down, holding Lily's hand.

"What do you want to hear?"

"He always seemed like he was looking for something. Do you think he found it? Was he content?"

Nadia wasn't sure what to say or what Lily expected, so she tried to be vague. Easier to gloss things over.

"He loved to laugh, you know that much. He was always joking around. I know we had a group of friends we hung out with…he always had a lot of fun with them."

If you wanted to define "fun" as getting blindingly drunk and having to call a cab home, then yes. He enjoyed himself.

"That's good to hear. And what about his paintings? I only

received one of them, but it looked amazing. I have it hanging in my house."

Nadia let her thoughts slip back to a happier time. When he found out she had moved to Toronto to attend school, they started hanging out again. The fight that sent her to Drew was forgotten like most of their fights were. She had thought he had changed because he had a regular job.

They didn't date right away. She was busy with her schooling, but they hung out on weekends. Nadia was lonely in the new, unknown city, and Arlen was a connection to home.

"He set up a studio in one room in his apartment. It had such perfect light, he always said."

It was a corner suite of a high-rise close to downtown Toronto, and Nadia couldn't imagine how much that condo cost. His job paid well, but she found out afterward that Lily helped him as well.

"I'm so glad he found that place," Lily said, running her fingers up and down the fold of the sheet. "When we looked at it, I knew it would be perfect for his art pursuits. He sent me a few pictures of what he was doing in the beginning, but then, not so much." Lily sighed again. "He could be so melancholy. A genuine artist's personality." She looked over at Nadia with a glimmer of hope in her eyes. "But he was happy, wasn't he?"

"I think he was." There were times he certainly was happy. That was accurate enough. Even working a job he hated, he found times to laugh and enjoy himself.

Drew's mother bit one corner of her lip, obviously unsatisfied with what Nadia told her. "Arlen's father often told me I spoiled him, that I would make him an unhappy person. But a mother loving her child isn't a bad thing, is it?"

A couple of tears slipped out of her eyes and down her cheeks, so Nadia grabbed a Kleenex and wiped them away. Then she gave Lily another careful smile.

"I don't think any mother can love their child too much."

"I don't think so either," Drew's mother agreed, patting Nadia's hand. "Do you have any other stories about Arlen you can share with me?"

Nadia wasn't exactly sure what Lily was looking for, but she dredged through her memories.

"I remember one time we were in downtown Toronto, and he decided we should go up the CN Tower. Just like that. We had to wait in line for tickets, but somehow, he got us to the front of the line." He had managed by flirting with the ticket attendant and slipping her a few bills. Arlen thought it was funny, but Nadia had to fight down a beat of annoyance. "We got to the top, and it was incredible. It was late evening, so we could see all the lights of the city down below us. Toronto is a huge city, and you really have no idea until you're up on the top of that tower, looking down."

"That would have been wonderful to see."

"It was, and it made a good memory."

Lily yawned, and Nadia knew she was done telling stories.

"I'll try to remember a few more. Maybe write them down so I can give them to you," Nadia offered.

"Thank you for that. I tried to stay in touch with him, but he was so distant. I loved him so much and miss him even more." Her voice slurred on her last words as her eyes drifted shut.

The pain pill was taking effect.

Nadia waited another moment, and then a gentle snore told her that Drew's mother was asleep. She got up and tucked the blankets around her in a fussy, motherly gesture.

Then she left, second thoughts trailing behind her.

If this was what taking care of Lily entailed, she would have to wall off her emotions, which was something she had struggled with for the past five years. She walked to the kitchen to make herself a cup of hot chocolate before she went to bed with a book.

She passed Drew, who was still tapping away on his keyboard.

It seemed rude to ignore him, though he was doing a good job of ignoring her.

"Do you want some hot chocolate? I am making some for myself," she asked him.

Drew shot her a quick sidelong glance, then shook his head. "No, I gotta get this done tonight."

"I know what a multitasker you are," Nadia teased. "I'm sure you can drink hot chocolate and type at the same time."

He shot her a puzzled glance, then tweaked out a reluctant smile. "I guess so. Thanks."

He turned back to his work, and Nadia pulled the mugs out of the cupboard. She set them on the counter, found the hot chocolate that she had bought the other day in town, and scooped some into the mugs. She added the water, set a steaming mug beside Drew, and then hesitated a moment. She felt bad leaving him here, alone.

Drew murmured his thanks, and without looking up, he took a sip of the hot chocolate, then spat it out.

"Should I have warned you that it's hot?" Nadia asked, feeling guilty.

"If I was a little kid, you probably should have," Drew said, pulling a napkin from the napkin holder and wiping his mouth.

"Well, you're not a child," Nadia reminded him. Giving into an impulse, she sat down across from him, cradling her mug between her hands. "Sometimes I wonder if you ever were a child? I always imagine you with glasses, hunched over a book, taking notes."

Drew leaned back in his chair, running his finger up and down the handle of the mug as he looked over at her, his expression vague and rather puzzling.

"I am not sure if you're teasing me, or if that's a compliment."

"Maybe a bit of both." Nadia blew on her chocolate, then took a careful sip. "I just know sometimes I was intimidated by how serious you were."

Drew huffed out a short laugh. "You? Intimidated by me? How in the world?"

"Oh, c'mon. You were such an outstanding student. You always got the highest marks in the class."

"How do you know that? We weren't in the same class together."

"No, but Burke was always talking about you. He often said that it was impossible to beat you when it came to marks. He was initially intimidated by you, too."

"But not intimidated by my brother, I'm guessing."

"No, not by Arlen." She couldn't help the melancholy tone in her voice at the thought of her brothers and Arlen hanging out together. When she first took Arlen to the farm, her brothers roped him into watching the hockey game with them, going horse-back riding, and helping in the shop with whatever they were fixing. He always obliged and was good at whatever he set his hand to.

"I have to apologize for my mother dragging you down memory lane," Drew commented, his expression serious, his voice quiet, sympathetic. "I'm sure it's difficult for you."

Nadia gave her hot chocolate another stir as she sorted through her thoughts and memories. "It is hard. In many ways."

She didn't want to say anything more. She abruptly stood, picking up her mug and giving him a tight smile. "Sorry to have interrupted you. I'm going to go to bed."

As she took her mug to the sink, his hand brushed hers, then to her shock, he caught it.

"Hey, I'm sorry. I know how much Arlen meant to you, and if it hurts too much, you don't have to talk about him with my mother."

Nadia wanted to snatch her hand out of Drew's, and, at

the same time, she also wanted to twine her fingers around his. His touch was gentle, comforting. Something she hadn't felt in a long time. Something she had always yearned for, but never seemed to find with Arlen.

She slammed the door on those memories and gently tugged her hand back.

"It's okay. I owe her and Arlen."

Before he could ask her another question, she turned and hurried to her room.

Her momentary sanctuary.

Chapter 3

Drew pulled up to his house, turned his car off, and gave himself a few moments before going inside.

While he was thankful Nadia could help him out, he hadn't considered how it would feel to see her every day in his house. He thought the years between them would have removed all traces of any feelings he had for her.

It was high school, for goodness' sake. It wasn't like they were married. Or even dating.

Though you could have been.

Grabbing his laptop case, he opened the door and strode up the walk.

He stepped into the house to the sound of laughter and the smell of something delicious wafting through the air.

Had Nadia made dinner?

"He promised me he would come back right away, but hours later, he still hadn't shown up. I was worried about him, so I went looking. That's when I found him downtown, sitting around with a few other artists and a sketchpad, selling pictures he drew of people to them."

"Why do you think he would do that?" He heard his mother ask.

They were in her bedroom. Drew walked to the kitchen to make himself some coffee.

But as he did, he couldn't help listening.

"I mean he didn't need the money, did he?" his mother asked.

"Of course not," Nadia scoffed. "He was still working at that investment firm at the time. I think it was the challenge. He called it instant art, and he loved the idea of making something quickly and then selling it."

"I always wished he had done a show in an actual gallery. I know he was getting ready for one."

"I wish the same," Drew heard Nadia agree. "He had so much talent."

Drew dragged his hand over his face, surprised at the twinge of jealousy Nadia's melancholy tone of voice created. She must really miss Arlen.

And why not? Despite their separation and divorce, they had been married for two years and dating for who knows how long before that.

"I always felt bad that we didn't go to his home to get his art supplies. Some of his unfinished work. I couldn't fly to the funeral. Drew went, though he brought nothing back with him."

Drew suppressed the self-reproach tingling down his spine as he dropped his briefcase on the table. After the emotionally wrenching memorial service, he had gone to Arlen's place to collect his personal items, knowing his mother would love to have anything to remind her of her son besides the ashes. Arlen's roommate, Foster, had said he didn't know of any pieces of artwork Arlen might have had lying around. As far as Foster knew, Arlen's art supplies were gone as well.

Drew suspected Foster wasn't telling the truth, but after checking Arlen's room, Drew saw no signs of any recent work in progress. No rags of paint, no paint-stained t-shirt like Arlen always wore. No sign at all that an artist had lived here.

However, before Drew left, Foster had asked if he might have some of Arlen's ashes. He had seemed genuinely upset at Arlen's passing, so without telling his mother, Drew agreed.

And Nadia?

Well, she couldn't even be bothered to attend the funeral of her ex-husband, even though Drew suspected she could have attended.

He closed the cupboard a little too hard, the sound reverberating through the kitchen.

"Is that you, Drew?" his mother called out.

"Yeah, it is."

After a pause, Nadia entered the kitchen. "I'm sorry. I didn't know you were home. I was just doing some exercises with your mother. Did you want some tea?"

"I can take care of myself," Drew returned, wishing he could keep the snappy tone out of his voice.

"I wasn't trying to say –"

"No, I'm sorry," he broke in, holding up a hand in a placating gesture. "Just a busy day at work."

"Of course," Nadia replied, folding her hands over each other. "But any time you want to eat, supper is ready."

"So that's what smells so good," Drew gave her an apologetic smile. His small way of making up for his snappy tone.

"Nothing special. My mom's macaroni casserole. It's all I could think of, given what I had to work with."

"Sorry about that. I'm a little shy on groceries. If you need anything in the future, just let me know, and I can pick stuff up after work."

"That would be good. If it's okay, I might put together a grocery list to give you for tomorrow, then."

"Of course, it's okay." He spooned some instant coffee into his mug and poured the boiling water in. "Sounds like my mom is in better spirits."

"Not too bad. She is tired now, of course. Just finished a

second round of exercises. We already did one set this morning."

"Did Patrice come again?"

Nadia shook her head. "I emailed her first thing, and she sent me a schedule of the exercises for your mother. Lily was pretty adamant about not having Patrice come."

"I'm surprised she was that upset about it."

Nadia glanced back at the room she had just come from, and Drew got a sense there was another layer to this story. Then Nadia took a step closer. Near enough that he could see the faint scar on her cheek she got long ago when she had fallen out of the barn onto a stack of lumber. He remembered how bad he had felt for her when her brothers teased her about it.

And when Arlen joined in.

But she had just laughed them off, and then he felt immediately jealous at how easily she could handle herself. How comfortable she was in her own skin – something he struggled with for so many years, living in his brother's flamboyant and exuberant shadow.

"She doesn't want Patrice coming because, apparently, Patrice had given Arlen a dressing down when he and his buddy Lee came in for Lee's physio session, and Arlen was joking around. Patrice told Arlen to leave. That this was serious business. Your mother hasn't been fond of Patrice since."

This time, Drew did roll his eyes. "Honestly. My mother."

It was all he could say.

"That about sums it up," Nadia returned, a dimple sneaking an appearance in the corner of her mouth as she smiled.

Drew had a ridiculous urge to touch it and let his hand linger on her cheek.

He spun around, almost knocking his mug off the counter.

"I should go up to my office. Do you need any help with dinner?"

He avoided looking at her, feeling dumb about his reaction to her. He had better keep a lid on it if he wanted her to stick around the next few weeks.

But when he opened his laptop to work on the case Aria had given him, he found he couldn't concentrate. He kept thinking about how close he had come to touching Nadia's cheek.

———

"HOW IS MY MOTHER DOING?" Drew asked when Nadia returned from the bedroom, where she had put his mother to bed. "She seemed exhausted at dinnertime."

To her surprise, he already had the dishes cleared off the table and had set aside the bowls holding what was left of the meal. She couldn't imagine her brothers doing the same without being asked.

"Long day for her," she returned, opening cupboards, and looking for containers to put the leftovers in. "But she's a trooper."

"Bottom drawer, left of the dishwasher," he said, sensing what she needed.

Nadia bent over, frowning as she opened the door to get the bowls. "Why are you doing dishes by hand when you have a dishwasher?"

"It's on the fritz, and I haven't had time to call a repairman."

Nadia pulled a few containers with matching lids out of the deep drawer, amazed at the organization. Bowls stacked, lids in a rack beside them. The glass containers were similarly organized.

"Is 'fritz' a technical term?" she teased as she set the glassware on the counter and tugged a couple of spatulas loose from a jar standing beside the stove.

"Yeah. It means, and I quote, 'For Repairman I'm Trying Zewaiting.'"

This made her laugh out loud in surprise. Drew's sense of humor was new to her. He had always seemed so intense and serious.

"How long is Zewaiting going to take?"

"Apparently, he's coming next week."

Still smiling, Nadia portioned the leftovers into the bowls.

"Are you really serving that again?" Drew asked, frowning her way.

"Yeah, why not?"

Drew caught his lower lip between his teeth as he turned, washed up a plate, and set it on the drying rack he had laid out.

"Mom doesn't do what she calls re-runs. Never did."

"What? Really? What did she do with leftovers?"

Drew gave her what looked like an embarrassed look. "She threw them away."

"Threw them away?" Nadia pressed her hand to her chest at such blasphemy. She remembered her mother saving even half a cup of leftovers, wrapping it up in plastic if necessary. They wasted nothing in their family.

"Yep." Drew's clipped response underlined his previous shame. As did how quickly he turned away from her.

"Well, your family could afford it, I guess." Too late, she realized how that came out, but she couldn't take it back now.

"We could, but it always bugged me." He shrugged, then shot a quick glance her way as he put another plate on the rack. "But if you can transform them into something she won't recognize, please keep them."

"I will amaze and surprise you with my inventiveness."

"You always did."

His comment was offhand, but it hinted at a layer of history that created a tiny shiver of awareness.

She wasn't sure what to say to that, so she finished cleaning up the leftovers in silence, then put them in the refrigerator. She reached for the tea towel hanging on the stove's handle just as Drew did. When his warm fingers brushed hers, she yanked her hand back, as if burnt.

"Sorry," he muttered.

"No, I'm sorry. You startled me."

Which wasn't too far off the mark. What had surprised her was her inexplicable reaction to his light touch.

Of course, Drew had always lingered around the edges of her awareness. A watchful, waiting presence she could never ignore. Even when she was with Arlen, who was more charismatic, charming, and exuberant, if Drew was around, she always knew exactly where he was. Being away from him these past years had smudged and eased away the memories, but it disappointed her how quickly they now returned.

He dried the dishes while Nadia left to check on his mother.

Lily lay on her back, a faint snore filling the silence, a sleep mask crooked on her face. Nadia entered the room and adjusted it, smiling at the silky pink mask Lily insisted helped her sleep.

Lily twitched at Nadia's touch but then lay still. Nadia waited a moment to make sure she was still sleeping, then returned to the kitchen to finish cleaning up.

When she got back, Drew was wiping down the empty counters. He glanced back at her as he rinsed the cloth and hung it over the tap.

"Is she sleeping?"

"Yes, and from the sounds of the snoring, fairly deeply."

"Don't tell her she snores." Drew's mouth shifted into a crooked smile, and once again Nadia felt her heart give a slow flip.

He'd always been attractive, even when he was nose-deep in a book, frowning, ignoring her. But age had lengthened his face and given more definition to his jaw. A faint slope to his eyes gave him a mysterious look. Changing from his suit, which created a stand-offish look, to a t-shirt and blue jeans, only enhanced his appeal. Add the scruff now shading his lean jaw, and he looked like he could be shilling for high-end cologne.

As if sensing her scrutiny, Drew's smile deepened. "What's up?"

Nadia tried to shake off her reaction to him, but the smile didn't help. "Nothing. Just...thinking...remembering."

He grew serious at that. "I imagine it will take time before Arlen isn't so heavy on your mind."

She figured it would be easier to go with that than to admit what she was thinking. Drew's rejection of her still created a pinprick of embarrassment. No sense putting herself through that again.

"Probably. Though I'm sure it's the same for you."

"It's been a tough year, but I'm getting through it. Mom, though, she's struggling."

"I sense that." She was quiet for a beat, not wanting to add too much more to the comment.

"I...uh...made some tea, if you're interested."

She hesitated, not sure she wanted to spend so much time with him, then decided she and Drew would be sharing this space for the next two weeks, minimum. May as well try to make it feel as natural as she could.

"Sounds good. I'm not ready to go back to my book yet."

"Not that interesting?" Drew turned away from her, pulling some mugs out of the cupboard and setting them on a tray. Another familiar gesture. Drew always liked to do things right. He was the complete opposite of his brother, who had often told Drew he needed to lighten up. Wing it once in a while.

Look how that had turned out for Arlen.

She pushed down the grating memory, hoping, one day, she could think of Arlen without the twist and tangle of emotions she couldn't sort out.

"It's...okay. Not what I expected when I bought it." She latched onto the topic. Safe. Easy. A love of books was something she and Drew had always shared.

"What had you expected?"

"More intrigue. More secrets."

"You always did like a good mystery," Drew agreed, adding a light chuckle as he picked up the tray and walked past her into the living room.

"I enjoy being surprised," she shared, following him into the spacious living room. A soft leather couch and loveseat faced each other, flanking a fireplace whose rough stone chimney soared up to the second floor of the open-concept great room. That's what Lily called it. At Nadia's place, it was simply the living room. And much living was done in it.

"Do you? Not me." Drew set the tray down, and Nadia followed, dropping into the love seat and curling her legs up.

"I know. You always liked things tidy and predictable."

"That makes me sound boring," he grumbled but added a faint smile.

"Not boring. Settled was what I was going for. Frank, maybe. Might need to pull out my thesaurus to find something more complimentary."

His chuckle at her attempt at humor made her feel better than it should.

Drew poured the tea, and as he handed it to her, their fingers brushed.

It was the lightest of touches, but Nadia had to stop herself from pulling back. Drew looked away, running his hands down the legs of his blue jeans, and Nadia wondered if he had been as affected by the touch as she was. He poured himself some tea and settled down across from her, resting his feet on an ottoman in front of the couch.

"How do you think Mom is doing overall?" He asked as he cradled his mug, blowing over the steaming tea.

Guess we're doing that then, Nadia thought with a flicker of dismay that they wouldn't be continuing their previous conversation. She loved talking books with Drew. It was a connection she enjoyed and, as she grew older, she came to appreciate and look forward to it more and more.

"It's only been a day, but I think she'll make a good recovery. She's determined to be mobile by the sixteenth, which seems an arbitrary date to pick."

"It's not arbitrary at all," Drew grinned. "That would be about four days before Ellen Bannister was up and about. One advantage of her being so competitive."

"Is she?" Nadia said with a frown. "Competitive?"

Drew leveled her a frank gaze. "Have you seen my mother's house?"

"Of course, I have."

"Well then, you know what that looks like. How fancy it is and how she loves to point out its advantages over, let's say, Jenna Burke's house."

"I always thought that was more of your father's doing. I know he was an ambitious businessman, at least according to my father."

Drew took another sip of his tea. "He was that," he admitted. "But he never cared how big our house was, or how fancy it was. That was all my mom's doing. The house was her plan."

"It is a beautiful house; you have to admit that."

"It is, but it never felt as much like a home as your place did," he said.

"Our house was always a disaster," Nadia lamented, unable to keep the melancholy tone out of her voice. "Way too many bodies and too much chaos."

"I remember a lot of laughter."

"I remember being embarrassed," Nadia admitted.

"Why would you be embarrassed?"

"I had been to your place enough times to draw comparisons. Your house had beautiful furniture, stunning art on the wall, classical music playing, and scented candles. It was always elegant and peaceful." She smiled, her mind slipping back to those happy memories. Arlen on his best behavior, his father and mother were warm and welcoming. Making her feel like she was one of the most special people in the world. How his parents would talk to her, as if she was an adult, rather than yet another child in the long line of bodies clambering through her home.

"Each to his own, I guess," Drew said. "I know Arlen liked it; me not so much."

"Arlen did like the finer things in life, despite his bohemian attitude. I had always figured he got that from your mother." Arlen's tastes always ran to the expensive, which ended up being a cause of friction after they were married.

In fact, they had done a couple of trips together, with his friends, and she found out how much he liked to throw money around. Always the nicest restaurants. He was generous and often paid for everyone, but she could never figure out how he could afford what he did, despite his good job.

"He did have an incredible apartment."

"He did that," Nadia agreed.

"I always wondered how he could afford it once he quit that job."

"He did well with his painting until…"

"Until you separated," Drew finished for her.

She nodded. "He didn't paint as much after that, which meant he didn't sell as much, which meant he didn't make as much."

She stopped herself there, unwilling to delve into Arlen's finances.

"I figured as much." Drew shook his head. "I also guessed that was why he was willing to move into that dumpy apartment."

Nadia turned her attention back to her tea, focusing on the steam curling up from it, picking through her thoughts to find the right thing to say. "After we divorced, he struggled for a while," she shared, feeling like she was defending her ex-husband, Drew's brother, and trying not to take too much on. "I know there were times he was short of cash toward the end." She wasn't sure if Lily had stopped sending him money, or if he was just spending more on his bad habits.

Silence followed that, and Nadia wondered if Drew knew what his mother had been doing. She wondered how Lily could justify the money she had sent to Arlen when she guessed Drew didn't get as much.

"I like how you embellish his life for my mother," Drew told her. "Arlen never communicated much with me, so I was never sure where he was at. But if he was having financial difficulties, I wish he had asked."

"Too proud, I think. It was bad enough that he got –" Then she bit her lip, cutting off the next words, wondering if she had said too much of the wrong thing. She felt as if she was picking her way through a minefield. Not sure where to put her foot, or how hard. The pressure of trying to juggle her own tangled emotions and telling Lily what she wanted to hear.

And now Drew asking his own questions.

"You're probably right. I'm sure he wouldn't want me to know what was going on in his life. Especially since he was the one everyone figured could conquer anything in his way. Overcome all obstacles. Storm the castle to save the maiden."

Nadia smiled at the admiration in Drew's voice. "You always looked up to him, didn't you?"

"I did. I often wanted to be like him." Drew leaned

forward, setting his mug on the table, and looking across at Nadia.

"You didn't need to think that."

She didn't look away, their eyes latching onto each other. Something indefinable arced between them, and her breath hesitated, her heart struggled to find its rhythm.

He was the first to look away, and Nadia glanced down, wondering again at this pull she felt around him. When Drew had turned her down, she had assumed he didn't care for her. At all.

But the look he had just given her…

She took a sip of her tea, reminding herself that talking about Arlen was creating this heightened awareness. That was all it was.

"He was a good brother," Drew continued. "I just wish he had been more careful. We all lost a lot because of his care-lessness. And the world lost a great artist. Though based on what you're telling me, he was having a hard time with his art before he died." Another quick glance her way, but this time his eyes seemed to skip over her features.

"I know he struggled emotionally," Nadia said. "His paint-ings weren't quite…" her voice trailed off as she swallowed down a knot of guilty sorrow.

"Weren't quite what?" Drew pressed, his voice gentle. Understanding.

"Not up to his usual standards. I see the painting you have in the living room, and I see the talent he…he once had." Nadia bit her lip, her heart quivering, tears hovering as she clutched her mug, fighting for self-control.

"Hey, you okay?"

She couldn't look at him. Not after the previous connec-tion they had unwittingly shared. She was afraid if she did, he would see the truth in her eyes.

She put her mug down and stood as if to leave, but Drew was right in front of her.

"I'm sorry if talking about Arlen has made you upset," he apologized, reaching out, his hand resting lightly on her arm. It was simply a consoling gesture, but his touch seemed to burn through the fabric of her shirt.

When he pulled his hand away, she realized he felt it, too. This unwieldy allure that, it seemed, neither knew what to do with.

Had he changed his mind about her?

Yet, despite how she felt, she couldn't dismiss the words he'd thrown at her when she had told him how she felt all those years ago. The sneer on his face when he said he wasn't interested in her. That he had some pride, after all. It had been enough for her to run away as far and as quickly as she could. The next day, she was in Toronto and looking up Arlen.

Nadia was about to excuse herself when her phone dinged at almost exactly the same time as Drew's did.

As she glanced down at hers, she saw Aria's number flash onto Drew's phone, and Lucas was calling her.

They separated to have their conversations.

"How are things coming with the party planning?" Lucas asked.

"Been kind of busy," Nadia told him, firing a glance Drew's way.

She heard him apologizing as well.

And for the same thing.

Nadia turned away, walking toward the kitchen and lowering her voice. "Is Drew supposed to be working on this party thing as well?"

How much were their lives supposed to intersect? Seriously.

"Yeah. Aria couldn't get Courtney to help, so she asked Drew. She's just checking in with him now and letting him know you're on the case as well."

"Perfect."

"Anyhow, I told Karissa and Burke that you would be coming to the farm sometime soon. Preferably Saturday."

"Of course, but I'm taking care of Drew's mother. She just had hip surgery."

"So I heard. She might like an outing as well by then."

He was probably right. Patrice had encouraged Lily to keep as mobile as possible. The drive to the farm wasn't that long. By then, she would be a bit more mobile, and it would be good for her to get out.

"Okay. I'll talk to Drew and see if that works for him."

She ended the call just as Drew ended his. Then she turned to look at him.

He was shaking his head.

"Guess we'll be spending even more time together," he said.

His grumpy tone was bad enough.

The sigh he added just made it worse.

Chapter 4

"So where should we put the tent?" Drew asked, looking over the yard of the Prins farm.

"I know Aria wants it by the lake," Nadia said, "But I think it should be closer to the barn. That way if it rains, we have more room for people to get away from it."

"But I thought that was the purpose of the tent."

Nadia shook her head, taking the folder from Drew's hands. Once again, her touch created very unwelcome reactions. "The tent is for protection from the sun more than anything and to give us something to hang the paper lanterns from."

"Paper lanterns?" Drew wanted to snatch the folder from Nadia's hands to check if she was right. "I don't remember reading anything about paper lanterns."

"I'm kidding," Nadia teased, tapping him with the folder.

He figured it was a coy gesture, but it rubbed him wrong; like she was patronizing him.

"Are you sure you don't want the tent by the lake?" Lily asked from her chair by the barn. "That way people can watch the sun set over the water."

"They can see it better from the spot I suggested," Nadia put in. "It's higher up."

"I suppose you're right." But Drew could tell his mother wasn't convinced. Then she folded her hands on the blanket, a pensive smile tugging at her mouth. "This is a beautiful spot for a party. Did you and Arlen ever think about getting married here?"

Drew couldn't help a quick glance Nadia's way. She was staring down at the folder as if looking for an answer there.

"Well, I'm sure Arlen would have considered this place for your wedding," his mother continued. "I know he often spoke with admiration about how beautiful it was, and I can see he wasn't exaggerating. You two must have sat on that dock often," she said, glancing over at Nadia, her voice breaking.

Nadia said nothing for a beat, and Drew shot a glance her way, once again wishing his mother would stop bringing up her relationship with Arlen.

Nadia walked over to Lily, her hand resting on his mother's shoulder. "We sat on the end of the dock and watched the sun go down. Waved to boats going by. It was kind of a family thing."

"He must have enjoyed spending time with your family. I think your cowboy brothers were more his type than Drew was. I'm sure he enjoyed their company."

"He did, but I know my brothers also liked spending time with Drew," she pointed out.

Her defense surprised him, as did the concerned look she shot his way. As if his mother's comments might have bothered him.

He gave her a light smile and added a shrug as if to say he was fine.

"What are some things you and Arlen did here?" Lily asked, predictably bringing the conversation back to his brother.

"We'd go canoeing and play with my brother, who seemed

to like Arlen as well," Nadia recalled. "If you look at that point over there, that's where our family used to go fishing if the motorboats weren't too plentiful. Arlen would do that with us."

"He must have so enjoyed being here." Lily sighed again, patting Nadia on the hand. "I'm sure you enjoyed being with him."

Nadia said nothing to that, and Drew restrained a flicker of irritated impatience.

"Now that we have chosen the spot for the tent, should we figure out how we can run power to it?" he asked, refocusing the conversation.

"Of course." Nadia stood, her lips pressed together as if her memories of Arlen caused her pain.

He felt like a jerk for the abrupt switch in topic, and when she passed him, he caught her hand, bringing her closer with a gentle tug. "I'm sorry," he said, keeping his voice low. "I should be more sensitive to your memories of my brother."

Nadia glanced back at his mother, then gave him a tight smile. "It's okay. I was ready to change the subject. It's difficult talking about him. I prefer to leave his memory in the past, but I know your mother wants to hear stories, so I give them to her. It's the least I can do."

"I understand, but you should think about your needs as well."

She gave him a probing look, which was followed by another glance his mother's way. "Thanks for that." She turned back to him, their eyes clinging just a few seconds longer, and when she pulled her hand out of his and walked away, he felt a sense of loss.

"You must be Drew," he heard a voice say.

He turned away from Nadia as a young woman walked toward him, favoring one leg.

"I'm Roxie," she told him, holding out her hand. "Nadia's little sister."

He was about to say that she didn't look so little to him. Thank goodness he caught himself in time. He had learned a few things since he was that awkward young man who wasn't sure how to talk to girls.

"I can see a resemblance," he went with instead.

"Prins blood is potent." She pushed her blonde hair away from her face. "Though RayAnn and I didn't end up with Nadia's thick hair or Celeste's aqua- colored eyes." Roxie blew out a sigh. "Just plain stringy blonde hair and watery blue eyes."

Now what was he supposed to say?

The truth, he figured.

"I don't know why you're putting yourself down like that," he managed. "You have a beauty all your own."

Oh boy, was he laying it on a bit thick? It sounded corny to him.

But Roxie just gave him a coy smile, curving a lock of hair behind her ear. "You think so?"

"Of course I do. I don't lie."

"But you're a lawyer. I know my brother Lucas always makes a joke. How can you tell if a lawyer is lying —"

"His lips are moving," Drew finished for her, shaking his head. "And somehow, Lucas still ended up engaged to one."

Roxie gave him a shrewd look, then laughed out loud. "You know what, you're right!"

"Lawyers are an easy target, but when you need one, you're not making jokes about them anymore."

"I can see that," Roxie agreed. "I know Aria gets annoyed with Lucas when he makes jokes about her work. But she can tease him back, so it's all good."

"For what it's worth, I'm not a talented liar, so what I just told you was true."

"Aria said you were a great guy."

"Really? When did she say that?"

"When the guys were talking about your brother. Arlen, I think his name was? How you two were so different."

"That we are," Drew admitted.

"I vaguely remember him coming here with Nadia. I was a lot younger then." Roxie made a face. "I didn't like him very much. He used to tease me and RayAnn. But not in a fun way."

Drew knew what she meant. Arlen, when uncomfortable, had a mean streak. Not wide, or deep, but it drifted to the surface whenever he felt threatened or unsure of himself. Drew had been on the receiving end of Arlen's anxiety as it switched to anger and was spent on whoever was near. Usually Drew. Sometimes their father.

Never their mother.

"What else do you need to go over?" Lily asked, her voice holding a chiding tone.

"I just need to decide where to put the pots of flowers Aria wanted," Nadia called out from behind him.

She walked up beside him and looked down at the folder he had opened to a plan Aria had drawn up.

"We'll have to change one thing off the top," Nadia said, moving closer to have a better look, a faint warmth driving off her body. Again, he caught the vague citrus scent of her perfume. "The row of flowering plants Aria wanted in front of the tent will have to be moved because of where we're placing the tent."

"Which row?" Drew asked, not sure what she was talking about.

Her arm brushed his as she pointed to a spot on the plan Aria had printed out. In triplicate, no less.

"Right there," she indicated, her finger tracing the line of leafy circles leading to the tent's opening. "If we put the tent closer to the barn, which I think we should do, then we won't have room for this lovely aisle of flowers."

"You could still do something like that if you shift the

opening of the tent here," Roxie put in, coming along his other side.

"But we won't be able to make it as long." Nadia's finger still lay on the paper, moving as if trying to figure out an alternate plan.

"You could put them here," Roxie suggested. "What do you think, Drew?"

"I'm not being paid to think. I'm just being paid to hold this folder."

"You're not being paid at all," Nadia teased, patting his arm. It was the lightest of touches, a grazing of her fingers over his shirt, but it created a jolt of awareness. "But thanks for being the folder holder. It's an important job while we consult."

Again, her gaze darted to his and he felt that low-level thrum of captivation. Her eyes grew liquid, her features relaxed, and her lips slightly parted.

"Um, are we flirting, or are we doing party stuff?" Roxie teased.

Drew snapped his attention back to the plans, clearing his throat like he tended to when nervous. A dumb tic from law school.

"Nadia is not flirting." Lily's tone was aggrieved, and Drew was surprised she heard or that she was even paying attention. But a quick glance his mother's way showed she was laser focused on what was happening.

"Oh, I don't know about that." Roxie laughed. "Celeste always said that Nadia knew best of all the girls how to lead a guy on."

"That's what you're going with?" Nadia responded, but she didn't sound put out. "And since when does Celeste confide in you? I thought you were annoyed with her?"

"Nah. We're getting along real good now."

"That's good to hear."

"Yeah, now that she knows I'm not eloping with Wade's

partner Vince, she and Wade haven't been all mother hen-ish."

"You were going to elope with Vince?"

"Of course not. It was just a silly joke."

"I'm sure Celeste didn't see it that way."

"No, but with me and Celeste getting along, I had to adjust my expectations of her."

"Speaking of adjusting expectations," Drew remarked dryly, annoyed by the give and take going past him. Like he wasn't even there. "I was expecting we would make party plans, not talking about peripheral and unimportant things."

Nadia nudged his arm in a teasing gesture. "Let's just call that a sidebar."

"An unimportant sidebar, I'm thinking." He tried not to sound grumpy, but it was a tad annoying to be talked past.

"You're right, that was rude. I'm sorry." Then, to his dismay, Nadia gave him a quick, one-armed hug, which he tried not to think of as patronizing.

"So, let's get back to where we're putting the plants, and I cannot believe I'm actually saying these words out loud," he grumbled.

"I'll leave you to it." Roxie gave Drew a sly wink as she turned and walked back to Lily, who was watching him and Nadia, a deep frown creasing her forehead.

He tried to shrug it off, but it was as if he could feel her disapproval washing over him. How dare he spend any time with her beloved Arlen's wife?

Ex-wife, he reminded himself.

Not that it should matter. He wasn't going down that road again.

But when she pulled him aside, asking him to check out the barn with her, he felt his determination waver.

Just a bit.

"SORRY ABOUT DUCKING AWAY HERE," Nadia said once they entered the cool, dim barn. "I just needed a bit of space."

Lily was making her feel claustrophobic, the way she stared at her, narrowed eyes locked on Nadia's every move.

"I get what you're saying," Drew agreed, still holding onto the papers Aria had given him. "I'm sure she's just missing Arlen."

Nadia shivered in the cool air of the barn, struggling with her own memories, not sure what to say or how to say it. When she took this job, she didn't think Arlen would be so much front and center in Lily's thoughts.

Or Drew's.

"Anyhow, I figured we could talk a few things over here without my family interrupting," Nadia said. "And we could look this over and try to figure out how we could use the space."

That sounded professional and in charge. On the surface it was true, but if she were honest, a part of her just wanted to talk to him alone.

The other night had been more enjoyable than she dared admit. Drew was always easy to be around, despite the awkwardness of their last interaction. Before she left Aspen Valley all those years ago.

Drew set the folder aside, looking around the space. "It's set up pretty nice. I'm surprised."

"We've had a few parties here, and since I left, Burke and Karissa have spiffed it up. I think she'd hoped it might be a potential event place. Who knows? But it works in our favor." They had cleaned the entire barn. Someone had ripped out the old stalls. The cement floor was covered with strips of pine wood, and the walls were stained a deep brown. The windows had been enlarged, making the entire space lighter, and the ladder to the loft had been replaced by stairs. Burke had installed a fireplace at one end of the barn, and a few older sofas bracketed the hearth.

"Looks cozy."

"We could set up the snacks and drinks inside, and then people could either sit outside or in here." She tapped her finger as she looked around the barn, smiling at the transformation from the dusty space she and her siblings used to play hide and go seek in.

"What's up here?" Drew asked, walking to the steps.

"I don't know anymore." Nadia hadn't been in the loft yet, but she remembered all too well scooting up the ladder only to be yelled at by one of the older siblings who had planned a romantic interlude with whoever they were dating.

In fact, she and Arlen had spent time up there as well.

Her cheeks flushed at the memory.

"Should probably check it out," he said, glancing back at her.

Was that a coy look?

She shook off her reaction, blaming it on an unwelcome heightened awareness of him. Drew had gained a confidence that enhanced the appeal of his now-rugged features. It didn't help that, once again, he was wearing blue jeans and a t-shirt that sculpted his defined chest and shoulders. Thankfully, he stepped aside for her to go up the loft ahead of him. Once at the top, she had to smile.

"Wow, this has changed a lot," she declared as she turned, looking at the now-stained exposed beams and the skylights that lit up the corners of the loft.

"We spent so much time up here," she continued, walking toward a door at the end of the loft. "This thing used to scare the dickens out of me," she admitted, still unable to suppress a shiver as she turned the handle on it. But instead of the yawning space that it previously opened up into, now she could step out onto a small balcony.

"This is perfect," Drew said from behind her. "Aria and

Lucas can wave to the populace below and share a balcony kiss."

Nadia chuckled at that but couldn't stop a shiver of vertigo as she looked down onto the yard below. She saw Lily and Roxie chatting away, which surprised her. Roxie usually couldn't be bothered to talk to anyone who couldn't either give her makeup tips or fashion advice.

My little sister is growing up, Nadia thought with a pang.

"I can imagine Lucas hamming it up," Nadia said. "I heard that he and Aria were in the community play together."

"Oh yes. A western version of Pride and Prejudice. Quite the Aspen Valley production. Too bad you missed that."

"I missed a lot," Nadia lamented with a melancholy tone as she looked over the yard at the lake beyond. A few more houses now edged the lake, a sign of the changing landscape of the community. The broad expanse of water still called to her, bringing back many memories of canoeing with her sisters and water skiing with friends whose parents owned fast motorboats.

"Do you regret your time away?" Drew had stepped to her side and leaned on the railing, and they both looked out at the landscape leading up to the craggy mountain slopes, which were now a muted blue-gray against the blue sky.

"I do in some ways. I missed out on so many changes. Brothers settling down, my sister married and having a baby. Oh sure, I came back for the weddings and the parties, but then I went back to work again or to traveling."

"You and Arlen made several trips, didn't you?"

Was that a tiny note of condemnation in his voice? Or was she just projecting?

"We did. We both enjoyed traveling." She tried not to sound defensive. She had worked hard to save money to pay for her part of each trip, even though she was still going to school. Even though Arlen always offered to pay.

She shook off the thoughts, spinning around to release

them, and almost ran right into Drew. She stumbled and would have fallen over, but he caught her by the shoulders, steadying her. He didn't remove his hands right away, and she stayed where she was, her heart leaping in her chest. They faced each other, inches apart. She saw the hazel flecks in his eyes, the thick lashes she had always envied. Their gazes locked, connection pulsing between them. His hands shifted from holding to caressing. Her hand, as if working independently from her brain, came to rest on his chest, her fingers curling against his shirt.

"I wish –"

"I'm sorry –"

They both spoke at the same time, so close that their breath and words intermingled. A sense of wonder and curiosity filled her heart, an urge to know and experience more.

Drew's hand came up to finger a strand of hair away from her face. She turned her head, just enough, leaning into his touch. Her fingers spread, caressing his chest, sliding to his back.

She wanted to lean into him, rest her head against him, and lose herself in his arms.

So close. He was so close. So inviting. She sensed him moving closer and could feel his warmth against her.

What are you doing?

Her brain shifted into "normal" mode, and she jerked her gaze away, stepping back from him just as his hand lowered.

She had to swallow down a flood of emotions.

You have no right. No right at all.

And with those words ringing in her ears, she hurried down the steps.

Chapter 5

He only had to get through today, and then he could return to the office. Back to his routine and the predictability of work.

Safe.

Drew wrapped his tie around his neck, making quick work of cinching up the knot. He ran a quick brush through his hair, still damp from his shower. He could hear Nadia talking to his mother on the floor below him in the house, where it sounded like they were doing her exercises. Even the sound of Nadia's voice created a low-level thrum in his chest.

He resented the fact that his home had become such an emotional vortex. His encounter with Nadia at the Prins farm yesterday had chipped away at his self-control.

Then, all the way back home, his mother had continued quizzing Nadia about Arlen's comings and goings. As if recounting even the simplest facts of his day-to-day life would satisfy the emptiness Drew knew Arlen's death had created in their mother's world.

So Nadia complied. She talked about his favorite coffee, the art shop where he bought supplies. Places where he liked to hang out. Movies they had watched. Trips they had made. Arlen's dissatisfaction with work. All interspersed with sighs from his mother about how the world was poorer for Arlen's death.

An artist snuffed out on the verge of his greatest works.

Drew had let the words slide over him, focusing instead on the case he was working on, planning his strategy. As soon as they got home, he hightailed it back to the office, muttering vague comments about having to catch up on work, when he was already caught up.

Now, he just had to get through church and then the lunch afterward that his mother always insisted on. But this time, he would leave right away afterward, instead of sticking around to play the games that she enjoyed.

Today he was visiting Courtney and Cole so that he could catch up with them. He had talked about buying a horse, and Courtney had thought she might have one for him. Today would be a perfect day to check that out.

He heard the clink of cutlery downstairs and the smell of toast and coffee brewing. Breakfast time, which meant he couldn't put off going downstairs any longer.

A quick glance around his room showed him there was nothing else to do. Bed made. Closet tidy. Floor clean.

Okay, Lord. Going to need your help here, he prayed, slipping on his suit jacket.

He didn't like the feelings Nadia created in him. Especially because he suspected she was still grieving for his brother.

His mother sat in her wheelchair, pulled up to the table, drinking her coffee, chatting with Nadia.

Lily was discussing the quilt she was half-done making. Karissa, Nadia's sister-in-law, was helping her with it.

"Did you ever do any sewing?" his mother asked Nadia as Drew made his way into the kitchen, heading to the coffee pot.

"No, it's not something I enjoy doing. My mother did. In fact, I think she sewed most of our clothes, but none of the girls took after her with that. She loved making our Sunday dresses."

"I don't think I would want to sew dresses, but I often wished for a girl I could buy cute clothes for. The boys were so basic. Shirts. Blue jeans. Basic sweaters and those horrible hoodies." She glanced over at Drew, giving him a warm smile. "Though I don't remember you wearing hoodies that often, Drew. You preferred sweaters and shirts."

"And doesn't that make me sound like a total geek?" Drew chuckled. He walked over to her and brushed a light kiss over her cheek. "How did you sleep?"

"Not great. I had so many dreams. Not pleasant dreams either."

"It's probably the pain medication," Nadia sympathized, spreading jam on her toast. "It can do funny things to your brain."

"I think talking about Arlen didn't help," his mother admitted, her voice pained.

"Maybe you should talk about something else, then," Drew couldn't help saying.

Nadia's mug hit the table with a *thunk*, and Drew shot a frown her way just as he caught her biting her lip. He wondered if she'd had dreams about Arlen as well. Wondered if he had been as insensitive as his mother, at times, accused him of being.

Just get through this, he reminded himself, wishing, not for the first time, that he could have found someone other than his brother's ex-wife to take care of his mother.

Which was a foolish wish. Lord knows he had tried.

He grabbed his laptop and sat down at the table. It looked rude, but right now he needed the security of hiding behind it.

"Reading the news?" his mother asked, wiping her mouth and pushing her plate away.

"Yes. Not looking good."

"Does it ever?" Nadia put in.

He glanced over the top of his screen at her, but she was focused on stirring sugar into her tea. At least, he assumed it was tea from the tag and string hanging out the side of the cup.

"Aren't you having breakfast?" His mother asked him, wiping her mouth with her napkin.

"Not hungry."

"Now, my dear boy, you know breakfast is the most important meal of the day."

"Hasn't been proven," he muttered, scrolling through the news, then switching it off to go through his mail.

He frowned as he noticed a message in a mailbox he hadn't used for a long time. One he kept meaning to delete but kept around because he wasn't sure which accounts it was connected to. He ran the mail through a virus scan. No attachments. It came from a Gmail account. Not a familiar name.

The subject line jumped at him. "Is this Drew Rozak?"

He hesitated. Seemed scammy to him. But most of his spam came to his current address. He rarely got anything sent to this e-mail. And if he didn't click any links, he'd be okay. So, curiosity made him open it.

"Hello, Drew. At least I hope this is Drew Rozak," the e-mail started out. "You don't know me, but my name is Carrie Bukowski. I'm friends with Darnelle Jacobs from Port Alberni. I need to talk to you. Please send me a text so I know I got the right person." Then she gave him her cell phone number.

His chest hollowed out when he read Darnelle's name. She was a shadowy figure from a past he had dealt with, then put behind him. A lapse in judgment.

"Is everything okay?" The concern in Nadia's voice made him jerk his head up, hoping he didn't look as disconcerted as he felt.

He gave her what he hoped was a reassuring smile.

"Yeah. Just got something I need to take care of."

He wasn't taking care of it here in front of his mother and Nadia.

"I'll have to go to the office for this. Sorry."

"You won't be taking us to church?" His mother's tone was peeved, and her look held a note of condemnation. "How will we get there?"

He blew out his breath. Right. He forgot Nadia didn't have a vehicle. Guess he would have to handle this here. Otherwise, it would be nagging at him until he did. "Sure. Of course, I am."

He closed his laptop with a snap. Without another glance at his mother or Nadia, he tucked his laptop under his arm, grabbed his phone, and went upstairs.

As soon as he closed the door behind him, he texted the number Carrie had given him.

> This is Drew Rozak. I'd like to know what this is about.

He hesitated before sending it.

Normally he would have assumed it was a disgruntled ex-client or connected to an older case, but Darnelle was a name he knew all too well.

And she had nothing to do with any case he'd ever worked on.

He hit "send," and then waited.

It showed as "Delivered," then "Read."

He waited for the bouncing dots to show him a reply, but nothing. A few more minutes, but still no reply.

Hoping he wasn't getting set up for a scam, he turned his phone on silent and tucked it inside his suit jacket pocket.

For a moment he stood still, his mind sifting backward, still trying to sort out the emotions the memories of Darnelle created.

Forgive me, Lord, was all he could say.

Maybe going to church was exactly what he needed to do today.

‎——‎

"MAY the Lord bless you and keep you: the Lord make His face shine on you and be gracious to you. May the Lord turn His face toward you and give you peace."

Pastor Muller held his hands out in blessing.

Nadia had to swallow a sudden and unexpected knot of emotion at the memories flowing over her. Sitting in the Prins family pew, flanked by her siblings, her mother listening intently to the pastor, as if to absorb his words and let them give her strength for the week ahead. With ten children, who could blame her? She needed every scrap of encouragement and energy she could eke out of the sermon and the songs.

Nadia used to enjoy coming to church, but then she moved away from Aspen Valley, determined to redefine herself, which also meant, in her mind, staying away from church.

Her loss, she realized as she let the pastor's blessing soak in along with the song they were now singing.

"Go now into the world,
taking God's love and strength and peace,
Find your hope in the Lord
And in his arms, release.
Your guilt, your fears,
No longer yours
They are removed by God's pure love
Which forever and ever more endures."

Nadia closed her eyes, letting the words ease into her troubled soul, her hands clenched against a heart that had held too much pain and regret.

Could it really be taken away?

Could she really release the burden she'd carried the past few years?

Yes. You can.

The words whispered into her mind, sliding around the edges of her consciousness, offering comfort.

But she couldn't grasp it. Not yet.

She pulled in a deep breath and lifted her head, catching Drew looking at her in her peripheral vision.

Could she tell him? Would he understand?

Would Lily?

A heavy lid slammed down on the box holding her questions. Lily would never understand. Or forgive.

She swallowed again, struggling to regain the moment of peace she felt after the pastor's blessing and during the first few bars of the song.

All her life, she'd been told that God forgives. She had accepted that truth as easily as a child accepts a parent's love. It was natural. Ordinary.

But when faced with an actual situation, an actual test?

A little harder to blithely accept.

"Are you okay?" Drew asked, his hand resting on her arm.

Her gaze slipped to his, and in his eyes, she read concern. His hand resting lightly on her shoulder underlined the sense that he, of all people, might understand.

"You seem upset," he continued, keeping his voice low.

Though her eyes were locked on Drew, Nadia was also aware of Lily watching them both.

"Maybe later."

As the words slipped out, she felt as if she had committed herself to something she might regret. Did she want to see Drew's gaze shift? The past few days she had felt a growing attraction between them. Yesterday, inside the barn, she had come so close to kissing him, and she knew, deep in her soul, that he would have kissed her back.

He's Arlen's brother. Arlen, the beloved one.

The words were like acid dripping into her already vulnerable soul.

So, she turned away.

The service ended, and people greeted each other. The mother of the young family beside her was reprimanding the youngest, who had been wiggling beside Drew the entire service.

The older woman in front of her turned and said hi. Nadia couldn't place her.

"Debbie Properzi," she offered in a helpful voice. "I'm Karissa's aunt. I used to own the store that Karissa does. I remember your sisters and mother coming in to buy fabric. She loved making stuff for you."

Nadia sifted through her memories and slowly one returned. Herself as a young girl, staring at bolts of fabric, wondering why this lady had so much.

"Yes, I remember. I loved looking through all the fabric. Though I loved the notions too."

"Your mother made you and your sisters some pretty cute outfits."

Another memory resurfaced. Coming to church and trying not to be embarrassed because she and her sisters all had the same skirt and ribbons in their braided hair.

"All matching," Nadia added.

"Cheaper for her that way."

Nadia chuckled at that, and then someone else was vying for Debbie's attention, so she turned back to Lily, who was also talking to someone Nadia vaguely remembered.

"I'll have to come and visit sometime," the attractive woman said, then smiled over at Nadia. "And how lovely to see you back as well."

"Nice to be back," Nadia murmured, returning the smile, a bit too embarrassed to ask for her name.

Then Drew's voice, low and soft, whispered in her ear, "Mary Cosgrove. Mother to Kip Cosgrove. Also had surgery."

She tried to suppress the shiver dancing down her spine at the feel of his breath on her ear, his voice low and almost intimate.

"You're welcome to come any time, Mrs. Cosgrove," Nadia added. "I'm sure Lily would be encouraged by stories about how you recuperated from your own surgery."

"Well, now, I sure hope I can be of some comfort," Mary said, beaming at Nadia. She patted Lily's arm, then walked away.

Lily glanced over at Nadia, her smile less bright. She looked tired.

"We should get you back home," she said, stepping into the aisle and grasping the handles of the wheelchair to turn her around. But before she did, she couldn't help a glance in Drew's direction, and she mouthed a quick, "thank you," netting her a grin and a faint wink.

Which didn't help her determination to keep her distance at all.

Chapter 6

Drew closed his laptop and checked his phone one more time.

Since this morning, he'd heard nothing more from Carrie. He'd had to resist the urge to check his phone every few minutes, but his watch would notify him if a text came through.

He'd have to sit down with Nadia tonight to discuss the preparations for the party. Today he'd gone to Cole and Courtney's place for lunch. Afterward, he and Cole went out riding, a test run of the horse Courtney wanted to sell him. Now he was stiff, but it was worth it all to be away from the house, his mother, and Nadia.

Things were shifting between him and Nadia, and he wasn't sure what to make of it. It was as if he couldn't keep himself from looking her way, finding obscure reasons to touch her. And he had the uncanny notion that she felt the same.

How else to explain the magnetism that sparked between them, almost as real as a touch?

Of course, falling for her again was never in the plans. He was determined to keep his distance. Especially the way she was always going on about Arlen.

He knew part of it was because of his mother, but he couldn't shake the feeling there was another agenda behind her conversations about his brother. Some unknown emotion he couldn't put his finger on. The last thing he needed or wanted was to have his brother's ghost haunting his changing relationship with Nadia.

He gave his head a shake, not liking the way his thoughts meandered.

He'd avoided his mother and Nadia long enough. After returning from Cole and Courtney's, he'd taken a shower and changed again. He'd dawdled as much as he dared. Time to go down and make nice.

His mother's wheelchair was pulled up to the dining room table, a Scrabble board on the table in front of her and Nadia, who sat with her back to him.

His mother looked up when he entered. "So, you finally decided to join us?"

A little too much emphasis on the "finally," but he let it go. His mother could do passive-aggressive better than most.

"Yes. I got lonely up in my room," he joked as he walked past Nadia, bent over, and dutifully brushed a kiss over his mother's cheek. When she smiled up at him, catching his hand and giving it a light squeeze, all was forgiven.

He often had to remind himself of all his mother had lost. Her husband, her son, her mobility. She'd never been an especially patient person, so of course she would struggle with dissatisfaction.

"How are you doing with the game?" he asked, standing by his mother and resting his hand on her shoulder. A moment of mother and son bonding.

"I got the word 'nannies' on a triple word score, emptied my rack, pluralized off another six-letter word, so pretty good, I'd say."

"I would say so, too," Drew agreed, looking down at the

tangle of words on the board. "But you might be stuck with that Q."

His mother tapped his hand in reprimand. "Don't give away my letters."

"Doesn't matter. I know you have it because we're almost at the end and it hasn't shown up yet and I don't have it," Nadia said.

"Thanks for coming to my defense," Drew added, giving Nadia what he hoped was a casual smile.

Then she glanced up at him, and there it was again. That feeling that time had lost its shape, and they had shifted back to that moment, that one kiss they had shared. A kiss that marked a huge turning point for Drew. When he knew beyond a doubt that he would never care for anyone the way he cared for Nadia.

In fact, it had been part of the reason things hadn't worked out for him and Aria.

Or him and Darnelle.

"Any time," Nadia returned, turning her attention back to the game. She put some words down and added up her score.

Drew noticed that she had left a "U" accessible. He wondered if his mother would notice. She hated being patronized.

"Ah. There. The perfect spot for my Q," Lily crowed as she put her tiles down, spelling the word Quick. "And on a double word score, no less."

"Good eye, Mom," Drew said, stifling a smirk. Her competitiveness overcame her dislike of being helped along.

Once again, his gaze meshed with Nadia's, and he felt the lapping of emotions he didn't know if he should explore.

"Did you get your work stuff sorted out?" His mother asked. "You seemed worried about it."

For a moment, he wasn't sure what she was referring to, then he recalled what he had said when the text on his phone came in this morning.

"Not yet, but I'm not too concerned." Which was another lie. Unease had been nipping at him all day.

His mother laid down the last of her tiles and sat back with a grin of satisfaction. The game was over, and she had won handily.

Then she rolled her head, yawning. "I'm tired now. I'd like to turn in for the night."

"If you need any help to get her into bed, just let me know," Drew said, his gaze once again skittering over Nadia.

"I think we'll manage, but thanks for the offer." Nadia rose and was about to clean up the game when Drew stopped her.

"I'll clean up. You go take care of my mother."

Another tight nod and a few moments later he heard his mother talking, Nadia giving her instructions.

He dropped the tiles into the velvet bag that they had always used, feeling a glimmer of nostalgia. He and Arlen used to play, and his mother always complained at how noisy they were. How much they laughed. They would make up nonsensical words, sometimes stealing each other's tiles.

The memory created another pang as he put the game away. He knew it would take time before his memories of Arlen would cause him to smile, rather than make him feel twinges of guilt and pain.

Having his mother and Nadia constantly revisit their recollections of Arlen didn't help.

He walked into the kitchen to plug in the kettle. He had a hankering for a cup of hot chocolate. Maybe throw a shot of Baileys in it, too, if he was feeling adventurous.

Twenty minutes later, Nadia came down the hallway and paused at the entrance to the living room, as if she wasn't sure whether she should enter.

Drew put his mug down and stood. "I made myself some hot chocolate. Do you want some? I can throw some Baileys in if you like."

"That sounds amazing," she said as she lowered herself

onto the loveseat across from the couch. She looked tired, but Drew knew better than to say anything. No woman likes to be told she doesn't look her best. Drew had found that out the hard way.

He made her drink and brought it back to her.

She had already kicked off her shoes and curled her feet up under her, looking comfortably at home. It made him feel good to see her so at ease in his house.

She took the mug from him with a sigh of gratitude.

"Long day?" he asked, feeling a flicker of guilt at leaving her with his mother all day.

"Not too bad. Your mom had a long nap this afternoon, and so did I." She took a grateful sip of her hot chocolate, closing her eyes in bliss. "This is delicious. Thank you so much."

Drew dropped onto the couch across from her, resting his feet on the coffee table between them.

"I bet you wouldn't dare do that if your mother was up and about," Nadia teased him.

"This is my house," Drew protested. "I can do whatever I want."

Nadia didn't reply, just arched a questioning eyebrow at him, and he shrugged.

"I concede. I wouldn't dare do this in front of my mother. Even though it's my home and I paid for everything here, my mom still wields a heavy influence."

Nadia chuckled, "And how was your visit at Courtney and Cole's place?"

"It was good. Had a great time. Even did some riding."

"I imagine that hasn't happened in a while," Nadia returned.

"Sure didn't do any of it when I was living in Toronto."

"How is the baby?"

Drew shrugged, not sure what to say. "Sleeping?"

"What? You didn't hold the precious infant?"

"I don't do babies well." But he smiled to ease any misconception she might have. After all, who admits to not connecting with babies? May as well say you don't like puppies.

A silence rose between them, but it was gentle, comfortable.

"What made you decide to come back to Aspen Valley?" she finally asked, cradling her mug in front of her.

Her question surprised him, but he figured it wouldn't hurt to have some casual conversation. Maybe it would ease some of the tension he felt around her. "I got tired of the city. I got tired of the cut and thrust of the law firm where I was working. I came back for a visit to see my mother and father. Then Aria and I spent an afternoon catching up. When she told me that her law practice was getting busier, I didn't say anything, not wanting to put her in a tricky position. Later on, she offered me a partnership."

"You used to date her, right?"

"Yeah, a while back. After she and Lucas broke up. But we were more friends than anything. We decided it wouldn't work. Probably the only amicable split I've ever had with a girlfriend."

"You've had more?"

Was his overactive imagination reading a note of jealousy in her voice?

"Of course I have." As he spoke the words, his mind ticked back to the few weeks he'd spent with Darnelle. They had met in a coffee shop that they both frequented. She was new in town. Lonely. As was Drew.

She broke up with him when she moved back to Port Alberni. Said she wasn't into long-distance relationships. Though he had tried to contact her, she never replied, and then she faded out of his life.

Until now.

He pushed that sinister thought down, wondering when he would hear back from Carrie.

"I'm so sorry," Nadia apologized, breaking into his thoughts. "I was kind of kidding. It's no surprise to me that you've had other girlfriends. Just that you have found no one to share your life with."

"I'm picky." He smiled to show her that there was no harm done.

"Do you like being back here?"

"You sound surprised," he returned. "As if you couldn't imagine why anyone would choose to come back here. Does that mean your stay here isn't permanent?"

She shrugged. "Not yet. I love being back with my family, but I have spent so much of my life wanting to move away from Aspen Valley. I feel like it would take something major to make me want to stay."

"Major? As in life-changing?" he teased.

"Something like that."

"As for your question," Drew continued, "I am happy here. I like the fact that I can walk down the street and say hi to anyone, go into a coffee shop, sit at just about any table, and strike up a conversation."

"Are all your memories of Aspen Valley good?"

Again, that subtext, as if she was trying to tweak out something he hadn't told her yet.

"Most of them are good," he admitted. "But there is one…" He stopped himself, wondering why he even ventured there. Then shrugged as he took another sip of his drink.

"Just one? I thought there'd be more. I know people here didn't always treat you so well."

"I wasn't treated badly. Ignored mostly because Arlen seemed to use up all the oxygen wherever he went."

"He sure did that. Arlen was comfortable with attention. But you seemed content to keep the focus away from you."

"I wasn't that much of a wallflower," he protested.

"No, you weren't. You had your own quiet appeal."

He wasn't sure what to say to that as she looked over at him, her gaze seeming to delve into him. Again, looking for something. Finally, he decided to face the issue straight on. Maybe he was wrong, but some indefinable emotion was dancing between them, and he wanted it out of the way. Especially if they were going to be spending the next few weeks in each other's company.

Especially if she was leaving Aspen Valley again, as she said.

"Why do I have the feeling you want to tell me something?"

Nadia looked surprised at his straight-forward question. Then she tucked one corner of her lip between her teeth, lowering her lashes, now hiding her eyes. He saw her swallow, her fingers tightening on her mug.

"That time…that time when I came to you. And asked you…if you liked me. If you wanted to go out with me." She paused her halting question, but he kept his words to himself, waiting. Knowing she would fill the silence. She still kept her eyes down, as if afraid to show her vulnerability. "Why did you turn me down?"

He set his mug back on the table, then leaned back, his arms crossed over his chest. A defensive gesture? Maybe. But with her, he knew he had to be on his guard. She was his brother's onetime steady girlfriend, and now, widow and ex-wife. It had always been Arlen until that moment she came to him. Dating her, being with her, was something he had always wanted, and when she offered it to him, so to speak, he had been tempted. "I know I'm being a typical lawyer answering a question with another question, but why do you want to know? Is this important to you?"

She nodded slowly. "It is…it was hard for me. I was scared."

He heard a vulnerability in her voice that made him want to cross over to her, slip his arm around her and comfort her. But he stayed where he was.

"What were you afraid of?" He sounded like the attorney he was, probing her response for any weakness. Trying to discover the source of her fear.

"Being with you was something I really wanted, and you definitively turned me down."

"You wanted me? Really? You were dating Arlen. The golden boy. You came to me after he broke up with you. I thought for sure you were coming to me on the rebound. And there was no way I would be someone's second best."

It was hard to keep the frustration out of his voice. He was an adult, for goodness' sake. Why was that moment so intently seared on his mind?

Her eyes flew to his, wide, her expression shocked. "You thought I was coming to you on the rebound?" She stared at him, eyes wide, as if trying to make sense of what he was saying. "When I was the one who broke up with Arlen?"

Her question threw him for a loop.

"Wait, you broke up with Arlen?"

"Yes, I did. We had a fight, and I was tired of how high-maintenance he was. I told him it was over."

"You certainly wasted little time coming on to me."

She blinked, biting her lips. "I didn't waste any time because I was tired of wasting time. I had wasted too much time with Arlen. I knew you liked me, but maybe you never stopped to think that I always liked you. But you did nothing about it. So I waited while Arlen kept on after me. Sometimes I think he wanted to date me because he couldn't believe I might prefer you over him."

He was utterly perplexed.

"You never gave me any clue that you liked me," he said, struggling to find the right words.

"I did. You just didn't pay attention."

"Was I really that dense?"

"No. I think you just didn't think you could compete with your brother."

"Well, that's true enough." He scratched his temple with one finger, as if trying to sort through his confusion.

"You never gave yourself enough credit," Nadia told him, her voice quiet, reserved.

Again, he found himself at a loss for words. Not a place he was used to. Usually, he could think on his feet, pivot, retrench, and find a fresh approach. But this was too close to his heart. Despite the time that had passed, Nadia was too enmeshed in his emotions.

Drew stayed where he was for a moment, as if to absorb what Nadia was saying. He couldn't find the words to describe what he was feeling because he wasn't sure of his own emotions. What she had just told him turned everything upside down for him.

"But then you went back to Arlen."

She nodded, looking down at her hands, now twined together. "Yes, I did. After I realized you didn't want to date me, I applied to a college in Toronto. One of my friends was going there for school, so I figured I would follow. And, well, so did Arlen. My friend was busy with her life, and I was studying, but I was also lonely. Arlen and I got together, and old habits took over. We just fell into the old relationship. It was easy and comfortable."

"And then you got married."

Silence fell after his obvious comment, and it surprised him to see her press her knuckles to her mouth, nodding.

After a few more beats of silence that he wasn't sure how to fill, she pushed herself up. Conversation over.

"I better get to bed. Your mom gets up early."

She chanced a quick glance in his way as if trying to measure his reaction.

Drew stood as well, feeling like he had more to say.

As she passed him, he caught her by the arm.

"I'm sorry if I hurt you all those years ago," was all he could come up with. "I never meant to."

He thought she would pull away, but she looked up at him, and he was dismayed to see a glimmer of tears in her eyes.

His heart ached at her unexpressed sorrow.

He couldn't just stand there, trying to understand what was bothering her, so he gave in to an impulse. All the emotions that had been swirling around them, the exchange of looks, the touches, all coalesced into this moment.

He gently turned her toward him, his other hand coming to rest on her shoulder.

She swallowed and swiped at her cheeks and for a moment, he thought she would pull away.

Instead, her eyes delved into his.

They stood there a moment, like before in the barn, so close, their breath mingled.

"Oh, Nadia," he groaned.

Then he slipped his hand to the back of her neck, curling his fingers through her hair, his other hand sliding to her waist. It was coming. It was inevitable.

He didn't know who moved first, but then their lips connected, arms held each other closer, mouths moving over each other.

The power of their connection coursed through him, and he couldn't hold her close enough. Couldn't kiss her deeply enough.

He drew away just enough to look down at her, as if to make real what had just happened.

Then she caught him by the back of his head, pulling his mouth back down to hers. Warm, soft, seeking, passionate.

All his yearnings now coalesced into this moment.

He shifted his mouth, touching his lips to her cheeks, her temples, her forehead. Claiming each part of her face, exploring, seeking.

Her hand caressed his cheek, stroked his hair, then touched the corner of his mouth, as if claiming him for herself.

Finally, they drew back, catching their breath. Letting the moment settle, trying to find equilibrium.

Her eyes danced over his face, her fingers following her gaze.

"Is this really happening?"

"I'm pretty sure it is," Drew said, breathless. "My imagination's not that good."

A slow smile curved her lips as she leaned back in his arms. Her expression grew pensive.

"This...you and me..." she paused, as if sorting through what to say.

Then a harsh knock at the door broke into the moment. Shattering it.

Drew frowned, glancing at the clock on the wall behind Nadia.

"Are you expecting someone?" Nadia asked as she took the moment to lower her head and step away from him.

He wanted to recapture that fragile moment, angry at whoever decided to interrupt it. He tried to reach out to her, but another insistent knock resounded. Imperious. Demanding.

Stifling his annoyance, he strode to the door and yanked it open.

Then he frowned when he saw who was there.

A young woman, holding a sleeping toddler in her arms.

"Drew Rozak, right?"

Drew frowned, nodding, wondering what this woman could want.

"My name is Carrie Bukowski. Darnelle's friend. I'm the woman who texted you."

His attention was still ensnared by Nadia, who hovered in

his peripheral vision, so it took him a moment to recall who Carrie was.

Then it coalesced.

"Right. I remember now. You wrote to me. Said you had something to tell me." He realized he was being rude and stepped aside. "Come on in."

"I can't stay very long." With her free hand, Carrie bent over and picked up a suitcase that had been at her feet.

What was going on?

Nadia joined them, looking as confused as Drew felt.

The little girl lifted her head from Carrie's shoulder, blinking her sleep away, her eyes as blue as flax flowers. Her cheeks were a bright pink, and her blonde hair was a tangle of curls.

"I may as well get right to the point." Carrie heaved out a heavy sigh. "This little girl's name is Charlotte. Darnelle is her mother."

"Where is Darnelle?" Drew frowned.

"I'm sorry to tell you this so abruptly, but Darnelle is dead."

Drew just stared at her, trying to absorb this information. "When?"

"Couple of weeks ago." Carrie's voice broke again. "There's more."

———

NADIA COULD NOT CONTAIN her gasp.

Had she heard right?

She dragged her gaze away from Drew, who was now staring, open-mouthed, at the little girl still in the strange woman's arms. The toddler was yawning, rubbing her eyes with one chubby fist. Charlotte looked to be about two years old.

"She's my daughter?" Drew's voice cracked on that last

word, sounding as stunned as Nadia felt. "How can I believe you?"

"There is a letter in the suitcase," Carrie tilted her head toward the bag at her feet. "It explains everything."

"But her mother…Darnelle…where is she?" It sounded like Drew could hardly drag the words out.

Carrie closed her eyes, swaying as if overcome by emotion.

Concerned for the little girl, Nadia reached out to her and took Charlotte away from the young woman.

To her surprise, the little girl snuggled into her, resting her head against Nadia's neck.

"I firsty," she mumbled.

Carrie had one hand on the back of the chair in front of her, as if holding herself up.

"Darnelle…" Carrie's voice broke again, but then she swallowed, looking over at Nadia.

"She probably wants something to drink. It's been a long drive."

Nadia wasn't sure what to do, what thought to process first. But the little girl's needs were more important than trying to figure out what was happening.

So she carried her into the kitchen.

"Would you like some juice or water?" she asked Charlotte, bending over to get a better look at her.

"Firsty," she repeated.

Right now, Nadia wanted more than anything to be in the living room, to find out what Drew and this woman, Carrie, were talking about in hushed voices.

Instead, she poured some juice into the glass and handed it to Charlotte. The little girl grabbed it with both hands and chugged it down, almost pouring it over her face.

"You sure were thirsty," Nadia murmured. "Do you want some more?"

The little girl nodded, looking through the doorway of the

kitchen, as if she also wanted to know what was being discussed in the living room.

Nadia poured her some more juice, propping one hand on the kitchen counter, trying to catch her balance. Her confusion was a mixture of everything that had happened during the past few moments. *It was just a kiss,* she reminded herself.

But when it came to Drew, she knew there was no "just."

And then, this momentous interruption. What would happen now? Where did this little girl come from?

Was she actually Drew's daughter?

The questions nagged at her, with no concrete answer. She reminded herself she had laid out her plans. Deviating from them would turn her life in a direction she knew she had no right to go.

She didn't deserve Drew and all that he represented.

"Are you hungry?" she asked Charlotte, needing to focus on the present instead of on the uncertainty of the future, the teasing possibilities that were so far out of reach they may as well be Jupiter.

Another quiet nod. Nadia's emotions shifted from her own troubles to the poor little girl. Charlotte was tired and more than likely confused.

What was her story? How could Carrie possibly accuse Drew of being this little girl's father? Would she simply drop her off, expecting Drew to take her in?

Who was this Carrie anyway?

Wait. Just wait. This would eventually be resolved.

"Would you like some bread?" she asked, brushing Charlotte's tangled hair away from her face.

"Wif jam. Pwease."

Well, she had good manners.

Nadia picked her up and sat her on a stool by the eating bar. She was so small, just her head and shoulders showed above the counter, but Charlotte scooted onto her knees, as if she was used to this. Nadia made Charlotte a sandwich, cut it up, put it on a plate, and set it in front of her.

Then Charlotte folded her hands and bowed her head.

"Oh bwessa food and wink. Jesus sake, oh man."

Despite the drama of the moment, Nadia stifled a smile at the innocently mangled prayer.

Whoever raised this child had obviously prayed before meals.

Which only raised more questions.

Nadia took a chance and walked to the doorway of the kitchen, glancing back at Charlotte, who was eating her bread.

Carrie and Drew still faced each other, but their voices were lowered. Nadia couldn't hear what they were saying.

Drew lifted his hands in a gesture of surrender, shaking his head.

Carrie had one hand pressed to her chest, and Nadia could see that she was crying.

Then Carrie walked past Drew, past Nadia, into the kitchen to Charlotte's side.

The little girl looked up at her, her expression unchanging.

Carrie gave Charlotte a quick hug, then bracketed her face between her hands. "Love you, little bug. But Aunty Carrie has to get going. You're going to stay here for a little while. I'll come visit you soon."

She brushed a kiss over the little girl's head, but Charlotte just gave her a blank look.

"Bye-bye, Kewwy. I be good."

"You're always good, little bug." Carrie kissed her again, wiped her eyes, and with her head down, hurried past Nadia. When Carrie shut the door behind her, the click resounded like a crack.

Nadia heard Drew heave out a sigh, then his footsteps echoed in the heavy waiting silence as he came back to the kitchen.

He was carrying the little suitcase Carrie had brought.

He shot Nadia an anguished glance as she tried to decipher what he was thinking.

"What is going on?" she asked. "Why did Carrie leave? Is she coming back?" She caught herself, questions tumbling through her mind as, she was sure, they were for Drew as well. He looked as surprised as she did.

"Apparently, there's a letter in here that explains more." He glanced at Charlotte, his expression unreadable, his gaze slipping over the little girl, as if taking stock.

A trickle of unease slithered down Nadia's neck.

Drew set the suitcase on the table with a "thunk," unzipped it, and flipped it open. He pulled out an envelope tucked into a mesh pocket on one side, looking down at it.

"Is Carrie coming back for her?" Nadia whispered so Charlotte wouldn't hear.

Drew glanced over at Charlotte and put his finger to his lips as he shot her a warning glance.

"Charlotte is going to have a sleepover with us," he said, a little louder.

Charlotte looked back at him and held up three fingers. "Fwee nights." She announced, dragging her shirt sleeve over her mouth to wipe it, then yawning again.

Three nights?

Obviously, Carrie was coming back. But then what?

Nadia glanced over at Drew, who dragged his hand over his eyes then gave her a bleak look. Questions spun, crowding her head, but they would have to wait until she and Drew were alone. If, in fact, he was willing to answer them.

Drew walked over to Charlotte and lowered himself to her height. "You're probably tired, right?"

She nodded, frowning at him.

"Okay. We need to find a place for you to sleep."

He patted her on the head, then stood, blowing out his breath, looking around, frowning as if trying to figure out where to put her.

"She can sleep with me," Nadia quickly offered. She guessed Drew didn't have a child's bed anywhere in the house. "She shouldn't be alone tonight."

"If that's okay with you, that would be best for now."

"Let's see what's in the suitcase," Nadia said, walking to the table.

She unzipped one compartment, dug through the neatly folded clothes, and found a stack of pajamas. She pulled one set out, a pink ruffly top with matching pants. There were no diapers, so she guessed the little girl was fully trained.

"Should I give her a bath first?" Nadia asked, glancing over at Drew.

He lifted his shoulders in a shrug, looking puzzled. "She looks pretty wiped. Maybe put her straight to bed."

Then Charlotte let out a jaw-cracking yawn, underscoring Drew's decision.

"Can you help me get her changed for bed?" Drew asked, picking her up and taking ownership of the situation.

"Sure, of course."

A few moments later, Charlotte was tucked up in Nadia's bed with a cloth rabbit they had found in the suitcase, alongside a few other toys. Nadia sat on the bed, one hand on Charlotte's shoulder as the little girl lay curled up on her side, looking glassy-eyed. She blinked a few times, and then her eyelids drifted shut. Her breathing grew heavy, and Nadia guessed she was sleeping.

Nadia waited a few more minutes just to make sure.

Once she felt sure the child was asleep, she turned to Drew, who stood over both of them. "It might not be my place, but can you explain what's happening?"

Drew shoved his hands through his hair, then pulled up a chair, pulling the envelope out of the back pocket of his jeans.

"The woman who brought Charlotte here is Carrie. She is a good friend and roommate of Darnelle. Charlotte's mother." Drew pulled in a shuddering breath, and Nadia shot him a concerned look. "Who passed away a couple of weeks ago."

He blew out a shaky breath, looking down at the floor, and raking his hand across his face.

"I'm sorry to hear that," Nadia said, surprised at his sorrow. "Was she a friend of yours?"

"More than that. We dated for a couple of months, and according to Carrie, I'm Charlotte's father."

Chapter 7

Just saying the words aloud made it sound more dramatic. Terrifying, if he were honest with himself. Drew still couldn't believe it. He didn't trust Carrie, or Darnelle, for that matter.

But this little girl was here, and Carrie made it vehemently clear that she was not responsible for a kid that wasn't hers. And that Charlotte was definitively Drew's child. Even though Darnelle had asked Carrie to stay awhile to make sure Charlotte settled in, the woman had other plans.

And they didn't include this poor, lost child.

Short of running after Carrie and dragging her back to his house, there was little Drew could do for now.

File a Missing Persons report?

Charge Carrie with negligence or abandonment?

Trouble is, there was enough truth in Carrie's story that it resonated with Drew's memories.

"So Carrie brought Charlotte here?"

"Darnelle told Carrie to bring Charlotte here if anything happened to her, and I guess something did happen. Darnelle died of stomach cancer. Apparently, it was quick."

Drew couldn't look over at Nadia, didn't want to let her reaction determine how he felt about what had just happened.

He was still trying to absorb it all himself.

"But how do you know she's your daughter?" Nadia asked, her voice holding the same shock he felt.

"I don't know for sure. I only have Darnelle and Carrie's word," Drew admitted, slitting open the envelope.

He scanned the neatly hand-written letter, his eyes darting over the words, catching only the main points. Then he read it more slowly, this time letting himself absorb the contents. Thankfully, Nadia was quiet, giving him time.

Then he looked up at her, thinking of what she had told him before his life was split into Before and After. How she'd always cared for him. How he had felt when she told him that. As if everything he'd ever wanted was within reach.

And now?

He pushed the question aside. No time to dwell on possibilities now. He had heavier things to deal with.

"I'll read it aloud to you," he said quietly, shooting another glance toward Charlotte to make sure she still slept.

Then he smoothed the letter on his knee and began.

"Dear Drew,

I know this comes out of the blue, and I'm sorry. I'm sorry I didn't tell you the truth those times you asked if everything was good between us after that night."

Drew paused, his mind ticking back to that time. It had not been his best moment, but there was nothing he could do about it now. He looked over at Nadia, feeling the need to explain. "She's referring to what happened before she left to go back to Port Alberni. We'd been dating for a few months. Darnelle thought there was more going on than I did. We went to a party; I was struggling at school. Arlen was ghosting me. My mom was busy, and I was depressed. Drank too much. So did she…" he let the sentence trail off, wondering why he was dumping all this on Nadia, of all people. Maybe the need to confess, or the basic reality of explaining to her how Charlotte had, well, come about. "We were…intimate, for lack of a better word. We'd both been drinking, were rather irresponsible, so…"

"No precautions," Nadia finished for him.

He shook his head, still feeling a tremble of shame over that.

"She broke up with me the next day, and I tried contacting her a number of times to make sure she was okay. If something had…well…happened, I wanted to help her out. She never responded to any of my texts and didn't answer my calls or emails. It was like she just disappeared. I figured she would have let me know if she'd gotten pregnant, so I left it at that."

He sighed, looked back at the letter, and continued reading.

"…I didn't tell you about my pregnancy because I didn't want you to feel responsible. It was as much my fault as yours. I know you were a good and honorable man, and I was afraid you were the kind of guy who would want to get married and make an honest woman out of me. Or at least, be involved in our lives.

I liked you, but I would not do what my mom did. So I bailed. And I'm sorry to say, I wanted Charlotte all to myself. I didn't want to share her with anyone. My mother passed away, and I hadn't heard from my dad since he left my mother after I was born. Thankfully, I could afford to take care of her all on my own and so didn't need any financial help. I realize now it was selfish, and I'm sorry you missed out on the first few years of her life.

But I'm dying now, and there is no one to take care of her. Like I said, my mother is gone and I have no other siblings. Carrie can't.

So, I asked Carrie to help me find you, and when we did, to bring Charlotte to you. I knew, as her father, you had a right to be involved in her life. To take care of her.

Again, I'm sorry you have to find out this way. It took a while to track you down. And yes, I know Charlotte is yours. You were the only man I was intimate with. I'm sure you'll want to do a DNA test, but it will only confirm what I'm saying. I'm dictating this letter to Carrie from the hospital. I don't know how much longer I have. I'm sorry. So very sorry."

A faint sob curled up his throat as he read some of the last words from someone he remembered as very sweet and kind. Now she was gone, and her daughter, possibly *their* daughter, was here. Dropped into his life.

Darnelle was correct about one thing. They would not have worked out as a couple.

Because Darnelle never was and never would be Nadia.

"Oh, Drew, this is hard news," Nadia breathed, looking

down at the little girl, stroking her tangled hair away from her face.

It's beyond hard, he thought, glancing over at Charlotte. *It's life-shattering.*

"Do you believe her?" Nadia asked, keeping her voice quiet, almost tentative.

"I don't want to, but from what I remember of her, Darnelle was a sweet girl. She wasn't someone who would lie or play this horrible trick." He looked down at the letter again, struggling with his fluctuating emotions. "But I'm still doing a DNA test. Just for my peace of mind."

He turned the letter over to see if anything was on the other side, and he found a list.

"Charlotte's Routine" was written at the top. His eyes skimmed over the page, but after what he'd just read, nothing else registered.

"Did you want me to look that over?" Nadia asked, now standing beside him as if sensing his confusion.

He glanced over the list one more time. If he was Charlotte's father, he needed to know all this. But his head felt tight, and he didn't know which thought or question to grab and examine.

Nadia took it gently from his unresisting fingers.

"Here. I'll look it over, and we can talk about it later."

"Later. Okay. Okay. I can do that later." Another pull of air as he stood, catching the back of the chair to steady himself. Even as he did so, he chastised his weakness. Wished he could face this more like the man his mother always told him to be.

Wondered how Arlen would have reacted.

Nadia looked over at him and pulled in a breath as if readying herself to say something. Whatever it was, he wasn't sure he wanted to hear it. Didn't want to hear anything coming close to condemnation from her. Not with everything so messed up right now.

"I just need a moment."

"Okay. Let me know when you want to talk."

"Just give me five minutes."

It wasn't nearly enough, but he had to deal with this eventually.

He gave her a tight nod, then left, confusion and frustration trailing behind him.

⊏⊐

NADIA WATCHED DREW GO, her heart dropping like a stone into her stomach.

How could things have turned around so dramatically and so quickly?

One moment hope had bloomed, and possibilities lingered. Then a knock on the door and "maybe" turned into "after." Now Drew had withdrawn from her, and rightly so. She couldn't imagine what was going through his mind at this moment.

Her legs were still shaking with reaction.

However, she was surprised at how calm Charlotte had been after being dropped off at a total stranger's house. She must be either exhausted, traumatized, or a combination of both. The morning would tell how she would behave, but for now, thankfully, Charlotte was sleeping.

Nadia glanced down at the letter in her hands, looking over the cramped writing that filled the page. It was a carefully written schedule for Charlotte's day. What time she woke up, what time she had a snack, what time she had a nap, and what time she went to bed. Times she liked to eat.

Foods she liked to eat. A long list.

Foods she didn't like to eat. A very short list.

Toys she liked to play with and television shows she liked to watch.

Her preference in clothing and what her health was like.

At the very end was another note to Drew, another apology. *"I'm so sorry I didn't let you see her sooner. I'm sorry it took me so long to let you know. Charlotte is a sweet, loving girl. And I'm sorry I won't see her grow up."*

Nadia pressed her fingers to her lips, her heart wrenching at those last words from a mother whose heart must have shattered along with her health. She didn't know Darnelle but she got a sense that the woman had been a loving mother. What state she must have been in to know that she would not live to see her daughter grow up, graduate, or get married?

It was such a sad story, and now Nadia was dropped into it.

She felt confused and disoriented, and she knew that if she felt like this, Drew must be even more emotionally lost. She wanted to go to him, talk to him, feel him out. But she knew he wanted some space, and she wanted to give him time to gather his thoughts.

To her surprise, tears gathered in her eyes. It was such a sad and confusing situation. She looked for tissues, but couldn't see any on the end table. She opened the drawer, but all she found was a worn Bible.

Her fingers ran over the cracked leather cover, and she smiled at the sight of Drew's name stamped in gold. Every member of the church got this type of Bible when they turned eighteen. She had an identical one, also with her name stamped on it.

Except hers didn't look as worn.

She swiped at her tears with the hem of her t-shirt and then stroked Charlotte's shoulder.

The little girl stirred but then drifted off to sleep again.

Nadia felt she should stay in case Charlotte woke up.

But she also wanted, no, needed to see Drew. Besides, she wasn't far. If the little girl woke up, she could be at her side in seconds. Despite her lack of Bible reading, Nadia took a moment to send up a prayer for strength and wisdom as she left the room, leaving the door open.

Drew sat on the couch, his head laying on the back, eyes closed. He looked as if he had aged five years in the past half an hour. She hesitated, but the moment that had come so close to being life-changing in another direction still lingered.

What lay ahead for them now?

Charlotte for Drew.

And herself?

"Hey, you," Drew said, lifting his head as if sensing her presence. "Come, sit down."

There was room beside him, but Nadia chose the love seat across from him, and she could tell by the confusion slipping across his face that he would have preferred her closer.

The last few minutes were a stark reminder to keep her distance. Keep her life on the trajectory she had planned. The only one she deserved.

"I have to confess this was not how I envisioned the evening going," he said quietly, his eyes holding hers, delving into her as if seeking an answer to an unspoken question.

"Having a long-lost daughter dropped on your doorstep shifts things," she replied, sidestepping what she guessed he was looking for.

Disappointment glinted in his eyes. She didn't blame him. She had felt the electricity between them. The charged atmosphere. A remnant from the kiss they'd shared.

"So now I have to figure out what my next step is," he continued, his voice, thankfully, taking on a practical tone.

She could do practical.

"Take tomorrow off," she suggested. "Much as I hate to tell you that."

"Yeah, I need to set up a room for her." He blew out his breath, then pinched his lower lip between his fingers. "It would have to be an upstairs room for now. Close to me." Then he frowned, looking over at Nadia. "But would that be okay for her during the day? When she has a nap? What if she wakes up in the middle of the night, and I don't hear it, and she comes down the stairs?"

He released another sigh as he laid his head back against the couch. "I am so not the right person for this. How am I supposed to juggle all that I've got going? Work, my mother….this party?"

And now a daughter to take care of and get to know. Figure out how to fit into his life.

"I'll be around for now," Nadia assured him. "I'll help you as much as I can, and we can pawn parts of the planning of Aria and Lucas' party onto my family. I'll talk to the twins and Burke and Drake. I know they're busy too, but right about now, you've got enough going. I have a list of things we have to do. I can pass that on to them."

"I guess."

His reluctance to pass on a job that would take up too much of his time didn't surprise her. Arlen always said Drew was a man of his word, and when he said he would do something, you could count on him. Though Arlen always said that with a chuckle.

"No guessing needed." Poor Drew looked exhausted, and Nadia didn't blame him. She was tired, herself, just thinking of how Charlotte would affect his life.

But what if she wasn't his child?

It didn't matter. The little girl was here in this house, and he had to deal with it.

"For now, I think we need to be practical. We have to deal with the very first thing in front of us, and that's sleeping arrangements for her. I don't mind sharing a bed with her until she gets a bit more settled. I'm sure that will take her some time."

She said the words lightly, but they dug into that deep corner of her heart. She thought of her family, and how established they were. Each finding their place.

It's not what you wanted, the old voice taunted her.

But that voice grew fainter each year she got older.

And then there was that moment –

"We can make a list of the things she needs." Nadia jumped to her feet and strode to the dining room.

She returned with a pen and some paper she found, sat down, and wrote Charlotte's name at the top, as if reminding herself of the girl's presence.

"The first thing she needs is a proper bed."

"She won't need a crib?"

"No. Darnelle had written…" Her voice faltered for a moment, her heart aching at the thought of Darnelle making this list, uncertainty dogging the poor woman. Releasing her child into the unknown. "She wrote that she sleeps in a regular bed. We could just get a small one for her. And of course, she would need bedding."

"Does she have enough clothes? I should get her some toys."

"She has a lot of clothes for now," Nadia assured him. "Toys would be a good idea. Maybe some stuffed animals. Pictures for the walls. And we will have to get some other groceries. I have a list of the foods she likes."

Though she tried to be practical, Nadia felt a shiver of sorrow at Charlotte's mother, listing all this out. And anger at Carrie for not having the backbone to stick around and make sure the little girl would be okay. She could have been dropping Charlotte off at a crazy person's place, for all she knew.

"I guess that takes up most of tomorrow." Drew dragged his hands over his face, shaking his head again. "You know, this was not how I hoped the evening would go."

Again, their gazes locked, that attraction sparking between them.

Nadia lowered her head. Right now, there was no room in his life or hers for anything more to happen.

"I can go into town tomorrow and get some of this stuff,"

Nadia said, focusing on the practical and the current.

"I'll come with you."

"What about work?"

"Right now, I've got something way more important to deal with. Freya can help until Aria comes back."

Nadia knew what a sacrifice this was for him. He was still the "new" lawyer in town, trying to gain the trust of the people in Aspen Valley, who still saw him as a young kid, hunched over his books on the school bus.

"We can take your mother along. The outing will do her good," Nadia suggested.

Drew slowly shook his head, groaning.

"How am I supposed to tell her about Charlotte?"

The stark question hung between them. Nadia wished she could assure him that everything would be fine. However, she knew Lily would be even more confused than Drew was, and she would probably have a lot to say about the fact that Drew had a child out of wedlock.

"Well, I better get back to check on Charlotte," Nadia said, putting the list on the table as she stood.

She paused a moment, looking down at Drew, who was massaging the back of his neck. She wanted to comfort him. Slip her arms around him like she had almost done an hour ago. Instead, she turned and strode down the hall to the bathroom. Brushed her teeth, brushed her hair, and then entered the bedroom.

As she crawled into bed, she reached across the space to touch the little girl, who was now turned toward her. And then, in the solitary darkness, she allowed herself the release of tears. Just for a moment, she gave the sorrow space, then pushed it down. She turned on her side to face the little girl and tried to still her spinning thoughts.

Chapter 8

Drew sat on the edge of his bed, giving himself some time to let the dreams of the night slip away and let reality settle in.

Which it did, with a crash.

The girl he'd always loved, the girl he had kissed last night, now lay sleeping with the daughter he never knew he had.

Across the hall from his mother.

He was sure she would have plenty to say about what had happened last night.

"Okay, Lord, I do not know how this will play out. I feel like I'm driving down the foggy road, only able to see what's in front of me. I am going to need strength and courage and patience."

He let the prayer settle a moment, then got up to face what lay ahead.

He showered, shaved, and dressed, listening as he did so, but the house was still quiet when he was done. That meant his mother was still sleeping, and hopefully, Charlotte and Nadia were as well.

Lucky them. Last night, his dreams were troubled and chaotic, and when he woke up, his pillows were on the floor and his blankets were a tangled mess.

No rest for the wicked?

When he opened the bathroom door, he smelled coffee brewing.

Nadia was awake.

He paused a moment before going downstairs, his thoughts returning to last night - before Carrie and Charlotte had crashed into his evening and his life. When he and Nadia had exchanged a kiss that rocked his world, that fulfilled so many of the hesitant dreams he had spun around this woman.

Now, life had dumped him back into the box called "Reality."

He sent up another quick prayer, ran his hands over his hair, pushed aside his dread, and went downstairs to face the day.

Nadia looked over at him as she poured herself some coffee. "Hey, you," she greeted him, her voice quiet.

"Charlotte still sleeping?"

"And your mother. Want some coffee?"

"Gonna need it," he admitted, chewing his lower lip. "This is going to be one roller coaster day. But I'll first check on…my…on Charlotte."

He walked quietly down the hall and opened the door enough to peek inside. Nadia had left a bedside light on, and it cast the little girl's face in shadow. He wanted to go inside but was afraid he would wake her up. He wasn't ready to face that yet.

Charlotte probably wasn't either.

So he returned to the kitchen.

"She okay?"

"Yes. Still sleeping."

Nadia handed him a mug, and they sat down at the table across from each other.

He glanced up at her, only to catch her looking at him. For a moment, he didn't look away, their kiss from yesterday rising between them, haunting and taunting at the same time.

Well, that's not going anywhere, he thought, looking back down at his mug. Not that it would have, even had Charlotte not been dropped into his life. He had other responsibilities now, and Nadia still talked about traveling.

"How did…Charlotte sleep last night?" Her name still felt unwieldy on his tongue. A sound that was now connected to this little person he had just met.

"She barely moved."

"I'm thinking I'll have to head out and do some shopping today." Thanks to Nadia, his refrigerator was much better stocked than it had been, but they still needed things the little girl would enjoy.

"I don't mind coming along."

He tried not to read more into what she was saying than a simple offer to help. Until his life settled down and Nadia left, he had to keep his focus narrowed and stop letting her presence distract him.

Easier said than done. Even now, it seemed he was aware of every movement she made. Every breath she took.

"Your mother might want to, as well," Nadia added.

Which made him close his eyes and shake his head, wondering how telling his mother this life-changing news would play out.

Then a bell rang from Lily's bedroom, the noise like the clang of inevitability heading toward them.

"I better go," Nadia said.

"Let me know once you've got her in her chair, and I'll come to talk to her."

Nadia just nodded, but before she left, her hand lightly brushed his shoulder. Connection? Commiseration?

He didn't want the latter, and he couldn't give in to the former. He felt restless now, knowing that no matter how diplomatically he approached this, for his mother it would be a storm of shock, surprise, and probably some condemnation.

Most likely condemnation.

With a final chug of coffee, Drew stood and headed to Charlotte's room. To his surprise, she now sat up in her bed, eyes wide, staring at him, her thumb in her mouth, a stuffed rabbit clutched to her chest. The sight created a wave of sorrowful sympathy. She had no idea where she was or what was going on.

"Hey there," he said, keeping his voice quiet, non-threatening, as he closed the door behind him and walked to the bed.

He sat down by her feet and smiled at her. "You sleep good?"

Charlotte's solemn expression didn't change, but she nodded.

"Do you want anything to eat?"

She gave him no reaction to that.

Well, this father-daughter bonding moment was going well.

Finally, she pulled her thumb out of her mouth, still staring at him with those sea-blue eyes.

"Who you?"

The two simple words were like a dose of cold water. What to say?

When in doubt, go with the obvious.

"I'm your dad."

She frowned, shaking her head. "No. You not."

Hostile witness.

"Yes, sweetheart, I am." The endearment seemed to come easily out of his mouth. "Carrie brought you here because I'm your dad, and you'll be staying with me."

She tilted her head to one side as if to see him from another angle.

"Okay."

Just like that. He wasn't sure if she comprehended what was going on, but for now, he was thankful for her simple acceptance.

Then she pushed aside the blankets and jumped out of the bed. "Go bafwoom," she declared, blinking up at Drew.

Oh boy. This was a little out of his depth.

But he may as well get started on this father thing.

"There's a bathroom right here," he said, walking ahead of her to the en suite.

She trundled inside, then looked at the toilet and up at him. "You help me," she demanded.

Of course, she would need his help. So, trying not to feel like he was trespassing on her personal space, realizing he was her father and allowed to do this, he helped her onto the toilet.

"Dat's better," she told him. "I sweep good. I have dweams. You have dweams?"

Oh, he'd had many of them, but none that he was about to share with her. Too many of them had to do with her and the woman who was across the hallway now, helping his mother ready for the day. A day he dreaded deep in the pit of his stomach.

"Yes, I dreamed about cars." Which wasn't too far off the mark, mostly dreams about trying to stop his car and the brakes not working. Probably indicative of where his life was right now. A dream specialist would have a heyday with that.

"I dweam cars too. Dwiving, dwiving, dwiving." Though she was finished, she seemed in no hurry to leave, her elbows resting on her legs, her bare feet swinging back and forth. "All dwiving."

"And then you came here." He wasn't sure which topics of conversation would be appropriate.

"Yes. I stay fwee days." She held up four fingers to indicate this time. He was tempted to ask her what would happen afterward, but of course, she would not understand. Based on Carrie's hasty retreat, he had a good idea of what "afterward" would look like. She was staying here.

"Now I hungwy," she announced, jumping off the toilet.

"We should wash your hands first," Drew said. "And then maybe put some clean clothes on you."

"No, I have pajama day," she announced matter-of-factly as he ran the tap.

He paused, wondering where to go from here. Should he let her do what she wanted?

Like his parents did with Arlen? Then, when they realized what mistakes they had made, clamped down on Drew.

Obviously, he was facing his first test as a father.

Start as you mean to go on.

"But I'm not wearing my pajamas," he said, as he lifted her up to the sink so she could wash her hands.

He caught sight of their combined reflection in the mirror, and his heart clenched. He saw himself as a young boy in the curve of her cheek, the little bow of her top lip. Her eyebrows had the same slant.

Out of curiosity, he lifted her hair aside, checking her ear. His heart jumped as he saw it. A distinctive crimp in the top curve of her ear, just as he and Arlen had. Drew's on his right ear. Arlen's on his left. Just like their father had. If he had any doubts about his paternity, they were immediately quashed.

But he was still doing a DNA test. Because, well, lawyer.

"Okay. I get dwessed," she said, adding a heavy sigh.

He walked with her back into the bedroom, looking around for her suitcase, but it lay empty on the floor. Nadia must've put the clothes away.

He found them tucked into the drawer in his walk-in closet.

"What do you want to wear?" he asked, turning to Charlotte.

She wiggled her mouth as if thinking, then walked over to the drawer, and pulled out a pair of leggings and a sparkly t-shirt. He found the rest of what she would need. He was all awkward hands and thumbs, but finally got her dressed.

While he worked, she stared at him, as if puzzled.

CAROLYNE AARSEN

"You weally my daddy?"

Either the thought hadn't sunk in, or she had forgotten what he had told her earlier.

"Yes. I'm your father…your daddy."

Her gaze didn't falter, her sea-blue eyes still holding his.

"Okay," she announced, obviously satisfied with his reply. For now, at least. "Now I hungwy."

"Well, let's go to the kitchen then." He opened the door and heard Nadia in the bathroom with his mother. His heart stuttered at the potential confrontation.

Later.

For now, he had to figure out what to feed this little girl.

She climbed up onto the stool by the eating bar and rested her elbows on the counter as if she had been doing this forever. Drew walked over to the refrigerator, opened it, and scanned the items inside. "Do you like eggs? Toast?" He asked, glancing over at her.

"Yep."

Probably meant both. He pulled out the breakfast tray with the toaster and a loaf of bread on it. A few moments later, he set a piece of toast in front of her, cut into four triangles like his mom always did, with scrambled eggs on the side. He gave her a fork, poured her a glass of milk, then walked around and sat down beside her.

To his surprise, she folded her chubby hands. "Bwessa food and drink. Oh man."

He suppressed a chuckle at her prayer, but at the same time, warmth flooded through him. Darnelle had obviously taught her this.

Then she picked up the large fork, trying to stab her eggs with it.

"Do you need help?" He asked, his hand hovering.

"No. Do it mysewf." The slightly belligerent tone in her voice told him he should stay and supervise.

Somehow, she got some of the egg into her mouth. She

110

gobbled down the toast and slurped down her milk, swiping her arm, once again, over her mouth.

Memo to self, Drew thought, *get napkins.*

The bathroom door opened. He heard his mother's voice, and a sharp fist clenched his stomach.

"What have you planned for breakfast?" he heard his mother asking Nadia. "Smells like Drew has already had his toast."

Dear Lord, help me through this, he prayed frantically, as he got up and stood beside Charlotte, his hand resting on her shoulder. Protection? Ownership? Then Nadia pushed his mother around the corner and stopped within a few feet of where Drew and Charlotte were.

His mother frowned at Charlotte, then looked up at Drew. "What is going on? Who is this little girl? Where did she come from?"

Here it was. Moment of truth.

He could dance around it all he wanted, but he knew it was better to get to the point. Thankfully, his mother's heart was strong. He didn't have to worry about her having a heart attack.

"This is Charlotte. She's my daughter."

His mother's mouth dropped open, her head came forward, eyes wide with shock. Her hands clenched the handles of her wheelchair, fingers white with tension.

"Your…your daughter?"

He could barely hear her whispered words.

"Yes. She just arrived last night."

"And no one…I wasn't told…why didn't you?"

"It was as much of a shock for me as for you," Drew informed her. He glanced back at Charlotte, then turned back to his mother, lowering his voice. "I had no idea about her. None until last night when Carrie, a friend of Charlotte's mother, dropped her off."

"We thought it best if you got your rest before we dropped

this on you," Nadia explained, kneeling down, also speaking quietly. "That's why we didn't wake you up last night."

The use of "we" warmed Drew's heart. As if she was in this with him.

"You knew about this, too?" Lily's head whipped around, glaring at Nadia.

"I was awake when she came," Nadia said. "It was rather late at night."

Lily's gaze returned to Charlotte, her shock morphing into confusion.

"How...when...who is the mother...I know she's not Aria. Never saw her....never saw her expecting...so who?"

Her stuttering questions were a direct testament to how flustered Lily was.

Drew wasn't sure what to say or where to start.

"Tell me. Now." These were fired off like bullets, fast and sharp, and Drew's back stiffened at her now imperious tone. Obviously, his mother had gotten her spunk back.

A thick, oppressive silence followed this as he weighed his next words.

"I don't appreciate you talking to me like that," he said, delivering his words firmly and with authority, never breaking eye contact.

"I'm sorry. You're right." She drew in a deep breath, her eyes still downcast, stroking her cheek with her fingers. "It's just...I never thought of you...of you that way..." Her self-conscious sentence trailed off, and Drew sensed what she was trying to say.

A backhanded compliment in one way.

"Nadia, do you mind helping Charlotte finish her breakfast? I'm taking my mother into the living room."

She held his gaze for a few heartbeats, and he saw a glimmer of sympathy, which was followed by an encouraging smile. He fought down his frustration at the current situation between him and Nadia. A scant ten hours ago, he had kissed the woman who haunted his thoughts. Their shared emotions had allowed hope to bloom. Now both his mother and his daughter were in the same house as Nadia, and too many complications hovered between them.

Stifling his frustration, he wheeled his mother to a space by the couch and sat down facing her, bracing himself for an onslaught of questions. Not that he blamed her. He had hundreds spinning through his head as well.

"Tell me. Please. How did that child get here?" His mother demanded, then, as if remembering how Drew spoke to her just a few moments ago, held up her hands in an apologetic gesture.

"I'm sorry," she said. "I had no right to ask that. Especially not like that."

"First off, that child's name is Charlotte. She's two years old, and I'm ninety-nine percent sure she is my daughter."

"But not one hundred percent?"

"I am doing a DNA test, but I'm sure it won't change what I've been told and what I know. Charlotte's mother's name is Darnelle. She passed away over a month ago. I dated Darnelle for about four months, shortly after Aria and I broke up. Darnelle was a lovely girl, and I liked her a lot, but I knew it wouldn't last. However, despite that, one night we got intimate, and Charlotte is the result of that."

"How did you just find this out now? Why did this Darnelle woman not tell you earlier?" The belligerent tone had left his mother's voice, replaced, thankfully, by a quieter, confused one.

"Darnelle sent a letter along with Charlotte, explaining why she hadn't contacted me even though I had tried to get hold of her. I won't go into all that right now, but when Darnelle found out she was dying, she attempted to track me down. Unfortunately, her roommate only found me after Darnelle had passed away. She was the one who dropped Charlotte off last night." Explaining the situation to his mother made it even more real. The story was out in the open, and now it was a part of his life.

"And you're absolutely positive?" his mother repeated.

"Like I said, ninety-nine percent." He scratched his forehead with one finger, still trying to adjust to his situation. "She has the same crimp along the top of her ear that Arlen and I have."

His mother sucked in a quick breath, then relaxed back against her chair.

"Your father had the same thing,"

Drew nodded. "It's pretty distinctive."

His mother chewed at her lower lip, the knuckles of one hand moving up and down her cheek. Something she always did when stressed.

"So, I finally do have a grandchild..." Her voice held the tiniest note of wonder, and Drew clung to the faint hope that she would accept the situation.

"I had always thought Arlen would be the first one to give me a grandchild. I always thought he and Nadia..."

Drew pushed back a beat of frustration at his mother's assumption. But then, he could hardly fault her. Arlen and Nadia were married at one time. Having a child might have been part of their plans.

"It broke my heart when they separated," his mother said, shaking her head. "I still don't understand why."

Drew had his own questions about Nadia and his brother. But there had never been a time or opportunity to ask them. Any other time would've been presumptuous on his part.

And now?

"At any rate, Charlotte is staying here," Drew continued. "Now I have to figure out how to blend her into my life." It annoyed him that even during this life-changing event, he still had to bring the conversation away from his brother, back to his own situation.

He felt annoyed that it bothered him, and, if he was

honest with himself, annoyed that her constant talking about Arlen could still wound him.

"That little girl is going to make you very busy," his mother warned. "How do you propose to take care of her and still work?"

He couldn't believe she could even talk like this. Of course, their whole married life, his father took care of earning the money and she took care of the children.

But still...

"Lots of women work and have children. Many single fathers do, as well. I can either find someone to watch her here in the house or take her to daycare."

Lily pursed her lips, nodding. "It would be so much easier if you had a wife. If you were married."

This was going nowhere, and the last thing he wanted was yet another "discussion" about his marital prospects and how he wasn't getting any younger.

"Anyhow, that is how Charlotte came here." He stood and glanced at his watch. He had to call the office soon. Let them know he wouldn't come in for the next couple of days. Which would throw a huge wrench in the well-oiled machinery of Waldren and Rozak, but there was no way around it.

Right now, Charlotte was his priority.

And Nadia?

He pushed that lingering question aside as well. He had no right to expect anything from Nadia now.

⸺

"THIS WOULD BE A GOOD OPTION," Nadia said, standing by a small white bed with short side-rails.

"It's not too big?" Drew joined her, leading Charlotte by the hand.

Ever since Charlotte had woken up this morning, Nadia had felt surprised at how easily the little girl accepted her fate.

According to some research she had done about abandoned children, apparently, this could be labeled "the honeymoon phase," though that had been more applicable to older children moving into foster care. Still, it helped explain how docile she was, considering what a huge life change had just happened to her.

"I think it could work very well. She can sleep in it until she's about six, and then you can buy that for her to sleep in."

Nadia pointed to a canopied princess bed tucked in one corner of the showroom of the local furniture store.

Glittering gauze netting cascaded from a crown suspended halfway above the bed, flowing over the gilded headboard. The quilt covering it was decorated with shining stars and flitting fairies in pastel colors.

"Really?"

The pained look on Drew's face made her laugh. His house was all heavy wood and dark leather furniture. A man's abode. That princess bed would look as out of place as a fairy at a lumberjack convention.

"Maybe. Depends on what Charlotte's tastes run to." Nadia looked down at Charlotte, who stood by Drew, looking around, uninterested in the princess bed.

Her silence broke Nadia's heart.

"You weren't the fairy princess type, were you?" Drew asked.

"I had too many brothers to get away with that." She turned her attention back to Drew. "And I had to share a room with Celeste, who was way too practical for anything remotely resembling fairy stories."

Drew gave her a slow-release smile that shimmied down to her stomach, giving it a little clench of appeal.

"You sound regretful," he teased.

"I had my dreamy moments. Not too unusual." Then she turned back to Charlotte. "What do you think of this bed?"

Charlotte blinked slowly, looking from her to the bed, to Drew, as if trying to put it all together.

"I yike it."

"Would you like to sleep in it?"

She shook her head. "Sweep wif you," she said in a tone that left little room for discussion. She grabbed Nadia's hand, clinging to it as if establishing her claim.

"But it's a nice bed," Drew said, bending down to look at the little girl. "You can have the whole thing to yourself."

Again, that firm shake of her head. "Sweep wif her," she declared, leaning into Nadia.

Drew shot her a confused glance. "What do we do?"

"Just buy the bed," Nadia suggested, her hand curling around Charlotte's soft fingers. "We can transition her into it before I leave."

"Can I help you?" An older woman joined them, her hands clasped behind her back. She wore a pink blazer and floral pants, her crimson lips parted in a wide grin.

Nadia glanced over her shoulder and felt a tremor of long-forgotten shame. Della Parsons used to be a teacher's aide in high school. She worked with some kids who struggled in regular classes.

At one time, Nadia had been one of them. And Della hadn't liked Nadia.

"I think we're okay here," Nadia said, struggling to keep her tone even. It was silly that despite all the years that had passed since high school, she could still feel a chill encircling her gut at the sight of this woman.

Still feel that helpless onslaught of fear.

Then Della frowned, looking more closely at Nadia. "Well, well, the black sheep has come home. Welcome back, Nadia."

She said the words in a jokey manner, but Nadia sensed an underlying note of censure. Especially when her eyes shifted to Charlotte, still leaning against Nadia, her hand holding tight.

"Nope. Just stopping by. Not much to keep me here," she

shot back, the edge in her voice betraying the subtle jab at Della's comment.

"Oh?" Della scoured the group, her gaze bouncing from Drew to Charlotte and then to Nadia. Della gave Nadia a pointed look, as if saying she wasn't surprised that Nadia had brought a daughter back with her to Aspen Valley. She opened her mouth as if about to ask another question when Lily made her appearance, pushing her walker.

"Well, hello there, Ms. Parsons," Lily greeted her in a tone that made it clear the two weren't fond of each other. "I didn't know you ended up here."

Nadia tried not to grin.

Ms. Parsons wasn't the only one who could do passive-aggressive.

"It's lovely to see you up and about," Della replied. "I hope the surgery was successful. I heard you were staying with Drew and that Nadia and…" once again her eyes flitted to Charlotte, still looking confused. "Nadia is taking care of you."

"And she's doing a wonderful job," Lily returned. She turned to the bed they had been considering. "I think that could work for little Charlotte. We'd need some bedding for it, I would imagine."

"And Charlotte is…" Della asked, unable to keep her unabashed curiosity at bay.

"Two years old," Lily returned, not taking the dangling bait. "So, I think this could work well."

Nadia had to stifle a smile at the abject disappointment on Della's face.

"We'll take it," Drew said. "We'll need bedding for it as well."

"But we can figure that out on our own," Lily commented, her smile polite but dismissive.

Another smile, and then Della was gone.

Lily watched her go, then turned back to Nadia, shaking

her head. "The nerve of that woman. To imply that you would –"

"Let's not go any further with that, mother," Drew said, his tone dry. "After all, I did."

A flush slid up Lily's neck and tinted her cheeks. "Yes. Well, that is a surprise for sure."

Drew didn't look over at Nadia, but again, crouched down in front of Charlotte. "What do you think? Do you like this?"

Once again, the little girl pushed her thumb into her mouth and nodded.

"Okay, that settles it. Let's get the rest of what we need and get out of here."

Nadia sensed a faint tension in his voice, the way he held his head, the press of his lips.

Was it shame?

Older emotions spiraled up from the place she thought she had buried them. Regrets that still haunted her.

And yet, she felt an affinity with Drew.

She knew what he was feeling.

She'd been there herself.

Chapter 9

Drew struggled to get Charlotte ready for bed. It didn't help that she was wiggling around, resisting all attempts to get the pajamas on.

"See Nadia," she whined as Drew tugged her shirt over her head. It was small, so by the time he got it over her face, she was tossing her head back and forth in frustration.

"Nadia will come in and say good night," Drew assured her, trying not to feel frustrated.

He heard the door across the hall click shut, which meant his mother was settled in for the night. A faint knock on the door gave his heart a quick nudge, and he turned to see Nadia enter the room.

"Everything okay here?" She asked, glancing from Charlotte to Drew.

The little girl launched herself from the bed and ran to Nadia, clinging to her hand.

"You stay wif me."

"I will, but we need to tuck you in first."

Charlotte kept tugging at her hand.

"You tuck me," she insisted, and Nadia shot Drew a puzzled look.

"I'm okay with that," he said. Though saying that bothered him more than he wanted to admit. She was his daughter. Shouldn't there be some immediate biological connection between them? And yet, she clearly preferred Nadia to him.

"Let's go get some books, and we will read to you together," Nadia offered, bending over and swinging Charlotte into her arms.

After purchasing the bed and the bedding, they walked to the local bookstore and picked out some children's books. And once again, they'd ignored several questioning looks and raised eyebrows.

Drew was sure the Aspen Valley grapevine was vibrating by now. It shouldn't bother him, but it seemed those years of being so cautious, of doing everything right, were now obliterated by the presence of his young daughter. It shouldn't matter to him, but somehow, it did.

A few moments later, Nadia returned, leading Charlotte by the hand, a few books tucked under her arm.

"You go sit on the bed," Nadia instructed Charlotte, "and Daddy and I will sit on either side of you and read a story to you."

Daddy. The word still felt unfamiliar.

Charlotte shot Drew a distrustful look, as if she was also struggling with her identity as his daughter.

Drew shoved his hand through his hair, easing out a sigh of frustration.

"You don't seem happy." Nadia frowned.

"I just wish that at least the women in my life would want to be with me," he muttered. Then he realized how whiney that might end up sounding.

To his surprise, Nadia gave him a teasing smile. "I enjoy being with you."

Her tone was light, but it hearkened back once again to that kiss they had shared.

He had to keep that back where it belonged. His life was way too complicated right now.

And yet, as they settled down with Charlotte between them, he couldn't help dropping his arms across the pillows behind the little girl, his hand resting on Nadia's shoulder. And she didn't move away.

"We'll do this one first," Nadia said, picking up a book whose cover was sprinkled liberally with fairies and glitter.

She opened it to the first page, and Charlotte stuck her thumb in her mouth, leaning against Nadia. Nadia began reading about a lonely fairy, who thought her wings weren't pretty enough, and she wandered the forest looking for ways to decorate them and for people to help her.

Nadia read the first page, and then when she turned it over, looked over at Drew. "You read this page," she instructed.

"I have to read a story about an insecure fairy?" he asked but gave her a faint smile.

"It takes a real man to read about fairies with a straight face," Nadia teased.

He laughed at that, found his place, and began reading about the fairy's quest through the forest looking for leaves, spiderwebs, or moths, anything to make her wings look prettier.

Nadia took a turn, and then he did. He fell into the rhythm of the story and started reading with a bit more enthusiasm, making up the voices like his father used to when he read to him. However, as he read, he sensed a shifting in Charlotte. She glanced over at him from time to time, looking a little puzzled. As if surprised he knew how to do this. By the time they came to the end of the book, the little girl was smiling.

"I yike dat," she mumbled around her thumb. "Read more," she demanded, reaching past Nadia for another book.

This one she pushed toward Drew, obviously accepting his ability to tell a story.

A small gift, but it made him feel better. This time, as he read to her, he became more animated, and she even shifted a little toward him.

Small gains, but he would take it.

Two books later, she started yawning, nestling down in the bed.

Drew stayed where he was, looking down at her. Maybe it was his imagination, or maybe he was just projecting, but she just seemed to get cuter and cuter.

He and Nadia stayed at her side while she drifted off to sleep. Her rabbit was tucked under one arm, but this time she didn't suck her thumb.

"She seems to be settling better," Nadia said.

"Early days yet." Drew tried to be practical. "I'm sure she's still confused, trying to figure everything out. I feel so bad for her."

He fingered a strand of hair away from Charlotte's face, slipping it behind her ear.

"Are you still doing the DNA test?" Nadia asked.

"The lawyer in me wants to tie up any potential loose ends. But I'm sure of what it will tell me." He ran his finger over the crimp in Charlotte's ear, smiling again.

"You sound pretty positive," Nadia returned.

"I am, and this is why. Do you see this little crimp here?" He put his finger behind her ear, lifting it so she could see better.

Nadia nodded, then Drew turned his head and pointed to his own ear. "Same crimp as I have. Same crimp as Arlen has. My dad had it too."

"That's too much of a coincidence," Nadia agreed quietly.

"I would say the biological evidence is pretty clear."

They were quiet for a moment, both looking down at the little girl sleeping between them. Drew's mind shifted, wondering if this would have been his life if he had accepted Nadia's offer all those years ago.

Would they have had a child together? Or two maybe? Would they have been a family?

The questions taunted him, but he couldn't indulge in that. His reality was that Charlotte was the daughter of another mother and that Nadia had been married to his brother. And seemed more than willing to talk about him.

Like any grieving widow might.

They waited a few more moments, then Nadia eased herself off the bed, and Drew followed suit.

"You want some tea or coffee?" she asked once he closed the door behind him.

Seemed like she wasn't shutting it down for the night, and the thought of spending some more time with her sounded far more appealing than holing up in his room with a boring book.

"Sounds like a good idea," he said, moving toward the kitchen.

"I'll make it. You sit down."

He didn't argue with that, then walked to the living room and dropped onto the couch, grabbing the folder for Aria and Lucas's party.

"I guess we'll have to go over a few things on this," he sighed, turning over the pages.

He looked them over as Nadia joined him, carrying a tray holding a teapot, two mugs, and a jar of honey.

She put the tray on the table, then sat beside him, taking some pages away from him.

"For someone who is willing to delegate, Aria sure likes her lists," Nadia grumbled.

"Thanks to your ability to delegate, we can check a few things off it."

"The twins sent me pictures of some flower arrangements they found at a local nursery."

Nadia pulled out her phone, and as Drew glanced over, he noticed she had a piece of Arlen's artwork as her screensaver.

He knew he had no right to be bothered by it, but it still stung. Just a little.

As if noticing his attention, Nadia held the phone a moment, looking at it as well.

"This was one of Arlen's better works," she said. "He had such talent."

"I've asked you this before, but does it hurt to talk about him?"

"He was a part of my life, and I can't deny that. Also, I was more involved in his art than I would have liked."

"What do you mean by that?"

"Even after we separated, he would come over to get my opinion on what he was doing. He made a few paintings of me." She gave him a wry look. "Everyone always thought he was so self-confident, but there was an insecurity that he hid. I don't know if he ever told you, but he always respected you. He was jealous of your ability to stay focused. To stay on task. That was something he struggled with."

Her criticism of Arlen surprised him. "When you talk about him with my mother, you always sound so admiring."

Nadia swiped the screen, closing out the picture. "You realize I do that mostly for your mother, right?"

Did he imagine that faintly bitter tone in her voice?

"Why is that important?"

Nadia ran her thumb up and down the side of her phone screen, making the icons jiggle. "I suppose it's a way of giving to her what I took away from her."

"What do you mean when you say, 'took away from her?'"

He sat close enough beside Nadia to feel her tense up. Her hand was now clenching her phone, her fingers growing white.

He knew enough to wait, hoping she would say something. Anything.

But she was silent, her head dipped now, her hair hiding her face.

He decided to come at things from another angle. So he waited as if to let her know he was changing the subject.

"I have to confess, I'm surprised that Aria and Lucas are eloping," he said, once again trying to sound indifferent. "I kind of thought she would want the big wedding. But then, maybe you would understand. After all, you and Arlen eloped as well."

It was a clumsy nudge, but considering what was at stake, it was the best he could come up with on the fly. He had always wondered why Arlen and Nadia had kept their wedding on the down low. The only people who had been invited were his parents. He wasn't sure if Arlen knew about Nadia's visit to him or if his brother was just being secretive, but Drew had not been asked to attend their wedding. Then again, neither had any of her siblings, and her parents were gone well before that.

"It was Arlen's choice, and I went along with it." Her voice was barely above a whisper, her head still hidden by the fall of her shining hair.

Then he gave in to an impulse and slipped his hand through it, gently pushing it aside. She didn't look up right away, but when she angled her head toward him, he caught a flash of pain in her eyes.

"What's wrong?" Despite the fact that she and Arlen had separated, did she still miss him?

"How do you feel about Charlotte?" she asked.

Her question seemed to fly in from left field, but he played along.

"It's an adjustment, for sure. I mean, you've got to admit, getting a little girl dropped into my life is pretty huge for anybody. But I believe she's my daughter, and I'm going to take care of her. To be honest, I thought I would feel some immediate engagement, and I'm a little disappointed in myself that I didn't, but I feel like that will come."

Shame flickered as he admitted his thoughts. But he had to be honest.

"Did you always want children?"

For a moment, he wondered if he had spoken his thoughts aloud when they sat reading to Charlotte. He wasn't sure where she was leading him, but her need to ask him these questions rekindled the faint flicker of hope.

"Yes, I always wanted children. I always wanted a family."

Her mouth twisted into a wry smile. "You are a good man."

"Why does that sound like a backhanded compliment?" He gave her a smile to show her he was teasing. And yet, beneath all that, a faint edge of disappointment ran over his soul. Good man? Was that the only way she saw him?

"Nothing backhanded about it. It's true. And it's a positive thing to be called that. There are few truly good men in this world."

Another hint, another glimpse behind the curtain.

She shifted a little, and he realized so had he. Once again, their faces were close enough that he saw the faint laugh lines fanning from the corner of her eyes, the glow of her pupils. He caught the citrus scent of her hair. He rested his hand on her shoulder and, taking a chance, he stroked one finger up and down the warm skin of her neck.

"I'd like to think I'm more than just a good man to you," he said, his voice tender.

Her face paled, but she didn't pull back.

"I'm not...I'm not who I used to be. I'm not...I'm not who you think I am."

Her hesitant confession puzzled him, but the yearning in her eyes told him more than her words did.

"All you have to be is Nadia. That's enough for me," he whispered.

"Is it?" she whispered.

"Yes. It is." He bent close, cradling her neck in his hand, waiting a few seconds for a sign from her.

Then her hand slid up to his shoulder, her other hand clutched the back of his head, fingers tangling in his hair, and suddenly, once again, they were kissing.

Seeking, tasting, touching.

The deep yearning that had shadowed him all these years slipped away with her in his arms. Their breaths intermingled, their mouths exploring. He drew back enough to rain kisses over her cheek, down her neck, then, hungrily, returning to her mouth.

This is what they were meant to be.

The kiss went on, melding them, making them one.

When he finally drew away, he rested his forehead against hers. His breath came in hard, quick gasps.

"This is who you are," he whispered against her mouth. "Loving, giving, caring. No less than that."

"But I'm not…"

Her voice came out in a strangled gasp, and he smothered a beat of fear at the despair in her voice.

"So much has happened since I left," she protested, pulling away just enough to create some distance between them. And yet, staying in his arms.

"Like what? Please tell me. I feel you've got this wall you keep putting up, but yet, you keep coming back to me, throwing out these vague comments."

"I know I shouldn't —"

"Why not?" he pressed.

"I don't deserve you."

Drew lowered his arms, feeling the need to create some distance as he tried to get through to her. He had tasted her, held her close. She hadn't hesitated. In fact, she had fully participated.

It was as if, once she gave herself some time to think, she

pulled back. But he wasn't letting her off. Not when he sensed he was close to a revelation. Something she was holding back that kept her away from him.

"How can you say you don't deserve me when I'm the one with the child I didn't know I had only a few feet down the hall?"

Nadia twisted a strand of hair around her finger, a sure sign of her discomfort.

"But you didn't know about her. And when she came, you willingly brought her into your home. You're trying to be her father. I know you weren't probably thrilled to find out about her, and yet, when I see you with her…I see that you want her. That you are willing to let her into your life."

Something in her tone showed him another layer to her protests.

"What happened between you and Arlen?" he pressed, sensing that was part of the secret.

He kept the question simple, hoping she would fill in the blanks that kept coming up in her conversation each time she pulled away.

She twisted her hair tighter, bit her lip harder, then looked directly at him.

"Please tell me. Trust me, I'm the last person to judge anything you might have to say," he said.

She released a light laugh, but it held no humor. "Okay. Here it is. I got pregnant while Arlen and I were dating, and I told Arlen. I told him that much as it shamed me, I had to move home to have this baby. He had made no kind of commitment the entire time we were dating, and I was thinking of breaking up with him before I got pregnant. He was upset, but said we had to get married. That I wasn't raising this child away from him, and he wasn't moving back to Aspen Valley. That's when he told me he loved me and couldn't live without me. I believed him and clung to this hope that I thought we could make it work, thinking it would solve everything, so we eloped..." Her voice broke, and Drew caught her hand, squeezing it, giving her what little comfort he could. He wanted to pull her into his arms again but sensed there was more to say. So, he kept his distance and waited.

She drew in a shaky breath, both hands clutching his now. "But after we were married, Arlen grew...morose...depressed. I tried to get him to tell me why, but he wouldn't. Then, three months after we got married, I lost the baby."

She paused there, her hands twisting around each other. Drew stifled his gasp and couldn't stop himself from pulling her close to him. Trying to comfort her.

She leaned against him, her head resting on his chest.

"How did Arlen react to that?"

She swiped at the tears on her cheek. "I was devastated, and Arlen pulled further into himself. He started drinking, staying away, and one night, when he came home late after yet another night out with his friends, he was in a foul mood. I'd rarely seen that side of him, but it was coming out more and more. That night, he accused me of trapping him into marriage. Then things got really ugly when he admitted that he never wanted to have the baby. He said it worked for the best because he wasn't ready to be a father, despite all his declarations to the contrary only a few months previous. I knew he could be erratic, but when he said that, I was so upset. So angry." She released a harsh laugh. "As if anyone is ever ready, no matter how longed for or accidental the child is." Then she pulled back, looking up at him. "And even though I know you were probably not ready to be a father either, I see you with Charlotte, I see you trying, and I realize how much better you are than you think you are. If that makes any sense."

"I'm so sorry for you," Drew said, surprised at the surge of grief he felt for her loss. He'd had no idea. Not even an inkling. His brother mentioned nothing in the few texts or phone calls they exchanged.

"I was sorry for me, too. But I made vows, and even though all I wanted was to come back to Aspen Valley, I stayed with him. He seemed to have turned a corner after that. He quit his job, started painting full-time, and produced some beautiful works. I thought I could find my way through this, until, well…"

"Until what?"

She nodded. "Until I couldn't. I tried. I really did. It was enough work being with Arlen when he was sober, but when he was drunk…" she let the sentence drift away, and Drew filled in the blanks, fighting down anger with his brother for what he had done.

"You always talk about him so positively to my mother."

He dropped the comment quietly into the conversation. Just a casual observation, hoping she could explain that to him. Which made her pull her hands out of his. Made her turn away, looking ahead a moment, then she stood.

"I'm sorry. I'm tired. I'll look over all this tomorrow. I thought the girls sent pictures of the flowers, but I can't find them."

Another brush-off. This time, he let it go. He had pushed hard enough. Found out more than he wanted to and yet, it explained so much.

Even though he sensed there was still more to her and Arlen's story. He had grilled enough witnesses to know when there was still something waiting to be told. But she wasn't going anywhere, and the moments they had shared gave him enough hope to think he would discover what he needed to in time.

"I'm sure I have them somewhere," she muttered, scrolling through her phone.

He put his hand on hers to stop her and, thankfully, she didn't pull away.

"It doesn't matter," he assured her. "We can go in person to the greenhouse tomorrow after work. I wouldn't mind seeing them for myself." Again, he aimed for casual. No big deal. Just checking things out for his friends' wedding party. Due diligence and all that. "You and Charlotte don't need to come, but I thought it might be a nice outing for my mother."

Nadia blinked, still not looking at him. He waited, wondering if he was being way too obvious, which he probably was, but he wanted to spend time with her. Wanted to keep up the connections he knew were building between them.

"I think I'd like to come along," she said. "It would be good for Charlotte and me to get out of the house as well."

Then she gave him a careful smile, her hand still holding his. She gave it a light squeeze, then got up, leaving him and the tea tray behind.

He leaned back, watching her go, curiosity fighting with a general impatience.

He knew one thing for sure. He wasn't giving up on her again. If there was a chance, he wanted to make sure he didn't let it slip out of his hands. If only he could figure out what else she was holding back about Arlen. Because it seemed to hover like a ghost he couldn't pin down.

Chapter 10

Nadia hesitated at the door of Drew and Aria's office, looking down at Charlotte, who clung to her hand, her rabbit tucked under her arm.

They were in town to visit the nursery and look at the plants the twins had already scouted out. They also intended to give Drew some more time with his daughter during the day.

Yesterday, while Charlotte napped, Nadia had gone through Lily's exercises with her. While Charlotte was awake, Lily's friend, Lorna McLure had picked her up for an afternoon away from the house.

Nadia was thankful for the break, as it gave her a chance to spend one on one time with Charlotte without feeling torn between doing what she was paid to do, which was take care of Lily, and doing what she wanted to do, which was play with Charlotte.

Drew had come home for lunch to be with his daughter. He read her a couple of stories and tried to play with some blocks with her. She engaged for a little while but then sought out Nadia. Nadia had felt bad for Drew, but they both surmised that she was missing her mother and wasn't used to having a man in her life. They both knew it would be a while before Charlotte accepted Drew and grew accustomed to her new life.

Poor munchkin.

Now she would probably be overwhelmed by attention once they stepped inside Drew's office. Lily hadn't wanted to stay in the car with Charlotte while Nadia went inside to fetch Drew. She was itching to get to the Grill and Chill so that she could chat up some people there.

Nadia also guessed that Lily still wasn't too keen on being with Charlotte one on one. Lily seemed to do little more than tolerate the little girl. Nadia would have liked to call her out on it, but she didn't feel it was her place. After all, Charlotte wasn't her daughter, and Lily wasn't her mother.

But Lily's reluctance meant that Nadia now had to take Charlotte with her into Drew's office.

She pushed open the door and stepped inside.

Louisa looked up from behind the reception desk, smiling politely. Her expression shifted as she recognized Nadia. Then her eyes widened when she saw Charlotte.

She looked like she was about to stand up, and Nadia's hand tightened protectively around Charlotte's hand. She hoped that Louisa would be discreet. Thankfully, Louisa could read the room and sat down again. Instead, she smiled at the little girl. "Hello, Charlotte, welcome to...your dad's...office."

It seemed Louisa was also getting used to the idea of Drew having a child.

Charlotte leaned closer to Nadia, turning her head against her leg.

"She's rather overwhelmed right now," Nadia explained, bending over to pick the child up and give her a quick cuddle.

"No doubt. Poor kiddo." Louisa shook her head. "I'm sure Drew is feeling the pinch as well."

"I'm sure he is," was all Nadia said. She didn't want to say too much in front of Charlotte. Though the girl was only two years old, Nadia wasn't sure what that little mind understood or processed.

"I'm guessing this is Charlotte?" Aria came out of her office, smiling as well as she took in Nadia with the little girl. She kept her distance, trying to catch Charlotte's eye. "Hey little one," she said. "Good to meet you."

Charlotte just turned her head, tucking it into Nadia's neck.

Aria smiled, turning her attention back to Nadia. "Does Drew know you're here?"

"I just checked in with him," Louisa put in. "He's finishing up a phone call, then he'll be right out."

"What's on the agenda for today?" Aria asked Nadia.

"Greenhouse. The twins found some pots they want us to check out for the party."

Aria pressed her clasped hands against her chest. "I'm so excited. I want to come with you."

"You can't," Drew said, stepping out of his office and slipping on his suit jacket over his shirt. "That was the whole point of delegating, no?"

His gaze paused at Nadia for a heartbeat, then skipped over to Aria, his mouth curving in a wry smile.

"I know, but – "

"You still want some input?"

Aria chuckled and waved off his question. "You're right; I handed it over. I'll just get back to my client's files. Need to get lots done before we leave."

"You do that. And I'll help Nadia take care of your party."

Again, Drew's gaze slid to her, and the longer their eyes held, the less breath she seemed to have. His look was as tangible as a touch. An energy hummed between them, and she couldn't look away. Then Charlotte stirred in her arms and her heart twisted.

"Let's go," she said, spinning around, but not before catching Aria's lifted eyebrows and curious glance.

Don't blush, Nadia told herself, lifting her chin and giving Aria look for look.

Thankfully, Aria just grinned, turned, and walked back to her office. But just before she closed the door, Aria pointed two fingers to her eyes, then flipped them back to Nadia as if to say, "I see what's going on," and then closed the door.

"Did you want me to take her?" Drew offered, holding out his hands to Charlotte.

"Sure," Nadia agreed, shifting the little girl in her arms toward Drew.

"No. Stay wif you," Charlotte protested, clinging like a little monkey to Nadia.

Nadia shot Drew an apologetic look, but he shrugged off Charlotte's reaction, walking ahead of them to open the door.

As he did, Nadia caught a look of pain in his eyes.

He walked ahead of her down the stairs, and once they reached his car, Nadia set Charlotte down. Thankfully, Lily was already walking toward them, so they wouldn't have to go looking for her.

"What a perfect day," Lily said, her smile wide, eyes bright.

"And what new gossip did you discover?" Drew asked, a note of humor now in his voice.

"No gossip," Lily protested. "But I have some plans in the making."

Nadia sensed that was all Lily was saying about that. She caught Drew's vague shrug, and they exchanged a smile.

Once again, Nadia felt as if she had to drag her gaze away from Drew's.

"THESE ARE BEAUTIFUL," Nadia said, looking down at the pots of flowers Rika had pulled for them at the greenhouse. "It's like you custom-made them for Aria."

White lilies nestled in beds of alstroemeria, a perfect contrast to the yellow-green of the sweet potato vines surrounding them and flowing over the black pedestal pots.

Rika had a dozen of them.

Simple and elegant.

"They were for another party that got canceled," Rika said. "I figured I could sell a few piecemeal, but I prefer to sell them all in one shot, so this works out great."

Rika pinched a random dead flower out of one pot, then arranged the vines in another.

The greenhouse was humid and warm and buzzing with bees coming and going. Colorful pots of geraniums, pansies, and petunias hung in rows from the bars of the roof, and the wooden benches overflowed with more plants and flowers.

The sight made Nadia smile.

What also made her smile was watching Charlotte ambling alongside Drew as he pointed out flowers to her, lifting her from time to time to let her sniff some. The sight warmed her heart, especially after Charlotte's rejection of him at the office.

When they arrived at the greenhouse, the little girl seemed to relax and toddled off with Drew when he held out his hand to her.

Lily was on another aisle of the greenhouse, smiling as she looked around, chatting up whoever passed her by.

Probably passing on tidbits of the gossip she picked up at the Grill and Chill, Nadia thought.

"So? What do you think?" Rika asked her.

"I think we'll take all of them. This is amazing and very fortunate. But we can't take them home right now."

Rika shrugged, adjusting her ball cap on her graying hair. "No biggie. I'll drag them to the other greenhouse so other customers don't snag them."

"I'll call one of my brothers to come and get them in a day or so." Nadia pulled out her phone to make a note.

"If you're looking for white plants, I've got more white pansies and lilies, some white lobelia. A few of the wave petunias are nice and full. Look around. Let me know."

Then, before Nadia could say anything else, Rika was off to deal with another one of the many customers vying for her attention. Nadia let her eyes flow over the explosion of colors, inhaling the heady mixture of flower scents, dirt, and moisture. After feeling cooped up all day at the house, taking care of Lily and Charlotte, this was like a balm to her soul.

Again, as if unable to stop herself, her eyes were drawn to Charlotte and Drew.

Nadia had to resist the urge to join them. It was good to see Charlotte with her father. Though, she had to admit, when Charlotte preferred her to Drew that moment in the office, she had felt a flicker of attachment and possessiveness. It was wrong, and she had no right, but it ignited the deep sense of motherlove she had felt those few months she had been pregnant.

Pushing that gut-wrenching memory down deep, she turned in the opposite direction, using her phone to snap pictures of other flowers they might buy to send to the twins.

One deep breath and she had control back again.

This afternoon she had verified with the caterer the time and date. Nadia just had to confirm with another rental agency for the delivery of tables, chairs, and tablecloths.

Burke had taken over the delivery and placement of the tent. The twins had picked out a playlist, and Shelby had lined up a DJ. Drake had agreed to be the Master of Ceremonies.

Things were coming together.

All that needed to be done now was to go over the invitation list that Aria and Lucas had put together. Aria had set up a website for people to reply and had given Nadia the password.

The job that had once seemed too large was feeling more controlled.

She found a few smaller arrangements that they could use on the tables and made note of them. As far as she could tell, they were still well within the budget.

"You look pleased with yourself," Drew teased as he came around the corner, Charlotte still clinging to his hand.

As soon as she saw Nadia, Charlotte pulled away from him and toddled toward her, holding one arm up, with her rabbit still tucked under her other one.

"Go with Daddy," Nadia urged, the sight of that little girl coming to her resurrecting the old, unwanted memories.

"No. See my Mommy."

Nadia sensed, this time, it wasn't her that Charlotte was referring to.

The little girl's simple words tied a knot of pain in Nadia's chest. What was she supposed to say? That Mommy isn't here and never will be?

"Why don't we look at some more flowers," she suggested, hoping to distract her.

Charlotte shook her head, her blonde curls getting tangled in the tears now spilling out of her eyes.

"See Mommy. Want Mommy." Her little voice broke on the last word.

Nadia shot a panicked glance at Drew, who held his hands up in surrender, also at a loss. She picked up the sobbing little girl and held her close, rocking her. There was nothing to say, so Nadia simply stroked her back.

Thankfully, the little girl settled down. Drew also put his hand on Charlotte's back, his and Nadia's hands touching. She paused, their fingers intertwining, connecting. They looked at each other and then could not look away. The moment stretched out. Nadia didn't even realize they had moved closer until she felt the warmth of Drew's arm as they brushed.

"I see you found some – "

Lily's voice broke off, and when Nadia glanced over, it was to see Drew's mother frowning at her, eyes narrowed.

Nadia wanted to pull away her hand, which was still holding Drew's, but she stopped herself. She had done nothing wrong.

Despite that self-talk, she couldn't stop a shiver of betrayal at the look in Lily's eyes.

"I think we'd better get going." Lily lifted her chin as if challenging Nadia. "I was hoping to stop at my house and see how the renovations are coming. I was told they might be finished by the end of the week." Then, without another look at her son or Nadia, she pushed her walker past them, her gait steady and even.

Drew ran his index finger up and down Nadia's hand before he pulled his away. She suppressed a small shiver at his touch, feeling a knot of uncertain emotions.

"She seems snippy," he remarked.

"That she does," was all Nadia could say.

Charlotte sniffed and lifted her head, looking around. "Pwetty fowers."

"She seems better," Nadia said.

"Better than my mother," Drew grumbled.

As they followed Lily out of the greenhouse, Nadia felt a sense of inevitability taking over. Eventually, she and Drew would have to talk about what was happening between them. But even as she thought this, she felt a flush of panic.

Because with that came the need to tell him everything else.

Chapter 11

Drew turned off the car and climbed out to help his mother, but she was already opening the door. She waved off his offer of help, turning in her seat as Nadia brought out her walker.

"I'm tired," she announced as she grabbed hold of it. "I'm going right to my room." Then, without another backward look, she marched up the walk to the house and up the makeshift ramp Drew had made for her convenience.

As the door fell shut behind her, Drew exchanged a concerned look with Nadia.

"What's her deal?" he asked.

"I dunno," Nadia replied with a tight shrug, walking around the car to Charlotte.

"I'll get her," Drew said, putting a hand out to stop Nadia.

Charlotte was fast asleep in her car seat, and Drew unbuckled her, easing her floppy hands through the straps. Her head fell back as he took her out of the car seat, but she still didn't wake up.

He curled her against him, warmth radiating off her damp hair. She smacked her lips as he cuddled her close. He straightened, his hand on the top of her head to make sure he didn't bump it against the frame of the car. Nadia watched him with a quizzical expression that he didn't want to delve into at the moment.

"Her rabbit is on the seat," he murmured. "Do you mind getting it for her?"

Nadia nodded, then Drew walked up to the house, shifting the little girl so he could open the door. As he stepped inside, he heard the muffled tone of his mother's voice. Probably talking on the phone.

She didn't seem happy.

He should care, but he didn't.

He shouldered the door of his bedroom, currently serving as Nadia's room, and walked to the bed. He laid Charlotte down, tucking a blanket around her. She snuffled, wrinkling her nose, then snuggled down on the pillow and drifted back to sleep.

He watched her for a moment, smiling at the memory of her holding his hand, walking alongside him at the greenhouse. As if she was slowly accepting him.

But behind that, he recalled her plaintive wail for her mommy.

"Oh, muffin," he murmured, stroking her hair away from her face. "This is going to be a hard road for the next bit, but I promise you, it will get better."

Then he bent over and brushed a gentle kiss over her warm cheek. To his surprise, a faint smile curled her lips.

He stroked her hair again, then turned, stopping short when he saw Nadia in the doorway, holding Charlotte's rabbit.

"She sleeping?" Nadia whispered, handing it to him.

"Yes. I think she'll be down for a while." He tucked the rabbit in her arm, then left, easing the door shut behind him.

As he did, he glanced across the hall at his mother's room. From her murmured conversation, he guessed she was still talking on the phone. For a beat, he wondered if he should go in and speak with her.

And say what?

I'm falling in love with Nadia, and I think you know it.

"Will your mother be okay?" Nadia asked, frowning as she glanced at the door to Lily's room. "She seemed upset."

Drew blew out a breath, shrugged, then walked toward the kitchen. He leaned back against the counter, keeping the island between him and Nadia, crossing his arms.

"I don't know about my mother. And, frankly, how upset or not she is shouldn't matter so much. I have to learn to separate myself from what she thinks because of how I feel about..." he let the word drift away, feeling a flare of disloyalty.

"How you feel about what?" Nadia prompted, elbows resting on the island between them.

How was he supposed to articulate what he was feeling?

"You seem at a loss for words," she said, looking puzzled.

"I am. Because words, once spoken, are out in the wild. And they can't be taken back."

"And actions? What about them?"

He frowned, holding her steady gaze, and realized what she was getting at.

"Actions definitely have an impact."

The truth of their own actions hovered between them, and he couldn't help a faint smile.

"We need to talk," was all he could say.

"Yes, we do."

Again, that silence. But this one held anticipation threaded with the reality that what they had to say would have repercussions for them and for Charlotte.

Because he had her to think of now.

Drew pulled in a breath to begin when his mother's door opened.

"How about some tea?" his mother announced as she marched into the kitchen.

Drew clenched his hands, holding back his frustration. Was his mother listening? Waiting to disrupt this moment?

Because it sure looked like that right now.

He sent up a prayer for patience. Then, so she couldn't see the frustration on his face, turned to fill the kettle. But he said nothing. As his mother sat at the dining room table, he pulled out some mugs, sugar, and honey.

"Have you heard anything more from your friend about Arlen's art show?" she asked Nadia.

"No. I haven't replied."

"Why not? I thought for sure you would want to attend."

"I'm taking care of you," Nadia returned. "I can't just take off when I want to."

"But you want to go, don't you?"

"I'm not sure – "

"Here's the tea," Drew said, breaking into the conversation.

"I think you should go." Lily took the mug of tea that Drew offered her, but she fixed her eyes on Nadia. "It would give you some closure. I'm sure you're still grieving Arlen's death."

Drew's gaze slid over to Nadia, watching her as she chewed her lower lip.

"There are a few things I need to…" her voice wavered, and she drew in a quick breath.

The confusion and sorrow in her voice were like a fist to his stomach. What was going on? He felt like it was two steps forward two steps back when it came to her relationship with Arlen. Some silly dance he didn't know how to follow.

You should walk away. Eventually, she's leaving.

NADIA FINISHED WASHING the dishes as she heard Drew's quiet voice reading Charlotte a story. She was perched on his lap, her damp curls curling around her face, her cheeks rosy, looking adorable in her blue ruffled pajamas. The ones Drew had picked out. He said he didn't know how to be a father, yet he was already such a natural.

The day had been busy. Lily had been a bit more demanding than usual. A bit more short-tempered. And, as if picking up on the mood in the house, Charlotte had been fractious as well.

Drew had come home for lunch, then, thankfully, took Charlotte out for a walk to the park close by. She came back tired and immediately went to sleep.

Nadia and Drew didn't have much time for each other because Lily hovered, asking questions about the party they were organizing for Lucas and Aria, and quizzing Nadia some more about her life with Arlen.

Nadia had answered her questions, catching Drew's puzzled glances. The promise they had made to each other to talk things through hadn't materialized, and she sensed it wouldn't happen tonight either. Lily seemed determined to stick around.

"Anudder one," Charlotte demanded, pushing a book Drew's way.

"You should make her say 'please,'" Lily grumbled.

Drew acted as if she hadn't spoken. He picked up the book and began reading.

Charlotte curled up against him, tucking her thumb into her mouth.

"And that's another thing you'll have to make her stop. It's bad for her teeth."

"So you said before." Drew's voice was even, as if he didn't care what his mother said.

Nadia turned back to the sink of dishes, surprised at how patient Drew was with his mother, which was something she had struggled with today.

As she grabbed a plate to dry it, it slipped out of her fingers and crashed onto the floor.

"My goodness, Nadia, what are you up to in there?" Lily asked. "You startled me."

Nadia glanced over her shoulder at Lily, who rested in her recliner, feet up, magazine open on her lap.

"Sorry about that," Nadia muttered.

But before she turned back, she couldn't help but watch the little group in the living room. Lily had turned her attention back to her magazine, quiet now. Drew was reading, Charlotte tucked against him.

Despite Lily's negativity, this was still a family, and Nadia couldn't erase the feeling that she was on the edge of it, looking in. She needed to go visit her own family. Connect with them and realize what she already had, instead of trying to imagine herself as a part of this one.

She finished the dishes, then put them away, wiped the counters, and set the leftovers in the fridge. She prepared the coffee pot for tomorrow morning, mixed up the porridge in the instant pot, and set the timer to go off so it would be ready when they got up.

Then there was nothing left to do.

"Are you going to come join me?" Lily asked, closing her magazine and setting it aside. "I'm fancying a Scrabble game rematch."

She would have preferred to join Drew and Charlotte, but this was part of her job. So, she just smiled.

"Of course," Nadia agreed.

She pulled the Scrabble board out of the cupboard and set it on the dining room table, then walked over to the recliner, supervising as Lily stood and grabbed her cane. She was getting more stable on her feet, but Nadia didn't want all her hard work to disappear with a fall.

"If you guys will give me a few minutes," Drew said, closing the book he was reading and setting it aside. I'm putting Charlotte to bed, and I can come join you."

"No bed," Charlotte grumbled, rubbing at her eyes, her rosy cheeks putting a lie to her protest.

"It's been a busy day for you," Drew said, standing and hiking her onto his hip. "Say good night to everybody."

She pouted for a moment, but then gave in, waggling her chubby fingers at Nadia and Lily, who were settling in at the table.

"Night-night, Nana. Night-night, Mama."

Nadia was startled at the words. She knew the little girl calling her that was unintentional, but they still hooked deep into her heart.

This little girl was worming her way into her life, and Nadia wasn't sure she could walk away as easily as she thought.

When she glanced over at Drew, that idea solidified even more.

They needed to find some time, just the two of them. But from the way Lily seemed to behave, Nadia guessed it wouldn't be tonight either.

LILY LAY ON HER BED, her hands folded over her chest, her eyes narrowed as she glared at Nadia.

The morning sun slanted into the room. The window was open, and birds sang. It was already a glorious summer day. But from the frown on Lily's face, Nadia guessed Lily's bad mood from yesterday had seeped into today as well.

While she wanted to quiz Lily about it, Nadia also got the sense that she might not want to know what was bothering her mother-in-law.

From the looks Lily had given them over the dinner table yesterday and this morning, and the few veiled comments she made about the "two of them," as she had said, Nadia sensed that Lily's mood had something to do with her and Drew.

Charlotte was napping now, which gave Nadia time to go over Lily's exercises without distractions. She kept the door open so she could hear if the little girl woke up.

"Can you lift your leg a little higher?" Nadia asked, trying to push Lily to work harder.

Lily did so, but again her resentment wasn't hard to read as she went through the motions.

Nadia couldn't stand the veiled antagonism any longer. "What's wrong? Did you not sleep well?"

"No, I didn't," Lily retorted.

"I'm sorry to hear that."

Lily pulled in a deep breath.

"I need to know. What is going on between you and Drew?" she snapped, avoiding looking at Lily.

The question felt like a lash, and Nadia tried not to recoil.

But her question validated Nadia's guesses.

"Two and One," she intoned, skirting the question as she fought the guilt that crept in behind Lily's accusing tone. "Your exercises are coming along well. I think in about a week, you won't need my help anymore."

"You're putting me off," Lily accused her. "I know something is going on. I've seen how you look at each other. Have you forgotten Arlen so quickly?"

Natalie released a harsh laugh. "I wish I could forget about him quicker."

"What do you mean? How can you say that?"

"I don't want to talk about Arlen anymore. I'd like to put him to rest."

"Seems to me he's at rest already," Lily said with a break in her voice. "And I'll never see him again."

Lily was being overly dramatic with her declaration. However, that all too-familiar fist of reproach squeezed Nadia's heart. In time, she hoped it would go away, but for now, she had to ride it out. Push all those horrible memories away. Lily wasn't helping, but eventually, Nadia would be finished working here and then…

Then…

At one time, she knew precisely what was coming after that. A shortened trip to Vancouver Island, then working for Liam. And after that, another trip away.

But now, as thoughts of Drew and Charlotte slipped into her mind, she wasn't so sure.

"At any rate, I'm feeling more and more uncomfortable here," she sniffed. "So maybe that time will be even less." Lily started the set of exercises on her other leg, still avoiding Nadia's eyes. "I called up Lorna McLure. She will come to my home to help me for the next week or so."

"I thought your house wasn't ready for you to move back," Nadia said, keeping her voice even and quiet.

"It's ready enough. The carpenters are just doing some touch-ups this week. Besides, I've taken up enough of Drew's time and space. I'd like to be on my own, and I hope that's not a problem for you," Lily sniffed, though her tone intimated that she didn't care if it was or not. "I know Drew hired you for at least another week, and I also know he's paying you. If you need the extra money, I'll gladly make up what you would've lost in wages."

Lily rolled to her side and pushed herself to a seated position, reaching for her cane.

Nadia wanted to argue that the money didn't matter, but it did.

"That would be nice," was all she could say, thankful she wouldn't have to talk to Drew about it.

Then, to her surprise, Lily grabbed her hand, her fingers tightening around Nadia's. "I wish…I wish things were different. I just wish…"

Nadia wasn't sure what the woman was referring to, so she just let the sentence hang, figuring Lily had something more she wanted to say.

"I wish you and Arlen could have stayed together. Could have lived here in Aspen Valley. I could have had my son back."

Nadia's thoughts veered from annoyance to pain, blended with self-recrimination. It was exhausting, this constant remembering of something she had hoped to put behind her. Forget. Move past.

"You know, Arlen would not have been happy here, even if he'd had the remotest thought of moving back," she said, keeping her voice quiet.

"I know. I just wish I knew why. I gave him so much, did so much for him. Was it wrong to hope for more gratitude?"

Trouble was, Nadia knew all too well all the things Lily had done for Arlen. She had her own opinions on that, but what did it matter now?

But the genuine pain in Lily's voice bothered her.

"Arlen was a complicated soul," was all Nadia could give Drew's mother as she extricated her hand from Lily's. "I think he needed to be with the people he chose to be with. He needed the inspiration he got there."

"I suppose," Lily conceded, blowing out her breath in a sigh. "And maybe I gave him too much. Made it too easy for him to stay there. I only ever wanted good things for him."

And around and around they went, and suddenly Nadia was tired of it.

"And what about Drew? Did you want good things for him?" Too late, Nadia realized how brisk and condemning her tone was. But the words were spoken, hanging between them like a cloud.

Lily's eyes grew wide, and she stared at Nadia as if she couldn't believe what she had just heard.

"How can you say that?" she demanded.

"It wasn't hard," Nadia said, deciding to go with it. "And it should have been said long ago."

Lily looked dumbfounded as if still trying to absorb what Nadia had said.

"I know you loved Arlen. I loved him too at one time. But I've also come to realize what a good man Drew is. And how much better he is than Arlen ever could be. I wish you would recognize that."

"But I love Drew…he's my son as much as Arlen was."

"I know that, and I respect that, but somehow, even when they were younger, Arlen seemed to be your favorite child. I'm wondering why that was. Especially considering what Drew has been doing for you the past while. What he has always done for you. Arlen was never and never could be as supportive as Drew is now."

Lily pressed her lips together, looking away from Nadia.

"That's unfair. Especially after losing Arlen like this. Of course, I would be thinking about him."

"It's more than that, and I believe you know that. It's something I've seen from the first day I came into this house."

"I don't understand why you're taking this tone with me." Lily lifted her chin in defiance. "Especially considering you did the same thing. Chose Arlen over Drew."

Once again, her words raised a flicker of guilt followed by remorse.

Nadia waited for a beat as she gathered her thoughts.

"You're right," she admitted. "I fell for the same lines that everyone else did. The same charm. But eventually, I was able to see Arlen for who he was." She stopped herself there.

"What do you mean by that?"

Nadia crossed her arms, scrambling through her memories to find the right words.

"Like I told you before, Arlen was struggling. And that struggle spilled over into our marriage. I saw parts of him that I had never seen before, but had gotten hints of. Things I didn't want to see before but were exposed to in our marriage. He could be…difficult. I think he was dealing with some depression. After he quit his job, his art wasn't selling the way he thought it would. Life wasn't panning out how he expected."

Not everyone saw his ability the same way his mother had, and that had been hard for him to accept.

"So you think Drew is the better man? Is that what you want me to say?"

Nadia waited, giving the question some time to settle. "I think I would like you to see how amazing Drew is. I think I would like you to see him as a faithful and loving son. Sometimes we project what we want a person to be on them, and we cannot see who they really are."

"And you think I did that with Arlen?"

"I think you did with Arlen, but I also think you did it with Drew. I think you wanted Arlen to be the faithful, loving son, and that's all you saw. And I think you wanted Drew to be convenient. So that's how you saw him, too."

Lily was quiet, as if absorbing Nadia's words.

Then the older women's shoulders slumped, as if in defeat.

"I didn't mean to… I love Drew. He's a wonderful son. As hard as it is to admit, I think deep down I know he was always the better son. He was always easy to be around. It's just that with Arlen…I felt as if I had to chase him down. So I tried harder with him."

Nadia heard the deep sorrow in her voice. The sense of loss on so many levels.

"Have you ever told Drew how you feel about him? How you really feel about him?"

"I think he knows." Again, that defensive tone in her voice.

"Even if he does, it never hurts to be told. He's dealing with a lot right now, and I think he needs your support."

Lily gave a tight nod, but then, without another word, she

grabbed the cane she had been using the last couple of days and left the room.

To Nadia's surprise, Lily pushed open the door of the bedroom across the hall. She stood just inside the doorway, and she guessed Lily was watching Charlotte as she slept.

Then, with her head bowed, she limped away.

As Nadia tidied the bed, she heard Lily talking on her phone, her voice low, quiet. Obviously, she didn't want Nadia to hear.

When Nadia was finished, she walked across the hall to the bedroom she shared with Charlotte, sensing that Lily wanted to be left alone. She had laundry to fold and put away.

A few moments later, as she put the last of Charlotte's small clothes in the closet, Nadia heard a faint knock on the house's front door, and Lily's call for whoever it was to come in.

Then she heard a woman's voice she recognized as Lorna, the woman who Lily would be moving in with. While the thought bothered Nadia, at the same time, it created a surprising sense of relief. Once Lily left, she wouldn't have to tiptoe around her feelings for Drew anymore. She wouldn't need to discuss Arlen anymore.

The thought made her smile, and she looked forward to Drew coming home later that afternoon.

Then reality lifted its ugly head.

Would she still be here if she wasn't helping Lily anymore?

She would have to deal with that later.

She was about to say hello to Lorna, but by the time she got to the front room, it was empty. Lily and Lorna were already in her car, driving away.

An hour later, Charlotte was awake. Nadia brushed her hair and then got the keys to the car, ready to leave. But before she could go out to the car, she saw that Lily had returned. Her friend backed her car out of the driveway, and Lily came into the house. She looked troubled, and Nadia was afraid she would have a repeat of the morning's disagreement.

Thankfully, she had an excuse to leave.

But to her surprise, when she came into the house, Lily gave her a gentle smile.

"Good. You're still here. I was hoping to catch you before you left. I can watch Charlotte while you go to get groceries."

Nadia frowned at this sudden change of events.

"Are you sure you'll be okay with her?" Nadia asked, trying to figure out what was happening.

"I'll have to be, won't I? She's my granddaughter."

While Nadia still struggled with her surprise, Lily's admission created a glimmer of happiness.

"Yes, she is that. But I was referring to your mobility."

"It's fine. It's not like I have to chase her around the room, now do I?"

"Not quite," Nadia admitted.

"Perfect. You can go on your own. I don't mind, and I'm sure it will be easier for you to shop without your little tagalong."

Nadia nodded, glancing over at Charlotte, who was rifling through the box of toys tucked in one corner.

"Are you sure?" She still was trying to wrap her head around the sudden change in Drew's mother.

Lily didn't hold her gaze, nodding. "I wouldn't offer if I wasn't."

"All right then. I'll leave. Text me or Drew if you need anything or if Charlotte gets upset."

"I will." Then Lily looked directly at her. "Don't worry. It will be fine."

Nadia nodded, acknowledging her comment, but even as she left, she couldn't help feeling that something had changed with Lily, and she couldn't put her finger on it.

Chapter 12

Charlotte dug a shovel into the sandpit and pushed it into a pile in front of her.

Sand sprinkled her blue dress and her hair was a tangle, but Drew didn't care. Charlotte was chuckling as she dug. Something he hadn't heard from her since she got dropped off at the house.

She had found a small plastic shovel laying on the park bench where his mother was now sitting, and ignoring his mother's warnings about germs, Drew let her play with it. He was still trying to figure out what his mother wanted. She had called him an hour ago, asking if he could come home early from work. All she would say was that she wanted to talk to him.

She gave him no hint of what it was about, but he sensed an urgency in her voice. So he put aside some of his work, planning to return to it after dinner.

This was not how he had envisioned his evening going, either. The conversation he hoped to have with Nadia hung between them, waiting. When he arrived home, his mother wanted to walk with him and Charlotte to the park.

Now he sat in the sand with his daughter, knowing his suit

would have to go to the cleaners after today. But again, he didn't mind. Charlotte's joy was infectious and made him smile.

"She'll get worms," his mother sniffed. "I wouldn't trust that sand."

"Aren't you a ray of sunshine?" Drew teased, shooting his mother a grin.

"Don't be flip. I'm serious." Her aggrieved tone made Drew wonder, yet again, why she had asked him to take her and Charlotte to the playground.

From the time she sat down on the bench, she had complained about the wind, the noise of the other children playing, and how hard the bench was.

"Maybe the exposure to the germs will be good for her," Drew suggested, watching as Charlotte pushed herself to her feet and toddled off toward the swings.

He was about to follow her when she changed her mind and veered back to him.

This time, to his surprise, she sat down right beside him, leaning against his arm.

"Make sure she doesn't suck her thumb after playing in that sand," his mother warned. "You should probably figure out a way to make her break that habit. It's not good for her teeth."

Drew had brought a package of wipes along, and without even looking toward his mother, he pulled them out and cleaned Charlotte's hands as best as he could.

"I don't know why you bother. She's just going to get dirty again," his mother sniffed.

He ignored that contrary comment as well, sensing that no matter what he said, she would find something to complain about. While he knew that with his mother, he had to bide his time, he was growing impatient. Nadia would be home soon, and he wanted to see her again.

Charlotte picked up the shovel, continuing to enlarge the sand pile that she'd been building.

"That looks fantastic," Drew praised her.

Charlotte nodded, as if agreeing with him.

"She doesn't say much, does she?" His mother asked.

"I'm sure she's still adjusting to this huge change in her life."

"And are you?"

"It's taking time."

"You're certain she's yours? Did you do that DNA test? I mean, that crimp on her ear and all is pretty positive proof, but you might want to make for absolute sure."

"I sent the test away," Drew replied. He had felt disloyal doing it. As if by mailing it, he still had lingering doubts about his paternity.

"Mind you, when she smiles like that, she has the same dimple tucked in the corner of her mouth that your brother had."

Obviously, Lily had seen the resemblance as well.

"Speaking of your brother, Nadia doesn't want to talk about him anymore."

And here they were, back on the subject of Arlen again, which made him think this was her purpose for coming along.

"That's up to Nadia. I'm not interfering."

"But she clearly misses him," his mother argued. "She sounded so sad when she used to talk about him. The deep grief in her eyes. Lately, she's been saying less about him, and I think it's because it hurts too much."

"Maybe she doesn't say too much about him because she's tired of talking about him." That came out a little harsher than he expected, but he wasn't sorry he said it.

"How can you say that?" His mother asked with a shocked gasp. "They were married. They loved each other."

"It's important that you emphasize the past tense of that," Drew said, still keeping his eyes on Charlotte.

"I'm sure you'd like to push Arlen to the back of your mind," his mother sniffed. "You always were jealous of him."

There it was.

Finally, out in the open.

Maybe the way that they had spent more time together in the past week than they had in the past couple of years had finally made her reveal the thoughts that he was sure had been on her mind for a long time.

"I think the only thing about Arlen I was jealous of was his ability to talk to anyone he met. How comfortable he was around strangers. And his artistic talent. But overall, I'm happy with where I am and who I am."

"Are you happy because you are trying to romance Nadia now that Arlen is out of the way?"

Trying.

Nice of her to put it that way.

He fought down a defensive comment, knowing it was immaterial. And yet, despite his own confident comments, he couldn't stifle the faint pang of sorrow at how clearly his mother favored Arlen over him.

Of course, were he to even hint at it, she would rebut that, saying that his father did the same by favoring Drew.

"Do you think she'll want to take you on now that you have a daughter?" his mother continued, not ready to let this rest. "That's a lot to expect of her. I know she's talked so much about her travels and how she and Arlen planned trips. I know she has one planned for when she's done here. Do you think she'll want to tie herself down?"

Though he tried to slough them off, her comments were like drips of acid, eating away at his own self-doubts.

"Why are you doing this?" he asked, turning to face her.

"Doing what? What are you talking about?" His mother lifted her chin, trying to look hurt.

He chose not to respond because he saw from the tilt of her mouth, the flicker of shame in her eyes, that she knew exactly what he meant. He waited, holding her gaze, keeping his expression neutral even though deep inside he felt an unwelcome churning in his gut.

"It's just…" she hesitated, looking down at her hands now folded on her lap. "Arlen and Nadia were married. He was… well…hers."

"I don't think Nadia sees it the same way," he couldn't help saying. "This ownership. She's an independent woman. And don't forget, they were divorced before he died."

His mother only sighed in response.

"I guess…I never like to think about that. I thought…she would settle him down."

"Do you think anyone could have done that?"

He brushed some sand off Charlotte's shoulder, and she grinned up at him. Her smile was like a tug on his heart, and he stroked her head. She returned to her digging and piling, tongue sticking out of her mouth in concentration.

"And now Arlen is gone," his mother continued, still in her own world. "He won't come back and he'll never…"

Again, he didn't see the connection between what she was saying now and previously, but he also sensed that his mother was struggling to articulate a thought she'd been wrestling with.

"He'll never what, Mom?" he prompted.

"He'll never spend time here, with me. Never realize how much I cared about him. He'll never…finally tell me he loved me, and that I mattered to him."

Her words settled in his mind as he sorted through the implications of them.

"I mean, I always knew where I stood with you." Her voice grew quiet. Soft. She shot him a quick glance, then looked away, her fingers twisting her wedding ring around her finger. "I knew you cared about me. And I never knew that with Arlen."

Her admission shocked him, but behind his reaction came

a surprising regret. Regret at the reality that his mother seemed to feel she had to earn Arlen's affection.

His love.

"I'm sorry you had to deal with that." He glanced over at Charlotte, who was still adding to her pile of sand.

He was still dealing with having her in his life, and yet, each moment he spent with her grew the fascination he felt with his daughter. Increased his affection for her.

If he had other children, would he do the same thing that his mother did? Favor one over the other?

"Arlen was an elusive person," his mother continued. "Hard to pin down, and that made me seek him out even more." She eked out a sigh. "It wasn't right, and I'm sorry."

Then, to his surprise, he felt her hand on his shoulder. It was just a touch, momentary, and then gone, but he sensed that for his usually undemonstrative mother, this was an enormous step.

"Thanks for that," he said.

Then he turned his attention to Charlotte, curling his arm around her narrow shoulders, determined that she would always know his love. His care.

No matter what it cost.

"THIS STILL SEEMS SUDDEN," Drew said to Lily as he took his mother's suitcase to her bedroom in her home. It was on the main floor as well, so the stairs in the house wouldn't be a concern. "I hope you won't regret this."

"Living in your house made me realize how much I craved my space and privacy." She added a soft smile, which tempered her words.

"Just give me her cosmetic bag," Lorna said to Drew before he could respond to his mother's comment.

Drew handed his mother's overnight bag to Lorna, who took it with a reassuring smile.

"I'll take good care of her," she assured Drew.

"I'm sure you will," he returned.

He had his own thoughts about his mother moving out of his house. If he were honest, he was concerned with how things would look now that he, Charlotte, and Nadia were the only ones there.

And, even more importantly, would Nadia be willing to stay and take care of Charlotte? They hadn't talked about it yet.

"Um, can you catch that little girl?" his mother asked, frowning as she looked past him.

Drew turned to see Charlotte climbing onto his mother's pristine white couch, knocking over a throw pillow. He made a move toward her, but Nadia, who had just entered the house, saw what was happening, quickly set down the box she was carrying, and scooted over to Charlotte, picking her up just as Drew joined her.

She gave him an apologetic look and moved to give Charlotte to him.

"I'm sorry. I just saw – "

"Good catch," was all he said with a gentle smile, guessing at her discomfort. He caught her doing this more often. As if she was concerned about getting between him and his daughter.

She returned his smile, her eyes holding his as she shifted Charlotte in her arms. Once again, he had that sensation of time slowing, wheeling backward.

Giving them both another chance at this relationship.

"I think I've got everything settled into my bedroom," his mother announced, joining them, an unwelcome interruption. Lily glanced over at her couch and the messed-up throw pillows. Her lips pressed together, and Drew prepared to defend his daughter. Thankfully, his mother's expression relaxed, and she gave Drew a tentative smile. "Thanks for all your help. I appreciate it. I know I haven't always done so."

He caught her gaze and sensed an underlying tone, a subtext hinting at what they talked about yesterday.

Truthfully, he was still adjusting to their conversation. Still resolving where to put this information in the timeline of his life. He knew a single conversation wouldn't erase years of snubs and comparisons with Arlen, but he also knew how proud his mother was and how difficult it was for her to admit a mistake.

It was a first step on what he hoped would be a journey of healing.

"You've got everything you need?" Drew asked, feeling reluctant to leave. "There's nothing we can get for you?"

"I got groceries yesterday," Lorna said. "Not much else needs to be done."

"I'll be fine," his mother reiterated. "You needn't stay if you and…you and Nadia…have things to do."

"What are your plans for the rest of the afternoon?" Lorna asked Drew.

"Nadia and I are heading to the Prins farm to go over a few last-minute plans for the party next week." He was deliberate about linking his and Nadia's names after his mother's hesitation. Though he understood, he and Nadia were moving to another level in their relationship, and the sooner his mother was on board, the better for everyone.

"I'm sure that'll be very exciting. Have Lucas and Aria left already?" Lorna asked.

"I told you already," Lily put in, frowning at Lorna. "They were flying out this evening."

"Oh, right. I saw Aria and Lucas gassing up at the Co-op, but I thought they were leaving tomorrow."

"No. Because that would make time tight for them since they have to be back by next week Friday."

"I'm still surprised they decided to elope." Lorna shook

her head. "I thought, given what her dad was like, that Aria would be more traditional."

"He could be, though I've heard some unsettling things about him. He's not the paragon of virtue we all thought he was." Lily asserted.

"Really? This is news." Lorna said, her voice laden with curiosity.

Drew guessed this back-and-forth could go on for a while, and he didn't want to listen to them rehash old Aspen Valley gossip.

"I think Nadia and I will leave you to settle in," Drew said.

His mother just nodded, not looking at him. She still seemed uncomfortable with the two of them being together.

But despite that, he walked over, brushed a kiss on her papery cheek, then pulled back, catching a whiff of the perfume she had worn for years. It teased a raft of memories from the past, some that were good, blended with others.

"What's the matter?" his mother asked as if sensing his melancholy.

"Nothing, Mother," he said. "Just remembering old times." A flicker of pain crossed his mother's face, and he guessed she was yet once again thinking about Arlen.

Somehow, it didn't bother him as much as it once might have.

A few minutes later, he and Nadia were in his car on the way to the Prins farm. Charlotte had fallen asleep as soon as they pulled out of his mother's driveway.

For a few miles, the only sound in the car was the hum of the tires on the pavement, and the faint tick of Drew's keychain against the steering column.

"You okay? With leaving your mother in her house?" Nadia asked, breaking the silence.

"Yeah, I am." Drew gave into an impulse and reached across the console, holding his hand out to Nadia. She waited for a heartbeat, then her hand clutched his, squeezing gently.

He slipped her a sideways glance, pleased to see her smiling at him.

"We finally get to be by ourselves," he said.

"At least until we get to the farm."

"We could take the long way around," Drew offered with a chuckle. "Maybe make a stop at the lookout point."

"I have a feeling that expectation will clash with reality when we stop the car there," she said, her lips curling into a sweet smile. "Because I'm pretty sure Charlotte will wake up."

"Yeah. Guess I never thought that through." He glanced back at his daughter, smiling at the sight of her sleeping, her bow-shaped mouth pouting, her cheeks flushed.

In the last couple of days, she seemed more settled. Less antsy.

And she was worming her way into his heart and his life.

"Another thing I need to ask of you," he said, not sure how to broach the subject. "But now that my mother's gone, you won't be working with her anymore. However, would you be willing to stay a week longer? Take care of Charlotte for me? I'll pay you the same I paid you for taking care of Mom."

Nadia didn't reply right away, which made him think he had stepped way out on a very precarious limb.

"I would love to. I don't want to leave you and her hanging."

Relief flooded him, and he angled her a quick smile. "That's great. I'll have to look into something more permanent, of course, but this gives me time to do that."

"I can look into that for you. See which options are available."

"I'll accept that offer. Hopefully, we can give her a smooth transition." He didn't want to think about what that next step would look like for his daughter. Yet another new thing he would have to deal with. Juggling his work and her care.

One day and one event at a time, he reminded himself, blocking his thoughts out. Trying to keep Nadia separate from Charlotte's care.

"What do you think she'll remember?" he asked, feeling a glint of concern. "About her mother? Being brought to a stranger's place? About you?"

"Hard to know. What's your very first memory? How old were you?" Nadia asked.

Drew bit the corner of his lip, thinking. His mind cast back over the years, then he smiled as a memory surfaced. "Me and my dad in a canoe on Aspen Lake. I had to squint because the sun was glinting off the water. I have a vague impression of scratching at mosquito bites, but overall, a sense of peaceful happiness."

"It was just you and your father?" Nadia asked.

Drew nodded. "I don't remember Arlen being with us. My father and I went for more canoe rides, just the two of us. Neither Mom nor Arlen ever wanted to come along."

"It's wonderful to have those memories of your father," Nadia said, giving his hand another gentle squeeze.

"What about you?" He asked. "What's your first memory?"

Nadia ran her index finger up and down his, looking contemplative. "My first real solid memory was also connected to the lake. I think I was about three and a half. It was summer, and my birthday is in late fall."

"November the fourteenth," Drew couldn't help putting in.

"You remember that?" Nadia sounded surprised.

"I remember a lot of things about you," he said, giving her another teasing look.

Their eyes met, held, and again that undeniable connection sang between them.

"Sorry for interrupting you," he apologized, dragging his attention back to the road.

"It's okay. Mine isn't as idyllic as yours, though the lake

features in it as well. Liam, Celeste, Burke, Drake, and I were playing on the pier. Just goofing around. I was the youngest one there, and they were teasing me, so I got mad. I'm not sure exactly what happened when. Each of the siblings has a different story, all defending their particular actions, but I fell in the water. I remember flailing around, then sinking down in the water, looking up at my brothers, who were pointing at me, eyes wide. I could see their mouths moving, the fear in their eyes. Then I looked down and saw this black hole coming up toward my feet. The next thing I remember was Liam holding me upside down by my ankles. I guess to drain the water out of me, I'm not sure. He wasn't the doctor he is now, so I don't think his first aid was up to date," she added with a gentle laugh. "But then he put me down and gave me such a tight hug, I thought he would squeeze out whatever precious air I had pulled back into my lungs."

"That must have been terrifying," Drew sympathized.

"At the time, I wasn't as afraid as my siblings were," Nadia said, sounding contemplative. "But it must have affected me on another level, because I know it took me until grade six to get over my fear of water, regardless of how many taunts I got from my siblings. I had to find my own way through the fear."

"And did you?"

"I did. One day, I grew tired of being teased and decided I would show my family I wasn't afraid. I waited until I was alone, though. I didn't want an audience. I pushed down my terror, went into the lake, and lay on my back in the water. Just floating, looking up at the sky, trying not to hyperventilate. It became peaceful, and I stopped seeing the water as something to fear, and I realized that it was holding me up. I relaxed, and shortly after that, I started swimming. My mom signed me up for swimming lessons right after that, and the rest is history."

"I didn't know this about you."

"Glad I have some secrets yet."

"Do you have more?"

He was teasing, but she didn't reply, and a heavy silence fell between them. When she pulled her hand out of his, he felt an unwelcome sense of foreboding. Part of him wanted to pursue it, but he also sensed whatever she held back would have to come out on its own.

"So going back to earliest memories, I'm guessing one would be about three or three and a half," he said, returning his hand, still warm from hers, to the steering wheel, adopting a breezy tone.

Another beat of silence, then, "You're probably correct. I'm not Googling it to check." In his peripheral vision, he saw her look back at Charlotte. "I'm hoping she might not remember what happened these past few weeks. And I think all you can hope is that there is not some unspoken or deep-seated trauma attached to her mother's death and subsequent separation."

"I guess I'll have to deal with that as it comes. Though I still struggle with what her mother did. With the fact that she took two years of Charlotte's life away from me." He sighed, puzzling this through. "I wonder what my life would have looked like if I had been a part of theirs."

"That's difficult for sure," Nadia agreed. "But I guess you can be thankful that you have her now."

"I am. I just struggle with anger at being deceived. At not being told the truth."

Silence rose between them, and Nadia was quiet for a few more miles, the quiet holding a layer of unrest that he wasn't willing to peel back. Not yet. Not when things between him and Nadia were moving from tentative to more serious.

Drew turned onto the gravel road that led to the Prins farm. No vehicles were behind them, and no plume of dust rose ahead to signal that vehicles were coming, so he slowed even more, looking at Nadia and taking a chance that it would help his sudden unease. "I'm going out on a limb and want to say how thankful I am that you're here. That you're back... back in my life."

Nadia pressed her lips together, her one hand coming up to touch her mouth. He caught the faintest glimmer of tears in her eyes.

"Are you okay?" he asked, concerned. Had he pushed too hard?

She nodded, blinking as she dashed her hand across her cheeks, swiping at her tears. "I'm fine. I'm just kind of overwhelmed. I feel like I don't deserve what you just told me."

"Why would you think that?" He asked, sensing they were hovering closer to whatever still lingered.

Another beat of silence. Then she reached over and caught his hand. "Just being silly. Trying to reconcile past and present. But you need to know I'm so thankful for you as well. You have always been a part of my thoughts and, well, my dreams."

"I'm glad to hear that," he said, wanting to kiss her.

He drove another mile, knowing the Prins farm was getting closer, closing the window of opportunity on any privacy they would have for a while.

Making an impulsive decision, he pulled the car onto the side of the road. He stopped, put it in park, and reached over the console, cradling her face in his hand.

"I don't think I've ever forgotten about you," he breathed. "Despite what happened after you left. After you married Arlen. I never forgot about you."

Nadia swallowed, then reached over, looping her hand behind his neck, pulling him close, their lips meeting in a soft, gentle kiss. A hint and a promise of what was to come.

As he pulled away, Drew smiled at her, easing out a gentle sigh.

"You mean so much to me," was all he could say.

A noise from behind them made him look back and he felt

a flicker of shock. Charlotte's eyes were wide open, and she was staring at him, a faint smile curving her lips.

"I think we have a spectator," Drew murmured. Nadia jerked back, glancing behind her as well.

"Oh, dear. I wonder what she's thinking?"

"Well, considering we just talked about earlier memories, I'm thinking whatever is going on behind those adorable eyes, she might not remember."

"Good thing she can't talk yet."

"Who would she tell?" Drew teased.

"Your mother."

Drew cradled her hand in his, stroking her palm with his thumb. "Does that matter?"

"Not really, though I know she's not crazy about seeing us together."

"She'll just have to get used to it," Drew returned, unable to keep the sharp tone out of his voice.

"I hope so," Nadia said, sounding melancholy.

Once again, a hint of something else loitered, but he wasn't ready to delve into it.

Yet.

Chapter 13

"I think we've got a good handle on this party," Burke said, hands on his hips as he looked around the yard. "The tent guys came yesterday and marked off where they're putting it. I think you had a great idea having it closer to the barn."

"The flowers are getting delivered next Friday," Roxie put in, making a check on the clipboard she had been carrying.

"When are you going to put that thing down?" RayAnn grumbled. "You look like a wannabe wedding planner."

"Efficiency, my dear sister," Roxie replied, tucking the pencil behind her ear. "It's all about efficiency."

"You know there's a list app on your phone," RayAnn returned. "And that Aria had everything in a folder."

"I know, but I enjoy having pen and paper in my hand. I like being able to see everything all at once."

"Since when? You're always on your phone."

Nadia grinned at the sisters' give and take. That much hadn't changed while she was gone.

"All sister quibbling aside," Burke put in, cutting them off. "I think Roxie can check just about everything off the list."

"DJ booked and bringing a sound system, tables and table-cloths, caterer, cutlery, and plates booked, thanks to Nadia.

Flowers ready to pick up. Caterer is a go." Roxie went down her list, tapping on each item. "I think we just about got everything."

"I don't like the sound of the words 'just about,'" Nadia teased her sister. "Given that you've got that clipboard, I'd like something more definitive."

Roxie just rolled her eyes, a remnant of her young teenager behavior. "Okay, fine. Just to satisfy you, everything is done and verified. Drew, I just need you to send a few memories about Aria to me, as well as those pictures you promised."

"Pictures?" Nadia teased, giving him a nudge with her elbow.

"Yes. From when we were together."

Nadia knew that. His and Aria's brief relationship wasn't news, but somehow it still gave her a tiny stab of envy. Aria always looked like she had her life together. She knew what she wanted and went for it.

"You don't need to worry about that," he assured her, his voice quiet, lowered for her benefit.

His added smile eased away her momentary agitation. She knew she had no right to feel any disquiet about Drew's romantic history.

After all, she'd been married to his brother.

"All we need is Lucas and Aria to show up on time," Roxie continued. "Hopefully their flight doesn't get delayed, and they don't end up stuck somewhere between here and Cabo."

"Don't even say that," Nadia warned, holding up her hands as if to stop even a mention of glitches. "I'm sure they'll make it on time."

"At any rate, things are going great." Roxie turned to Charlotte, who still clutched Nadia's hand. She bent down, getting on Charlotte's level. "What about you, little munchkin? What are you going to be doing when we're whooping it up here next week?"

"I haven't thought that far," Drew said, answering for her. "But I'm sure we can figure something out."

"She sure is a sweetheart," RayAnn put in, joining her sister. "And I'm sure she's bored with all this wedding planning stuff." RayAnn bent down and held her hand out to the little girl. "Do you want to see our old swing set and sandbox?"

To Nadia's surprise, Charlotte caught RayAnn's hand and let herself be led away.

"Baby whisperer," Roxie marveled, with a wry tone in her voice. "If you guys don't need me anymore, I'm going to join them."

"I think we're good," Nadia said.

Roxie handed the clipboard over to Drew and gave him a pencil. "I'm giving you this because I trust you more than my sister or brother. Don't lose it," she warned, then jogged away, her ponytail bobbing behind her.

"Nice to see her more mobile," Nadia remarked, watching as Roxie joined RayAnn, who was pushing Charlotte on a swing.

Burke nodded, blowing out a sigh. "It's been going a lot better," he agreed. "But I'm not gonna lie, Karissa and I will be glad to have the place to ourselves once they leave."

"Don't tell me Jake is moving with them?"

Burke shot her a frown, then rolled his eyes. "Shoot. I forget about him when the twins are around, sucking up all the oxygen."

Nadia resisted the urge to give advice. She was in no place to remind Burke not to neglect Jake when she had been gone so long from the family. At the same time, she knew her family took good care of each other. No matter Burke's slip, Nadia knew Jake was loved and taken care of.

An insistent ring sounded from Burke's shirt pocket, and he pulled the cell phone out, smiling as he looked down at the screen. "Excuse me, this is Karissa. I need to talk to her about something." Without another word, he turned and walked toward the house away from them, his lowered voice taking on a gentle tone.

Once again, Nadia felt a glimmer of envy, but when she looked at Drew, it faded in the light of his smile.

"It makes my heart happy to see my daughter with your sisters," he said.

Nadia glanced over to where the twins were playing with Charlotte. RayAnn sat on the swing, Charlotte in her lap. Even across the yard, Nadia heard the little girl's squeal of laughter as RayAnn swung back and forth.

"You're blessed with your family," he continued.

The wistfulness in his voice reminded her of what he had lost.

"I'm sure you miss Arlen as well," she said.

"I didn't see him that much. You know that better than anyone, but I still feel like a piece of my life is missing."

You need to tell him everything.

The voice slithered into her mind, and she allowed it a moment of her attention. Then her hand went to her lips as if to relive the kiss she and Drew had shared only a few moments ago. A reminder of what they were rebuilding.

What would happen if she told him everything?

She shunted the thought aside, turning as she heard gravel crunching. A vehicle pulled into the yard, parking beside Drew's car. Shelby climbed out, pausing a moment, stretching her back, one hand on her pregnant belly.

Again, Nadia felt a flash of jealousy. Her family was settling. Things were moving in a good direction after the tragedies they had dealt with.

"You look pensive. Is everything okay?" Drew asked.

She glanced over at him, then smiled. "Coming home has been a bit of an adjustment. Sometimes I feel like I'm still on the outside, looking in. But I know Celeste said the same thing, and she seems to have found her place." It didn't hurt that she had found the love of her life in Wade Hicks.

"That'll be another wedding in the family, won't it?" Drew asked.

"Yeah. Not sure when it will happen, or where I'll be." The words slipped out, her automatic protection or reaction in any situation. Always giving herself an off-ramp. But even as she spoke the words, she caught the shadow of concern flicking across Drew's face.

She wanted to explain, but Shelby joined them before she could formulate her thoughts.

"You guys get everything organized for the party?" Shelby asked.

Drew looked down at the clipboard he held. "According to all the checked boxes, I'm suspecting it is. I know Aria had asked me to take care of this, but things have gone well with little input from me."

"That's what happens when you get more than one Prins on the job," Shelby said with a chuckle. "There's enough bossy people in this family that if one doesn't take over, the other one will."

"I'm glad for it. Took a load off my shoulders."

"I imagine you needed the respite." Shelby glanced over to the twins, who were still playing with Charlotte, the creak of the swings echoing across the yard. Then a bark sounded, and Jake and his dog joined the girls.

"The twins seem to enjoy your little girl," she continued.

"Easy to do, she's a real sweetie," Nadia put in.

Shelby gave Nadia a wry smile. "I guess you would know, seeing as how you've spent the last little while with her."

"And with Drew's mother," Nadia added.

"Of course." Shelby turned to Drew. "You've had a lot on your plate the last little while. How is your mother doing?"

"Quite well. She got the okay to move back into her house, so that's nice for her."

"Nice for you two as well," Shelby said, with a sly smile.

Nadia swatted at her sister. "You just never mind."

Shelby gave her an arch look, and Nadia knew that anything she might say would be misinterpreted.

"You want to check out the infamous pier?" Nadia asked Drew, needing to get him away from her nosy sister.

Drew looked down at his clipboard, as if unsure what to do with it while they left.

"Just give it to Shelby," Nadia suggested. "I'm sure she'll take excellent care of it."

Nadia didn't even look back at her sister as she shoved her hands in the pockets of her skirt and sauntered past Drew toward the pier, hoping he would follow.

A faint breeze sifted off the lake, teasing strands of her hair loose from her ponytail. And then Drew was beside her, keeping pace with her.

"I knew you guys were a close family, but it sure is interesting seeing the interactions between everyone."

"Oh, trust me, there were lots of times I wished I had only one sibling like you did, or that I was an only child. But as I keep hearing from some of the in-laws, that's not ideal either. So, I just put up with them."

"But you seem to genuinely care for each other," Drew commented.

Nadia shot a glance back at her sisters. They had moved to the sandbox, and Jake was helping Charlotte dig sand with a pail and shovel. Shelby had disappeared, probably to the welding shop to check on some of their projects.

"We do, and I know that I'm blessed."

Nadia walked to the end of the dock and sat down, her legs hanging over the edge. The lake was lower than normal, and her feet hovered above the lapping waves. Drew sat down beside her, leaning back, hands resting on either side of him, his one hand brushing up against her thigh. She suspected he had done that on purpose, and it gave her a tiny thrill. These little connections, these small reinforcements, gave her a sense of an inevitable shift toward a place of no return, a place of settling in.

For a moment, a tendril of panic swirled around her heart. Could she do permanency?

For much of her life, even while attending school, she'd had so many plans for traveling, things she wanted to do on her own, things she knew wouldn't happen if she tied herself down. Even after marrying Arlen, they had traveled and made a wish list of places they wanted to go.

Then she looked at Drew, and he cocked his head and gave her a questioning look.

"You're looking pensive," he said, a thin note of concern in his voice.

Nadia snapped her fingers. "That's too bad. I was going for thoughtful."

Drew chuckled, then took her hand, his fingers tracing her palm as he looked down.

"What are the odds that you and I will be left alone here?" he asked.

"Why? Are you going to kiss me again?" Nadia tried to keep her tone light, but anticipation thrilled through her.

"I'd like to, but maybe this is our chance to talk a little. Because I sense once we get up from here, your family will take over again."

"You're right," Nadia returned. She bit her lip, looking somewhat self-conscious. "So, what do you want to talk about?" Nadia asked, going for direct.

"We've got Aria and Lucas' party organized. My mom is on her own. So, I think the only thing left to discuss is you and me."

Nadia's heart shifted, a sense of hurtling toward inevitability flowing over her.

"You and me as in…" she asked, being deliberately obtuse. Hoping he would make the first move.

Because she felt as if the path before them was still an unknown.

Would he still be able to accept her once she told him everything?

⸻

DREW KEPT his eyes on Nadia's face, even as she lowered her eyes.

"At the risk of sounding redundant, I mean you and me as in…well…you and me. Us. A couple." He wasn't sure how much more to say, sensing withdrawal on her part. Yet he couldn't deny anymore that he cared for her, that he wanted their relationship to be serious.

But did she feel the same?

Did he dare make himself that vulnerable again?

"I like the sound of that," she said, her voice quiet. "But yet…I feel like…" she sighed, her words like a sliver of ice to his heart. "Before we go any further, I need to tell you something." Then she looked behind her at her family's farm, the kids now walking toward them. "And it's too important to be interrupted. Can we talk tonight? When we get back to the house?"

He tried to still the thundering of his heart, wishing she would blurt out whatever was bothering her.

But he wanted to honor her request, so he nodded.

"Of course."

The girls joined them, holding Charlotte's hand. When she got closer to them, she ran toward Nadia. "Mommy," she called out.

Once again, Drew struggled not to take it personally. Charlotte was still confused. Nadia, to her, was the mother she had lost.

"Does she really call you that?" Roxie asked, frowning.

"It's just a thing she does," Nadia returned, giving Drew

an apologetic look as Charlotte grabbed her arm. "Doesn't mean as much as it seems. She's made me her mom substitute."

"That's gotta suck for you, right Drew?" Roxie put in, as she sat down on the other side of him.

"I don't think Drew needs to be reminded," RayAnn said. "I apologize, Drew, for my sister being Captain Obvious."

"Well, it's true, right?" Roxie insisted.

"I think this little one is getting tired," Nadia said, shifting Charlotte so she stood between her and Drew as she rose.

Drew took the hint and got up as well, taking Charlotte with him. Thankfully, she didn't protest, even slipping one chubby arm around his neck for support as they walked down the pier. Roxie and RayAnn stayed behind, but Nadia heard them whispering as they left.

"I understand what's going on," Drew said finally. "With Charlotte calling you Mama. It doesn't bother me."

"Thanks for being upfront about this," Nadia said, still feeling uncomfortable. "I know it's awkward."

"A bit, but understandable. I wonder if there have been any male figures in Charlotte's life."

"Well, there is one now," Nadia encouraged him warmly. "And for the record, I think you are an excellent father, given how quickly this was forced on you."

"Thanks for that. Means a lot."

She looked like she was about to say something more when the twins joined them.

"Are you guys headed back to town?" Roxie asked. "You're not staying for dinner?"

"No. We should get Charlotte back home on time," Drew said. "And I have some work I need to catch up on tonight."

"And some pictures to send me," Roxie put in.

"That too." He gave Roxie a quick smile and cuddled Charlotte close.

They walked back to the car, and Drew buckled Charlotte into the car seat.

"No, go out," she protested.

"Sorry, sweetie." Drew caught one of her flailing arms and held it for a moment. "We have to do this."

"No. Don't want to." She arched her back, fighting Drew, crying in earnest now.

Drew took her out of the seat and tried to settle her, but Charlotte kept squirming, then reached out to Nadia.

He tried not to feel hurt by it, realizing that it would take time.

So, he handed his daughter over to Nadia, who held her close.

"You have to go in your seat," Nadia insisted, her voice quiet but firm. "It's just for a quick ride. When we get home, we can read books."

This seemed to catch her attention, and she stopped crying. She looked at Nadia, her blue eyes still brimming with tears.

"G'night Moon?"

"Yes, of course. And *Good Night, Good Night Construction Site.*"

Charlotte nodded at that, and with a gentle smile, Nadia handed her back to Drew. Thankfully, this time she was quiet as he buckled her in.

He and Nadia got back in the car. As soon as he pulled out of the Prins driveway and onto the gravel road, he saw Charlotte had fallen asleep.

"Looks like we'll have a quiet drive back again," he said.

It was a rather clumsy attempt at giving her a chance to talk about what she had hinted at when they sat on the pier. Something he sensed was too important to put off. Then her phone rang, and Drew fought down a surge of frustration.

He reminded himself she said they would talk tonight. He just had to be patient.

Chapter 14

"Okay, I'll try to pick it up as soon as possible."

Nadia ended the call and turned to Drew, who was frowning at the road ahead. Something was bothering him, and she suspected it had something to do with the conversation she had promised she would have with him.

But she had other things to deal with at the moment.

"That was Alan at the mechanic's shop. My car is ready. Would it be okay to stop by and talk to him?"

She needed to know how much it cost, which would necessitate another awkward discussion with Drew about getting paid so she could cover the cost of the bill. It was borderline embarrassing, but it was her reality, and she had to face it.

"Of course. It's not far out of the way."

Which made her realize there was another potentially delicate situation she had to address.

"Um…if the car is ready…I'm thinking I might…might move back to the trailer in Celeste's yard. Now that your mom is gone."

She tried not to blush as she spoke the words. She knew, without a doubt, that nothing untoward would happen, but she also knew Aspen Valley. His mother and Lorna were two of the many contributors to the gossip grapevine, with its far-reaching tentacles. Nadia was sure most people already knew Drew's mother had moved out of his house.

And that Nadia was still there.

Best to quash any gossip that might come out of that. Drew's reputation was on the line. For someone who had spent so much of his life guarding his image, Nadia didn't want it sullied by assumptions.

No matter how wrong they might be.

"Probably better optics," he agreed, understanding where she was going.

Nadia couldn't help a quick sidelong glance, smiling as she caught his grin.

"I know Aspen Valley, and in this town, it only takes a tiny seed to grow into a monster plant."

He chuckled at that and returned his attention to the road.

"I'm also hoping you'll be willing to stick around until her bedtime. I'm sure it will be a change for her when you leave, but we'll figure that out."

Nadia quenched a flare of guilt. "I'll try to make it as easy as possible for her. Maybe stay until she falls asleep at night and try to come in the morning before she wakes up." They hadn't talked about how long Drew hoped she would stay, and she wasn't ready for that conversation right now.

The trip she hoped to make grew more vague with each moment she spent with Drew.

Drew frowned as if considering this. "That will make for a long day for you."

"Not any different from what it has been." She hesitated a moment, not sure how to broach the next awkward topic. She decided to jump right in, much as she would if she wanted to go for a swim in the lake. "I was also wondering if I could get an advance on my paycheck, so I can pay for the repairs on my car."

Drew shot her a look of surprise, then nodded. "Of course. I'm sorry I never thought of it earlier."

"It's okay. You're probably used to a regular payroll schedule in your office. This is just different."

"Yes, of course," he sounded flustered. "I never realized you needed the money right away."

He probably meant nothing by it, but his comment underlined her precarious financial situation. Something she wasn't particularly proud of.

"I'm managing," she said, struggling to keep the defensive tone out of her voice. "But it's just the car is an unexpected and large expense."

"I'll e-transfer you the money as soon as we get home," Drew said, giving her an awkward smile. "I should've thought of that."

"It's fine," she said, wishing this conversation would end. It emphasized the differences between them. And it made the consequences of her easy-going casual lifestyle come home to roost.

It wasn't all your fault.

Which was cold comfort right now as she tried to juggle expenses with income.

She looked away from him, not sure what else to say, watching as the landscape flowed past. He seemed to get the hint and said nothing more.

A few moments later, he pulled up in front of the mechanic's shop.

"I'll just be a minute," Nadia told him.

The sounds of impact wrenches assaulted her ears as she stepped inside, underscored by rap music beating out of a speaker somewhere in the main shop. No one was at the wide counter that took up the majority of the entrance. She looked past it through an open door and saw a car on a hoist, one of the mechanics wearing coveralls and working on it.

Then she saw Alan wiping his hands on a rag as he walked toward her.

"You've come for the car?" he asked, shoving the rag in the back pocket of his blue coverall.

"You said it was ready," she answered.

"Yeah, it is. Repairs went a little faster than I figured, which is good."

"I guess it's time for the moment of truth. What's the bill?"

Alan bent over, rifling through some grease-stained books filling a bank of shelves beside him. He found the one he was looking for, pulled it out, and laid it on the counter between them.

"I got a good deal on the U joints, and some of the other parts," he said as he flipped through it. "I found a car exactly like yours getting parted out at an auto wrecker in Edmonton. So that helped." He pulled a pencil out from a tin can sitting on the desk, ticking through the items. "Yep. Looks like everything's here."

Nadia's gaze skimmed over the bill, searching for the bottom line. She swallowed when she saw the final figure. Not much less than what he had originally quoted her. When he talked about getting a good deal, she had hoped it would reflect in the final price.

"Some of the parts we had to take out of your car were really hard because the bolts were rusted. We had to re-drill a few," Alan said as if he read her mind. Or maybe he knew how often customers complained about the final tally.

"Of course," Nadia said, waving off his explanations. "I trust you."

"Good to know. Not everyone does."

"There's only one small problem," Nadia said, shame warming her cheeks for the second time in less than twenty minutes. "I haven't quite got the money yet, but I hope to by tomorrow." Hopefully even sooner. "Can I pay you then?"

"Of course. No problem at all." Alan ripped the top layer of the bill off and handed it to her. "Besides, I know where Drew's house is."

"I'm not staying there anymore. At least not overnight." She bit her lip, realizing how defensive she sounded.

"I thought you were taking care of his kid now that his mother is gone?"

Of course, he would know all this, even though she and Drew had talked privately about it.

Lily and Lorna spreading joy and gossip, she presumed.

"I am." Nadia took the bill from him, folded it over, and shoved it in her purse. This conversation was getting more and more awkward.

"So if it's okay, I can take my car today?"

"Of course," Alan agreed, thankfully going along with her change in topic. He turned around, pulled a set of keys off the pegboard, and handed them to her. "Your car is parked on the north side of the shop. Let me know if everything works. We took it for a test drive and couldn't find anything wrong. But you never know."

Then his phone rang, and she was spared more conversation. She waved goodbye, then walked out to where Drew waited for her, the passenger window open.

"I'll take my car and meet you at your house," she said, bending down to talk to him.

Drew nodded, giving her a broad smile.

And as she walked back to her car, she hoped and prayed that he wasn't judging her. Goodness knows there was enough material in her life for him to work with once he found out everything.

NADIA HELD CHARLOTTE CLOSE, bouncing her up and down as she walked around the bedroom, the little girl's cries piercing her ears. For the past fifteen minutes, she had been inconsolable, almost as if she knew Nadia was leaving that night. Though Charlotte had been sleeping in her own bed for the past couple of nights, she now clung to Nadia, her damp face tucked into her neck, her sobbing interspersed with "No, no, no."

A light knock on the door, and Drew stepped inside the bedroom. "Doesn't sound like she's settling," he murmured, walking toward them both.

Since they came back home, he'd been on his laptop, catching up on some work, while Nadia heated leftovers from yesterday. Charlotte had been fractious during supper, and most of Nadia's attention was spent trying to get her to eat. After supper, Drew gave her a bath, but again she cried the entire time.

Nadia had taken over from him, and he muttered something about having to catch up on some work as he retreated. Not that Nadia blamed him. She was fighting a headache from Charlotte's constant tears. And not only Charlotte's tears but also the stress of wanting to finish what she had started as they sat alone on the pier.

An hour and eight books later, Charlotte had settled. Nadia sat on the side of her little bed, holding her twitching hand, as the little girl drifted off to sleep.

A few times Nadia tried to pull away, and Charlotte's eyes flew open, so she stayed.

Drew had come in twice to check on things, but they didn't dare talk, for fear of keeping the little girl awake.

Her breathing became deep and quiet, and Nadia gently tugged her hand free of Charlotte's grasp. Thankfully, this time there was no reaction.

Nadia shifted off the bed, still watching the little girl, then backed out of the room.

With slow and deliberate motions, she shut the door, then blew out a sigh of relief.

"Sounds like she's finally asleep."

Drew's voice over her shoulder made her jump, and she spun around, hand on her heart.

"Sorry about that," he apologized, giving her a gentle smile as he curved his hand around her shoulder.

"No, it's fine. I'm just a little tense."

"I'm not surprised," he said, ushering her down the hall toward the living room. "I don't know what got into Charlotte, but she sure glommed onto you tonight."

"Do you think she knows I'm leaving?" Nadia asked, stifling a yawn.

"Maybe, or maybe it was just an extra busy day for her."

"I feel like I'm just playing a guessing game with what she says."

"You want a cup of tea?"

Nadia couldn't stop a quick glance at the clock behind Drew. It was already 10:30, and she was exhausted.

"Yeah," he said with another gentle smile. "It's late. Maybe you should just go home."

She knew from the expectant looks he had thrown her way all evening that he had hoped they would have time to talk.

But his comment gave her an easy out.

"And while I want to know more about what you were saying this afternoon, I think we can put that off until another time," he added.

They were now standing close to each other. She could feel the warmth of his body and catch the scent of his cologne. Manly. Earthy.

She closed her eyes for a moment, allowing her senses to be tantalized by the thought of drifting into his arms and staying there. Of resting her head against the fabric of his shirt, feeling the strength of his body as she wrapped her arms around him, his arms holding her close and sheltering her, and then his warm lips on hers.

She didn't dare give in right now.

"Thank you for that," she said quietly, holding his gentle gaze. Then, giving in to an impulse, she cupped his face, stroking her fingers across the stubble on his chin. After a moment, she pulled her hand back and stepped away, giving him an apologetic smile.

"I'm sorry, but you're right. I'm done. I just hope Charlotte sleeps well tonight."

"If she doesn't, I'll just have to deal with it." Drew gave her a wry smile. "After all, I'm her father. I'll have to figure this out on my own."

She resisted the urge to give him a good night kiss and instead opted for a smile. "I better get going," she decided. "Deer like to come up this time of night, and after getting my car fixed, I don't need to hit one."

"Then I'll just pray that you get home safely," he told her.

Her smile shifted, her feelings drifting toward melancholy. "That means more than you might realize," she said. "That you'll be praying for me."

"Believe it or not, I've never stopped praying for you."

A gentle fist squeezed her heart as tears pricked her eyes. This wasn't some pious comment thrown out to appease her. It hearkened to a history between them.

Did he pray for her when she was with Arlen and struggling with her marriage? Was she on his mind when she and Arlen broke up?

When Arlen died?

"Thanks for that," was all she could whisper. Then turned and walked out the door to her car.

But as she drove away and saw him standing in the doorway, watching her leave, it was through a shimmer of tears.

Sorrow for what might have been.

And what she had to tell him yet.

Chapter 15

Nadia pulled into the driveway of the trailer, feeling a sense of déjà vu. Of time looping around, bringing her back to where she had started.

The trailer was dark and unwelcoming. While it had been adequate for her when she first arrived, leaving the cozy comfort of Drew's house made thinking about going back to living in the trailer borderline depressing.

Don't be a snob, she told herself as she shut the car off, glancing over to the log house Celeste had moved into.

Wade had tried to talk her out of that, but Celeste said she was tired of making do in the trailer and wanted to be in her house, with its solid walls.

Now, warm rectangles of light glowed from the house. Inviting and welcoming.

Despite the weariness that clawed at her, she wasn't ready to face being alone in the trailer.

Not yet.

She took a chance, turned on the flashlight of her phone, and walked across the uneven dirt of the as-yet unlandscaped yard.

When she knocked on the door, she heard Celeste call out

for her to come in. Her sister must have seen the lights of her vehicle coming down the driveway and guessed she might come here.

Nadia stepped inside as Celeste walked through the arched doorway from the kitchen. Music drifted out from a small speaker on the mantel of the fireplace.

"I just boiled some water for hot chocolate, my girl. Do you want some?"

"That would be wonderful." But she felt a twinge of guilt at accepting her sister's offer so shortly after turning down Drew's.

Different circumstances, she reminded herself as she walked across the unfinished rough wooden floor. She sank into one corner of the couch, her body melting into its comforting hug. Maybe it was being in her sister's house, maybe it was the fact that the couch was similar to the one at their parents' house, but it was as if the worn leather leached away the low-level stress of the past few hours.

She laid her head back, letting the music flow over her. Then her heart clenched as the words of the song caught her attention.

Let the pain of the past drift away,
As you surrender to the Father's grace,
Release your pain and unshed tears
Secure in his embrace

SHE CLOSED HER EYES, listening to the rest of the song, waiting for the chorus, and as it replayed, she felt shivering in her chest. Sorrow and reproach still clinging to her soul even as the words sank into her heart.

Can I truly do this, Lord? Am I allowed to let go?

"Are you okay?" Celeste asked, her voice slipping over Nadia's thoughts, pulling her back into the moment.

"Kind of," was all Nadia could say, utter weariness dropping onto her like a heavy blanket. She opened her eyes, sat up, and took the mug from her sister.

"You sound disheartened." Celeste settled into the opposite corner of the couch, feet tucked under her, cradling her mug between her hands.

Though it was summer, the house was cool. And Celeste looked cozy in her sloppy hoodie, flannel pajama pants, and fuzzy socks.

"I feel disheartened," Nadia returned, blowing over the mug of hot chocolate. "And confused."

"Tell Aunty Celeste what's on your mind."

Nadia chuckled, remembering many other times she would sneak into Celeste's bed in the room they shared, and her sister would say the same thing.

"Way too many confusing thoughts coiled together, each one calling for attention."

"Start with one of them." Celeste stretched out her foot and prodded Nadia's thigh, making a small connection. "The one that bothers you the most."

Nadia looked down at her mug, swirling it a little and watching the mini marshmallows Celeste always put in hot chocolate as they moved around. She followed their slow spiral, then blew out a heavy sigh.

"Drew and I kissed."

There. The words were out now, and Celeste was silent a moment, giving them the weight they deserved. Of all her siblings, Celeste knew her the best. Her struggle with Arlen, and her feelings for Drew.

"I'm not surprised it finally happened," was Celeste's gentle answer.

Nadia gave the marshmallows another spin around the steaming hot chocolate.

"More than once."

"I would imagine. I know he's been pretty crazy about you for a long time."

Her sister's words created a gentle warmth that chipped away at some of her concerns.

But only some.

"He also loved his brother," Nadia added.

"Of course he did. As I love you and all my siblings."

"But Arlen was his only brother."

"And…"

"Losing him was an immense blow. Not only for Drew but for his mother as well."

"I'm sure of that. From what I remember, Lily doted on Arlen. Didn't do him any favors, that's for sure. But he was a charmer, so I guess she can be forgiven."

"That he was."

Celeste was quiet for another few beats, then nudged Nadia again. "I never dared ask, and we were kind of going our own ways by then, but why did you end up marrying him?"

More guilt followed Celeste's question.

"You promise you'll just listen?" Nadia asked, afraid of what her sister might think.

"I will promise to try," was all Celeste could give her. "But I will interject from time to time because that's my love language."

"I just don't need any judging right now."

Celeste released a tight laugh. "Trust me, girlie, I am in zero position to judge you after the fiasco of my past." Another push, another reminder that Celeste was waiting.

And listening.

Nadia took another sip of her hot chocolate, buying herself some time as she tried to figure out what to say and how.

"After I broke up with Arlen, which I thought was for good, I worked up enough nerve to approach Drew, to tell him how I felt, and you remember how that went."

"I also knew how hard it was for you to be rejected by him."

"I wasn't cocky enough to think he would jump at the chance to be with me, but I was so sure there were some pretty strong vibes between us."

She was quiet another beat, then carried on. "I felt so rejected. I thought I had found peace and thought I had found someone I wanted to be with. Settle down with. But after he pushed me away, I knew I didn't want to stay in Aspen Valley, and that's why I went to Toronto."

"I thought you went there with Kelly, to go to school?" Celeste asked.

"I could have gone to Edmonton or Vancouver, but Toronto seemed far enough away. And when I found out Kelly was going there as well, figured this was my chance to get as far away from Aspen Valley as I could." Nadia's mind slipped back to that difficult and lonely time. "Trouble was, Kelly wasn't as serious about her studies as I was. She was gone lots. And when I took on a part-time job to help pay bills, we hardly saw each other. I got pretty lonely. And then Arlen moved to Toronto and looked me up." Nadia gave Celeste a gentle smile. "We started spending time together, two Aspen Valley ex-pats and it was like the old connection we once had came up again. I was hesitant, but like I said, I was lonely. And…well…things got intense." She bit her lip, looking down again at her mug, disappointed at how her hand trembled. Celeste was her closest sister, her confidant, and she knew she should be able to tell her anything. So she pushed on. "Long story short, I got pregnant. And Arlen and I got married. And then I lost the baby." She was surprised at how her voice hitched when she told her sister and Celeste's gasp of surprise underlined her aching pain.

Celeste put her mug down and scooted over to Nadia, pulling her into her arms. "Oh honey, we never knew. You said nothing."

Nadia let herself sink into her sister's embrace, thankful for the support. She closed her eyes against the tears that threatened. It had been a while, but somehow after telling her sister, it was like the grief was all new.

"Why didn't you say anything to us?" Celeste's sorrow underlined hers. But then Celeste pressed her lips together and shook her head, her hand stroking Nadia's shoulders. "I'm sorry. I didn't mean it to come out like that. I just wish we could've been there for you."

Nadia swallowed the threatening tears and nodded. "I do, too. I thought he was grieving in his own way when he quit his job and started painting. We realized we needed to reconnect and figure out where we were going. He took a break, and we went to Paris together. I graduated, and to celebrate, we took another trip to Belize. Trying to find each other again. It brought us together so, as soon as he said we could afford it, we went to the Netherlands after he quit his job. Whenever I asked him how we could pay for it, he lied to me. Said he had sold some paintings and got the money under the counter. But something didn't ring true for me. I pushed a little harder, asking him how much he sold the paintings for. That's when I discovered that his mother had been paying all the bills, even when he was working. That instigated one of our many fights. He started drinking, and things got way too difficult for me. I was working long shifts to pay back my loans. In one of our many fights, I found out he was glad I'd lost the baby. That's when I knew I couldn't be with him anymore. We got divorced a few months after that."

Nadia dragged her hands over her face, preparing herself for the next part of the story.

"He still kept coming over, asking for my advice about his painting. Apologizing for lying. Talking about maybe making another trip. Said he had made some actual sales. I didn't believe him, but it didn't matter anymore."

She paused a moment, still trying to sort out her thoughts.

"I remember being jealous of how much you traveled," Celeste recalled. "You had another trip planned, didn't you? After Aria asked you to come and help plan her wedding party?"

"I did, but then life got weird. I told Drew about all of this, but I didn't dare tell him the next part. The hardest part." She pulled in another breath, sending up another prayer, fighting for self-control. "Arlen and I had been apart for two years, and I knew he was slowly going further behind financially. He would come over, asking me to help him. Every time I said no, then I told him to leave me alone. At the time, I was working nights and sleeping during the day. One evening, Arlen talked the doorman into letting him into my apartment while I was working, telling him he was picking up some stuff I was giving him. While he was in my apartment, he took my laptop. I only used it for paying bills."

"And occasionally messaging us."

Nadia felt another flush of shame. "I'm so sorry I didn't connect more."

"I'm sorry for bringing it up. Doesn't matter."

"Anyhow, I didn't notice it was gone for a few days, and somehow in that time, he broke into my laptop. Because I was dumb and lazy, I had let my computer save my passwords for me, and even though I changed them, I kept forgetting to set up that two-factor authentication stuff. Anyhow, he could log on and empty the account."

Celeste's gasp brought back the anger and humiliation Nadia had gone through when she found out.

"I called him up and told him to give it all back. He was drunk when I called him, crying, feeling horrible about what he had done. Of course, that's easy to say after the fact." Nadia released a harsh laugh, shaking her head, still feeling ashamed of her lack of oversight. "He came to my apartment late one evening after I got off my night shift to apologize. To tell me he would get his mother to send the money to me. I said I was done with him and didn't want his mother's money. Though looking back, I wish I hadn't been so stubborn." Nadia stopped, pulling in a shuddering breath. "We had a fight, I got angry, and he left in a rage. A few days later, I found out he had died in a motorbike accident. After he left my place."

Nadia grew silent again, too easily remembering the twisting pain that she had felt when Foster delivered her the news.

"Oh, honey, that must've been so difficult," Celeste breathed, sorrow lacing her voice. "I can't imagine what you went through."

"What I went through was grief, sorrow, and a crushing burden of self-condemnation over his death." She stopped, her voice breaking.

Once again, Celeste pulled her close, comforting her.

For a long stretch, her sister was silent, then she drew in a long breath, eased it out, and began praying.

"Dear Lord, let your love wash over Nadia. Let it soothe her pain, ease her guilt. May your love give her strength and peace. May she know you love her, regardless of everything that has gone on in her life. Everything she thinks she has done."

A sob crawled up Nadia's throat and slipped out, followed by another. Soon she was crying in earnest. Grieving the losses of the last few years. Arlen, her baby, the love she thought she had for her husband. Their marriage.

And woven through all this, her fear of what would happen between her and Drew if she told him everything about his beloved brother.

Through this storm, Celeste just held her, rocking her.

Finally, after what felt like hours, Nadia's sobs eased, and she pulled out of Celeste's embrace, her face hot, her head aching.

She gave her sister a wobbly smile, swiping at her cheeks. "I must look a wreck," she murmured.

Celeste rose, walked to a side table, and brought back a box of tissues.

"You don't need to worry about that." Celeste handed her the box. "Grief doesn't make anyone look pretty."

Nadia wiped her eyes, blew her nose, and pulled in another shaky breath.

"Thanks for being here," was all she could say.

"We're family, that's all I need to say."

"I missed you guys so much. I missed you so much. I was afraid to come back here, broke, wounded, and not sure what to tell anybody. I was still grieving the loss of the baby and all the other stuff with Arlen, and I couldn't sort it out."

"I'm glad you told me," Celeste said. "Even though you hid it well, I often sensed something else was happening in your life. Even before you came home. Your texts, your emails, the few phone calls we had, were all light; like you were skimming over the surface of life."

"I'm sorry I waited so long," Nadia apologized. "I'm sorry I didn't trust you."

"Don't worry about that. You told me, and now we can help you heal."

Nadia wiped her eyes again, then leaned back against the couch, looking over at her sister.

"So what do I tell Drew?"

"What you told me. The truth."

Nadia held that thought for a moment, then nodded. "I suppose you're right." And yet, even as she agreed with her sister, there was another layer that she wasn't sure she wanted to explore.

"Like I said, I know he's crazy about you. He loves you dearly. And like Corinthians says, *'Love bears all things, believes all things, hopes all things, endures all things.'* You and I have heard that from our childhood. Now you just have to believe it."

Nadia nodded, accepting her sister's words, but on another level, she still wasn't sure.

Her phone binged, sending her heart banging against her chest and making her panic.

Drew?

"Who's texting you at this time of night?" Celeste leaned over to look at her phone.

Nadia's heart settled when she saw the name.

"It's Foster. Arlen's friend."

"What does he want?"

Nadia shook her head as she swiped over to read the text. Then she heaved out a heavy sigh. "He just landed in Edmonton. He wants to come and talk to me. It's about Arlen."

"What could he possibly want to talk to you about? Arlen has been gone two years."

"He's been in touch before. Something about an art show? But I feel like I should go."

"You still feel guilty about Arlen, don't you?"

Nadia gave her sister a wan smile. "I can't dump that so easily. I've been carrying it for a long time. But it might give me some closure. I haven't talked to Foster since that night."

Celeste sat back, her expression was serious as she held Nadia's gaze.

"I suppose. Just be careful that you don't take on more than you need to. I can come with you if you want."

Nadia gave her sister a guarded smile. "Thanks for that. But I need to do this on my own."

Chapter 16

"Nice place." Foster sat back in the Adirondack chair in Drew's backyard, looking around. "Obviously, Arlen didn't get the same cash Drew did."

Nadia gave him a level look. "Unlike Arlen, Drew earned the money he spent." She couldn't keep the acerbic tone out of her voice.

When Foster called, he had asked if they could meet at a local coffee shop. But Nadia didn't want to drag Charlotte around and interrupt her nap. Instead, she asked Foster to come to Drew's place. Now Foster was lounging across from her on the brick patio, sitting in the shade of the immense trees that surrounded the grassy area of the backyard.

Drew had a gardener come from time to time to take care of the lawn and the flower beds on the borders. It was a beautiful, calming place. Over the last few days, Nadia had dared let herself imagine this being a part of her life.

With Drew.

"Hey. Why were you so hard on your husband?" Foster said with a laconic smile. "Arlen was one of the good guys. He did good for you."

Nadia pushed down a sigh at his comment. "Ex-husband,

and he only did good because of the money his mother gave him."

And the money he stole from me.

Foster shrugged that off and reached into his pocket, tugging out a flask, but stopped when Nadia shot him a warning look.

"Don't even start with that," she said, her tone firm.

Foster had been one of Arlen's drinking buddies and had often teased Nadia about being boring and unable to cut loose.

"Sure, I get it. The usual Nadia," he said with a sly smile as he pushed it back into his pocket, then let his hands rest on the arms of the chair. "I remember all the times you used to come and get Arlen from one of our guys' nights." Foster leaned back in the chair, holding her gaze, unfazed by her warning. "We had good times together, me and Arlen. I miss him. A lot. I'm sure you do, too. I remember seeing you guys together and thinking, that, right there, that's what I want. You always had so much fun. Like that time you rented bikes and went biking on Toronto Island? I came along with some girl I was dating. You guys would laugh and joke. That was such a fun trip. All those little houses and cabins. So cool."

"I forgot about that trip," she admitted, her thoughts slipping back to that sunny, beautiful day. Those idyllic few months. It was before she had lost the baby.

And on the heels of that memory came other sorrows.

"Then there was that time, later in the year, in the winter, when the gang went skating on the Rideau Canal? I thought it would be so lame, but you talked me into it, along with – who was I dating? Some chick named Delta or Creek?"

"River. River Bailey," Nadia corrected him. "Long black hair in dreads. Wore yoga pants."

Foster snapped his fingers. "Yeah. All. The. Time." He rolled his eyes. "But she liked the skating." He sat back in his chair, smiling at Nadia. "Such fun times."

Then his smile shifted, and grief shadowed his expression, followed by a deep sigh. "Man, I miss that guy. And I miss you. I miss our talks. How you always tried to set me on a better path. Make me a better person. I know Arlen said you did the same for him. I think he tried to be that. For you. Because he loved you. So much. He told me that. Before he died. That was so freaking hard. To be with him in the hospital. To watch him breathe his last. But what an honor to be there."

Foster's voice broke on those last words, and Nadia felt a tremor of sympathetic grief shake her as he pressed his lips together and looked down.

Listening to Arlen's friend, the one who had been with him those last moments, coming so close on the heels of her talk with Celeste, brought up the old emotions.

"I'm sorry you had to deal with that," was all she could say.

Foster pulled in a shaky breath, then another as he tried to compose himself. "I know he would have liked you there. He talked about you over and over and said how sorry he was and how he missed you, and the mistakes he made. How he wished things were different. How he wished you loved him. He would have done things differently if you did."

Nadia knew he didn't realize what he was doing. Simply relaying Arlen's last words to her for the first time.

But they washed over her, erasing the sediment that time had laid over the pain, laying bare her remorse.

And her guilt.

Foster swallowed. "It was tough. Heavy." He sniffed, giving her an apologetic look. "I never talked about it with you, but I wanted to. So you'd know he was thinking of you."

"I know. It just never seemed to work."

"Yeah. Well, it was hard. Just bad karma and a confluence of tides and streams intersecting and keeping us apart. Life will go its own way, and we can't always determine the path it will take. Sailors on a stormy sea."

Nadia didn't want to remind him she had tried to connect with him, but he ignored her calls, and she had given up. She had to move on.

Speaking of, she needed to figure out what Foster wanted to talk to her about before Charlotte woke up. Despite the moment they had just shared, she also needed to move things along because Foster, once he started, could ramble for hours, mixing metaphors and reaching for obscure analogies. She was afraid that if he brought up Arlen's accident and death again, she might lose the self-control she was clinging to by a thread.

"So, what huge important thing did you want to talk to me about? Does it have anything to do with that art show you were talking about having?" she asked, sitting back in her chair, but on the edge as if ready to leave.

Half of her attention was now on the house. Though she knew Charlotte would sleep for at least another half an hour, she didn't want the little girl waking up with no one there.

Foster tilted his head to look over at her and grew serious.

"There's the Nadia I remember. Businesslike. Get to the point."

Nadia didn't see the need to belabor that point, since he was right.

"Actually, we canceled the show. We sold the paintings privately, me and the guy he'd been working with. His agent, I think it was."

"Was this above board or under the table?"

Foster frowned at her. "No. All legit and above board. Got some good money. Sucks that this couldn't have happened before he died. Arlen had been struggling for a while. He was broke. Then he got a bunch of money and made all these paintings. Sold a few. Started talking about making a trip. Nepal, Bali, Vietnam. I told him to ask you if you wanted to come along. Add you to the itinerary. Maybe see if you guys could resurrect that old magic."

Nadia's fists clenched in reaction to Foster's comment, guessing that Arlen's sudden stroke of good fortune was because of the money he had taken from her.

Foster continued. "But then the accident." For a few heartbeats, Foster said nothing, then sniffed, blew out another shaky breath.

"Sorry about the feels. I've been thinking about Arlen a lot lately. And I had a plan that I thought you might be on board with." He looked around the yard, then back at the house. "When you texted me after I told you about the art show, telling me that this job is only temporary, well, I figured you'd be pumped about this."

"This...being?"

Foster licked his lips, nodding as he leaned even closer.

"One last trip. I have some of Arlen's ashes, mixed with some of his paintings - he asked me to burn the ones that didn't sell - and we could spread them in Vietnam. Bring some of the peace he always talked about to another country."

Nadia could only stare at him, trying to sort out what he was saying, wondering if the people of Vietnam would appreciate the gesture.

"It would be an epic trip. I know you'll love it," Foster continued, mistaking her silence for approval. "Lane would be coming as well, and you know how he and Arlen always were such buddies, too. He asked me to tell you how much he misses you."

"He was, in his own way, a good friend," was all Nadia could give him. Yes, she'd had fun with Arlen and their group of friends, but it was just that. Fun. Not the kind of relationships she wanted long-term. The kind of relationships she had with her family and her friends here in Aspen Valley.

"The gang misses you. This could be such a great party. Spread Arlen's ashes. Spread the peace and spread the love."

Nadia tried not to grin at the old-hippie vernacular. But as she looked into Foster's earnest expression, she felt a glimmer of sympathy for him.

"You know that trip sounds fascinating."

"Really? I hoped you'd be on board with this. Hoped you would come along. I know you and Arlen had this in the works."

"It sounds pretty spectacular," was all she could give Foster.

"Spectacular? Sure. But it will be majorly intense. Sad, of course, but intense."

"Trouble is, I can't afford it right now."

Foster waved off her objections. "No worries there. Lily said she'd gladly pay."

Of course, she did.

"Well, I'm sure it would be amazing, and while I would love to go…" she paused a moment, catching a movement out of the corner of her eye. But when she glanced toward the house, she saw nothing. She walked closer to the window of Charlotte's room and peeked in. The little girl still slept, so it wasn't her. Probably just a curtain moving.

She walked across the cool grass to Foster and gave him a reluctant smile as she sat down again. "Intense as it may be, I'm not coming. I have no reason to go. My relationship with Arlen is in the past, and I don't want to accept any help from Lily."

"But you weren't even at his funeral."

All-too-familiar guilt slipped up, hissing its accusations at her. She pressed her quivering lips together, looking away from Foster, her mind letting the Bible passage she had read last night return with its comfort.

"No, I wasn't. I was gone and couldn't make it back in time." Not that she had tried very hard to return to Toronto. She could still feel bad about it, but she also had to respect her mental space at the time.

"This would be a great way to make up for that." Foster lifted his hands as if to underline his comment.

She turned his comment over in her mind but then shook her head. "I'm in another space now. And I have other things going on in my life."

Foster frowned at her. "Like what?"

"I don't want to talk about it now."

"Don't tell me Drew finally got to you?"

Nadia frowned. "What do you mean?"

"You know. Arlen was always saying how Drew liked you and wanted to date you, but he knew there was no way it could happen. I mean, really? Drew? By the book, boring Drew?"

Though they had just shared a very emotional moment, or maybe because of it, Nadia's fists were clenched in reaction.

"Drew is anything but boring," she countered, steel edging her voice. "He's caring and kind. And he was the one sticking around to take care of his mother while Arlen lived off her money. Arlen didn't seem to have any problem taking other people's hard-earned cash."

She stopped there, still ashamed to talk about what Arlen had done to her. Foster probably had no idea.

Foster held up his hands in a gesture of defense. "Whoa, whoa. No need to get all frosty with me."

"Maybe not, but I don't want you talking about Drew like that. He's the best person I ever met, and I don't need to defend him to you. His actions speak for themselves." She pushed herself to her feet, glancing over at the house, then looking down at Foster.

"Your body language tells me you want me to leave."

He stood, shoving his hands in the pockets of his jacket, shuffling his feet. "I didn't mean to offend. You know. Just repeating what Arlen always said."

"I get it, but that part of my life is in the past. You have your own memories, and I don't want to tarnish them. Right now, I have a little girl I have to check on and a job to do."

Foster held her gaze a moment, then lifted one shoulder in a laconic shrug. "Of course. I get it." Then he looked around the property one more time and let his eyes drift over the house. "And honestly, I can't blame you for wanting this. It's a lot better than that dive me and Arlen lived in for so long. And truthfully, nicer than the place you and Arlen lived in together toward the end."

"You know, I would've been happier there if Arlen had been a better husband. The house is only a building, but it's the people who live inside it that make it home."

"True that." Foster grinned. "Oh. Almost forgot. Duh." He pulled his phone out. "I need your e-mail address."

"What for?"

"Don't need to sound all suspicious." He gave her a wry grin. "I have some money for you. If you're not coming on the trip, then I should give you your share of the funds from the sale of the paintings."

"I don't want any of the money. It should go to Lily if anyone."

Foster frowned at that, then shrugged. "Sure. But Arlen had a will, and it said that money had to be split between you and his mom. Said something about paying his debts."

Nadia wasn't sure what to think about that. If she even wanted anything from Arlen.

"It's okay. Give it to Lily."

"Can't. Lawyer told me I had to follow what the will said."

"Fine. Here's my address." She took his phone and plugged it in. When she got the money, she could give it to Lily.

"Excellent. Was good to see you." Then he gave her a quick hug, and together they walked through the French doors to the front of the house.

Nadia couldn't stop a quick glance through the side

windows at the front of the house, still sure she had seen someone in the house. But the only vehicles in front of the house were her car and the one Foster had rented.

"I wish you the best," Nadia said to Foster. "I'm glad you stopped by. Please say hi to the gang, tell them I think of them once in a while."

"Only once in a while?" Foster asked.

"I have other things to keep my mind occupied right now." Better things, if she were honest, but once again she didn't want to put down Foster and the people she used to hang around with.

Foster nodded, then with another smile, he opened the door and left.

Nadia watched him get into his car, then turned and almost stumbled over Drew's briefcase. She frowned, looking down at it, trying to remember if he had taken it with him this morning. Then she heard Charlotte talking to herself, and with a shrug, she walked past it and toward the bedroom.

Chapter 17

All the old clichés about eavesdroppers swirled inside Drew's head as he pulled up in front of his office.

But it wasn't eavesdropping. He had left work early to get home, to spend time with Nadia and Charlotte. He thought they could pack a picnic lunch and go to the lake. Sit on the benches and feed the ducks and geese. Maybe take Charlotte wading in the water.

Family stuff.

When he saw the double doors open, he assumed Nadia was reading on the patio, as she often did. But he paused when he heard a conversation between Nadia and a man. Nadia hadn't told him she was expecting company. Not that it mattered. He didn't need to be privy to all her comings and goings.

He had set his briefcase on the floor to get a drink of water and then left.

But when he looked out the window and saw her embracing this unfamiliar man, he couldn't stop a burst of jealousy.

Especially when he heard what they said.

"I wish I'd known," he heard Nadia say. "I should have been there."

He thought he heard a sound coming from Charlotte's room, so he walked over, and opened the door, but she was fast asleep, clutching her rabbit.

He took a moment to watch her, smiling at the sight of her so content, now sleeping in her own bed. His thoughts shifted to Nadia, sitting in the garden with this stranger.

Shaking off his apprehension, he returned to the kitchen to put the cup away.

"You know that trip sounds fascinating," he heard Nadia say.

"Really? I hoped you'd be on board with this. Hoped you would come along. I know you and Arlen had this in the works." The guy sounded excited. "Just think how beautiful it would be. Spreading Arlen's ashes, mixed with his paintings over the ocean."

"I'm sure it would be amazing."

He pulled away from the window, angry at the old insecurities slipping back as he walked back to the door.

He knew Nadia had talked about making another trip after she was done here.

A trip with old friends to spread Arlen's ashes?

He quietly opened the door and walked to his car, hoping she wouldn't hear him leave. Bad enough that he had overheard this conversation; he didn't want to get caught doing so in front of Arlen's old friend.

He drove back toward the office, but then changed his mind, veering toward the lake. Parking his car in the half-empty angle parking lot by the boardwalk, he got out, waited for a couple of moms pulling their kids in chariots to pass, then strode across the path, down a set of stairs, and stopped at a bench.

From here, he could look out over the lake, take in the rolling water, the hills protecting this long lake. As he followed the shoreline, he caught a glimpse of a couple of piers. One, he assumed based on what he knew, was at the Prins farm.

He thought of his time with Nadia, sitting on the edge, enjoying the afternoon warmth of the sun.

Talking…

His thoughts screeched to a halt as his heart raced.

Nadia, saying she had something important to tell him.

How it was too important to be interrupted.

And, of course, they hadn't had time because they had been interrupted.

Ice seemed to flow out of his chest to his hands.

Was this what she was talking about?

Going off on this trip to spread Arlen's ashes?

Was her ex-husband still that important to her?

And, even worse, would she come back?

He recalled every time she had spoken about her travels. The doubt that slipped into her voice when she talked about the job Liam was offering her. The question in her voice, as she wondered whether she was doing the right thing.

But that was then. So much has changed between the two of you.

He clung to the encouragement, but even as he did, he couldn't unhear the yearning in her voice just a few moments ago.

What did he have to offer her compared to a spectacular trip and freedom?

A solid, staid life. A steady job and security.

A child.

He felt guilty seeing Charlotte as an obstacle, a negative. He was growing to love her more and more each day, and sometimes the fear that Carrie might try to come back to claim her would haunt him.

Not that she had any chance. The DNA test had come back some time ago, and it showed, beyond a doubt, that Charlotte was his daughter.

So, she wasn't going anywhere.

But Nadia might.

Drew scrubbed his face with his hands, as if to erase his desperate thoughts. But they spun around his mind, twisting and turning in on themselves.

Lord, this matters so much, he prayed, trying to shut down the mental picture of seeing Nadia leave.

Yes, he cared for Nadia. Loved her, in fact.

Shouldn't he be able to let her go?

He had to get back to work. Focus on something concrete. On his way back to the office, Freya called him in a minor panic. One of their clients was having a meltdown and needed some face-to-face handholding as she went through the details of her divorce settlement. Freya couldn't do it, and Aria was still gone. Could Drew drive down to Lethbridge and walk their client through what she had agreed to and then agree to amend?

It was one of their more high-maintenance clients, and Drew didn't want to deal with Francine right now. Yet, as he drove back to the office, it might not be a bad time to leave for a couple of nights. Give himself some perspective. Some space.

And Charlotte?

Hopefully, Nadia wouldn't mind staying overnight again. She had done it before.

He parked, then walked up to the office.

Freya stood by Louisa's desk and practically jumped on him when he came into the entrance.

"My hero."

Glad someone saw him that way.

He pushed the self-pitying thought down.

"I'm here to help."

"You don't mind going down there?" she asked, her voice holding a desperate tone. "I know it's close to the party."

"That's all under control."

"Excellent. We're down to the wire, and Francine is

getting all edgy. Seriously. I don't know how much more we can do for her."

"Go down and walk her through the final settlement, I guess," Drew said, his tone dry.

"You are a man among men," Freya announced, then turned to Louisa. "He is, isn't he?"

"One of the good ones."

"How to condemn with faint praise," Drew returned.

One of the good ones. Such bland words to describe a man with a bland life.

Okay. Enough. Man up.

His father's words slithered into his subconscious, and, shaking off his self-doubt, he entered his office, closed the door, and pulled up the file. A few phone calls later, he had the trip arranged, a place to stay, and a time and place to meet Francine.

The only thing he had left to do was call Nadia.

He picked up the handset of his office phone, then set it down again. Shaking his head at his indecision, he picked it up again and hesitated again. Blowing a sigh of frustration at his own weakness, he rang up Louisa.

"What?" she asked in a teasing tone when she answered. "I'm so far away you can't come out and talk to me?"

"I pay you to answer the phone. May as well get my money's worth," he returned. "Can you call Nadia and ask if she would stay a couple of nights to take care of Charlotte? Tell her I need to head out on a business trip."

"You can't tell her yourself?"

"I'm busy."

"You can't be that busy. You're talking to me."

"While you're making calls, give Frank Dillon a call and ask him if he wants to come in right away. I've got time. If he can come in, please print off the contract we set up for him and bring it in. Triplicate please." He hung up before Louisa could give him any more grief. *We really need to hire another guy,* he thought. Getting bossed around by women was eroding his self-esteem.

A few moments later, Louisa opened the door, announcing Mr. Dillon's arrival and bringing the papers Drew asked for.

Drew asked her to show him in.

"Hello, Frank, glad you could make it earlier," Drew greeted him. "Do you want some coffee?"

"That'd be nice."

Drew walked over to the percolator. Louisa always made sure it had fresh coffee. Drew poured him a cup, then sat down.

"I thought we could take some time to go over the corporate structure you want to set up for your venture with Celeste Prins," Drew said. "Make sure what we've drawn up is in line with your vision."

"I'm sure it is, but I appreciate the pass-through."

Drew handed him one of the copies and took one himself. The other he set aside, and soon he and Frank were working through nuances of phrasing and legal structure, things he was eminently comfortable with. Language he understood.

Chapter 18

"So you'll be back in time for Lucas and Aria's party?" Nadia asked, watching as Drew set his suitcase on the floor by the entrance.

"I'll be home Friday afternoon."

"Okay."

Nadia wanted to say so much more, but since Drew came home, he had been distant, distracted.

When Louisa had called her to ask if she would stay overnight to take care of Charlotte, Nadia had been surprised and disappointed that Drew hadn't made the call himself. Disappointed that she wouldn't have the time she had hoped to be able to talk to Drew about Arlen. Explain a few more things. Admit a few more things.

Maybe it was just as well. After Foster's visit, she felt agitated and out of sorts. She was tired of the guilt that dogged her and concerned about Drew's reaction to what she had to say.

"I'm just a call away if you need me," Drew said, setting his briefcase beside his suitcase.

Nadia frowned, looking at the black satchel. "Did you leave that behind this morning?"

Drew started, as if surprised at her question. Then he shrugged. "I must have."

But he needed it for this visit, Nadia thought, still feeling a moment's confusion. His off-hand and abrupt answers pushed that aside.

"Well, I better get going," Drew said, shooting a quick glance at his watch.

He gave her a tight smile, slung his satchel over his shoulder, picked up his suitcase, and opened the door.

Nadia stood, watching, waiting.

He hesitated a moment, then turned back to her. "Like I said, if you need anything, just call."

She nodded, concern twisting her heart at his detached expression. The polite smile curving his lips, the way his eyes slid away when she looked at him.

Had she done something wrong? Said something wrong?

"Is everything okay?" she asked, unable to keep her concerns quiet.

"Just got a few things on my mind." Then his smile shifted, but not enough to reassure her. "You take care."

With those bland words hanging between them, he left, closing the door behind him.

Nadia opened the door, unwilling to let him leave like this. What could she have done?

But Drew was already in his car, and pulling out of the driveway, his wheels squealing on the pavement.

Nadia pressed her hand to her heart, trying to stifle the sudden panic.

Why wasn't he talking to her?

She didn't know what to do, what to think. It was as if he was completely shut off from her. She pulled a long slow breath, then went back into the house and called Celeste.

But her sister couldn't shed any light on what might have happened. And all she could advise her to do was to be patient.

"Sometimes it's not all about you," she teased. "You know Drew. He is conscientious and careful. He's probably just thinking about the case he has to go deal with. Whatever that might be."

"Yeah, he didn't tell me anything about it." Not that he would. Drew was the epitome of discretion.

Nadia made herself a cup of tea, turned on the television, and tried to lose herself in the nature documentary she had been watching. But it didn't hold her interest, so she flipped to another television show. A murder mystery.

Another no-go.

She tried to read her book, but when she read the same page for the fourth time, she gave up and put it down.

May as well go to bed.

Nadia got up and, without thinking, walked to her bedroom and opened the door.

She was already inside the room when she realized Drew had moved back in after she left. She caught the faint scent of soap and aftershave. A subtle, earthy scent that he always wore.

She felt like an intruder, but the way Drew had spoken to her before he left made her feel disconnected from him. She wished she could put it down to distraction, but she sensed that something else was bothering him.

Call him. Ask him. Tell him what you need to say.

But anything she wanted to talk to him about, she wanted to do face-to-face.

One of his shirts lay on the bed, and she picked it up, holding it to her nose, inhaling the scent. Her heart clenched, as a slow fear spiraled up from her stomach.

She swallowed it down and, still holding the shirt, she got up and walked down the hall to Charlotte's room.

The little girl was fast asleep, one hand clutching her bunny, the other lying beside her face, her fingers curled.

A wave of love shivered through Nadia. This little girl was

working her way into Nadia's heart and very being. She bent down and brushed a butterfly-light kiss over Charlotte's cheek. To her surprise, the little girl smiled but stayed asleep.

"Good night, sweetheart. May angels watch over you."

For a moment, Nadia allowed herself to dream. She imagined herself living full-time in this house as Drew's wife and Charlotte's mother. The dream had been fragile at first, an ethereal thought floating around the edges of her mind, but during the last few days, it had become more solid, more real.

But now? After Drew's dismissive behavior?

She shook her apprehension off, reminding herself of what Celeste had said.

It wasn't always about her. Drew was probably distracted and had things on his mind.

But when she went to bed that night, she kept Drew's shirt on the pillow beside her.

The next day was dark and dreary, overcast with rain threatening, perfectly mirroring her frame of mind.

Nadia had called Drew just to check in, but again he was reserved and distant. When she told him that Charlotte was okay and his mom was fine, he quickly said goodbye. Charlotte was fractious, which didn't help Nadia's dejection, either.

Thankfully, she had to help at the farm today with the final setup for Lucas and Arias' party.

Something to keep her occupied and not focused on her worries.

When she got to the farm, the men who had put up the tent yesterday were back, double-checking the tautness of the ropes, putting up a few panels, going over everything one more time. Charlotte had slept on the drive, so she was feeling better when they arrived.

Nadia helped Karissa set out the flowers that she had picked up that morning from the greenhouse. The lush pots of flowers were a happy splash of joy that lightened Nadia's mood.

Jacob had stayed home from school, and he helped entertain Charlotte while Nadia and Karissa spread the tablecloths on the tables, put the arrangements of flowers on each, and decorated the head table. With each addition, the enclosure became more welcoming and festive, and despite the concerns about Drew that dogged her all day, Nadia got pulled into the expectations for the party tomorrow night.

Burke, Shelby, Beth, and the twins showed up in the afternoon and helped set up a backdrop of gauze netting and sparkly mini-lights. The table for a guest book was set out, complete with a picture of Aria and Lucas sitting on the pier, the sun setting behind them.

"Where's Drew?" Burke asked while Nadia fussed with the bouquet by the portrait.

"He's in Lethbridge, taking care of some last-minute stuff with a client he's working with."

"I thought for sure he'd want to be here for the setup."

"I thought so too, but work is work," Nadia said, adopting a breezy tone. Hoping her brother didn't notice the uncertainty she felt.

"Are you okay?" he asked, frowning at her.

"I'm fine. Why?"

"I don't know. You seem kind of down."

"It's the weather."

Burke looked her over, shaking his head. "Nah, I think it's something else. Everything okay with you and Drew?"

"Yeah, sure. It's all fine."

He shot her a look of disbelief and looked like he was about to say something more when a sudden cry from Charlotte made her spin around.

The little girl was screaming, laying on the ground by an overturned chair.

Nadia rushed over to see what had happened.

"She was playing on a chair, and I told her not to," Jacob said, sounding defensive. "And she fell."

CAROLYNE AARSEN

"It's okay, buddy," Nadia assured him, giving him a gentle smile as she scooped Charlotte up. "If she doesn't listen, then that's not your fault. She just fell on the grass, so I'm sure she's okay."

She looked Charlotte over but couldn't see any injuries. However, the little girl's red cheeks clearly showed how tired she was. She needed a nap, but Nadia didn't feel like driving all the way back to town.

She picked her up and carried her out of the tent, where she found Karissa fussing with some ribbon bows she was trying to attach to a signboard.

"Can I lay her down in the house?" she asked.

"Of course," Karissa agreed. "You can put her in Jake's room. Your old room."

A few moments later, Charlotte was settled in Jacob's bed. Nadia smiled as she lay down beside Charlotte, looking around her and Celeste's old bedroom. Nadia was seventeen when Jacob was born, and she moved out not long after that. Celeste was already gone, so Jacob had taken over this room.

Memories crested over her as she curled up beside Charlotte. Times she and Celeste would stay awake, well after everyone was asleep. Times they would sneak out, she to see Arlen, Celeste to just find someone to hang out with that wasn't family.

Nadia pulled out her phone and checked to see if Drew had texted her, but there was nothing. Her fingers hovered over the screen as she tried to think of something to say, but all she could come up with was, *What's happened? Why are you so distant?*

Hardly words to encourage a conversation with someone when they were being distant.

She put the phone away. Drew was dealing with something. She just had to wait until he returned to talk to him.

But as she curled herself around Charlotte, she couldn't

stop a prickle of nerves at the idea that he might be regretting spending time with her.

———

DREW SWITCHED OFF THE RADIO, the noise annoying him.

His nerves felt raw and jangled, and he was tired of listening to songs of heartbreak and beer.

He didn't feel like listening to classical music either, with its moody cello solos and frantic violins.

You are in a mood.

He had been since he stumbled into the conversation between Nadia and her friend.

Arlen's friend.

He sighed, wishing it didn't matter so much. Wishing he felt more confident about his relationship with Nadia. He felt like a high school kid all over again, with Arlen still dominating his life. Determining his behavior.

You're a big boy now, he told himself with a shake of his head. *Forgive me, Lord, for being so weak.*

But was it weakness or simply the vulnerability of loving?

He knew that since Charlotte had come into his life, he felt even more open to the "what if's?" What if something happened to her? What if she was hurt?

What would he do to help her through whatever she was dealing with?

Floating behind all that, he struggled with the "what if's" of his relationship with Nadia.

Drew eased out a heavy sigh, one of many that he had emitted over the past few days. He had prayed, had tried to let go, had tried to find a way through all of this. He had the feeling that Nadia had something to say to him that could fundamentally change the nature of their relationship, and he didn't want to hear it if it had anything to do with Arlen. He was tired of living in his brother's shadow...of wondering how much of Nadia's heart was still engaged by his brother. Despite all the things she had told him, Arlen was still a presence he couldn't get rid of.

Talking to his client hadn't helped matters, either. Despite being the one to initiate the divorce, as he understood Nadia had, his client still pined after her ex. Still wished he could have changed. Been a better person.

She still loved him, despite what he put her through.

Did Nadia struggle with the same second thoughts? Was that why she sounded so excited to go on this trip, so she could re-live some of what she had shared with his brother?

Was she still pining after him?

And if so, how was Drew supposed to compete with a ghost?

When his phone rang, he glanced at his car's display, and when he saw Burke's name, he answered it, relieved he had a distraction.

"Hey, what's up?" he asked.

"You sound distracted. You okay?"

No, he wasn't.

"I'm fine. Everything okay over there? Is Nadia there with Charlotte?"

"Yeah, she is. Just wondering why you didn't come and help us today. I thought Aria roped you into helping her."

Relief flowed like a river over him. Charlotte was okay. Nadia as well.

"I had a meeting with a client."

"That's what Nadia said, though she seemed peeved when I asked."

"Peeved?"

"Well, kind of. She was slumming around like someone kicked her favorite dog. Except, of course, she doesn't have a dog. Everything okay with you two?"

"Why do you ask?"

"You sound as snappy as she did when I asked her. What's going on?"

Drew frowned at his question.

"What do you mean?"

"Okay, dude, don't pull that lawyer stuff with me. Answering questions with questions. Just tell me straight up. My sister is walking around grumpy and miserable when two days ago I thought she was inflated with helium, she was flying so high. I figured it had something to do with you and her finally getting together."

Finally.

He latched onto that word but caught himself from asking about it and pulling more lawyer stuff on Burke.

His brain was tired from spinning around, chasing his own questions. Sure, Burke was Nadia's brother, but he was also a friend. And right about now, he could use one of those.

"She got a visit yesterday from an old friend. A friend of hers and Arlen's." He paused a moment, trying to figure out how to articulate what he was thinking.

Think like a lawyer, he reminded himself. *Don't incriminate yourself. Know the answer to the question before you ask it.*

"I caught the tail end of their conversation," Drew continued. "The guy was asking Nadia to go along on a trip with him to spread Arlen's ashes in Vietnam. I know it was a trip she had talked about taking, and I know how much she loves to travel. I just thought…"

Again, he struggled to keep himself from sounding like a whiny teenager, agonizing over his crush.

"And you thought she might want to go along?"

"I didn't just think it. I heard her say it. She used words like 'amazing, sounds like fun,' and she sounded very enthusiastic about it and said that she would love to go."

"I thought she'll be working at the hospital? I'm pretty sure she doesn't have the cash to do this trip."

"Apparently, my very generous mother is more than

willing to sponsor the cash." It still set his teeth on edge that his mother was more than willing to dole out cash to solve problems.

"I can't see Nadia taking that," Burke said, adding a snort. "I know she hated how much help Lily gave Arlen all the time."

"You know about that?"

"Yeah. She let it slip once. I wasn't allowed to tell anybody, so I kept it to myself, but I figured you knew as well."

He hadn't, but Burke didn't need to know that.

"So, you think my sister wanted to go on this trip?"

"I heard her say it," he repeated.

"Did you ask her about it?"

"No. Because I didn't think I wanted to hear the answer. It's a classic lawyer gambit. Don't ask questions if you don't want to hear the answer."

"Well, maybe you better ditch the lawyer persona and find out what's going on with her. I know you always liked her, but you know what? She always liked you, too."

He thought back to what she had said about marrying Arlen, about how trapped she had felt.

"Do you believe that?" Drew asked Burke. "And what else do you know about my and Nadia's relationship?"

"I don't know why you two can't figure this out."

"Are you telling me you and Karissa always had smooth sailing?"

"Of course not. But I got some help along the way. And as a friend of yours and a brother of a woman who is sulking around the day before my other brother is coming back from his honeymoon, and as co-organizer of this shindig, I want happy humans tomorrow, so I'm helping you get through this muddle."

Drew tweaked out a smile at Burke's run-on sentence, spoken in his gruffest, take-no-prisoners voice.

"And what help are you going to offer?"

Burke heaved out another sigh at his question. "You and the questions. Okay. I think you and Nadia need to have a face-to-face conversation about what is happening. I think you need to tell her what you heard and the conclusion you drew –"

"No conclusion. I heard what she said."

"Did you hear the entire conversation?"

"I heard enough."

"Really? And you won't get some context for the situation?"

"Have you been studying law in your spare time?"

"I'm married, I'm farming, and I'm taking care of the twins and Jake and a bunch of cows and horses and a welding business. You think I have spare time?"

Drew chuckled at the comment. "I guess that was a kind of stupid thing to say."

"You've said worse, I guess." Then a beat of silence and Burke said, "Just a minute. Karissa's telling me something."

He heard a muffled conversation, then a laugh, and Burke was back on the line.

"Charlotte and Nadia are staying here for the night. So if you want to talk to her, you'll have to come to the farm."

His unease shifted up a notch, apprehension skating up his spine.

"The farm?"

"Yeah. You know, the place Nadia grew up? Where we're having the party tomorrow night?"

Drew shook his head at Burke's tone.

"See?" Burke commented. "You're not the only one who can do questions."

"Okay, I got the message. I'll stop at home before I come and be there as soon as possible."

"I promise you won't have an audience," Burke assured him.

Drew doubted that, but he knew he couldn't carry on the way he had for the last twenty-four hours.

"See you later."

He ended the call, chewing at his lower lip.

Then he took the car off cruise control and pushed on the accelerator.

Chapter 19

Nadia rinsed off the plate and set it in the dishwasher.

"You don't need to help with the dishes," Karissa said as she brought the rest of the plates to the sink.

"You made supper. It's the least I can do," Nadia shrugged as she picked up another plate.

"I can take care of this," Karissa said, nudging her aside with her hip. "Why don't you go outside? Enjoy the summer evening. The twins are entertaining Charlotte, and I don't mind cleaning up."

Nadia shot a frown at her sister-in-law.

"I don't either."

Karissa dropped her hands on her hips, tilting her head to one side, her mouth pursed as she shook her head. "Stop arguing with me. Please, just go outside."

Nadia glanced over at Burke, who had joined them.

"I'll take over," he told her, hooking an arm around hers and pulling her away from the sink. "I think you should have a look at the plants. Make sure they've gotten enough water."

"I watered them this afternoon before we came in."

"Well, check again," Burke insisted, giving her a tight smile.

"What's going on?" she asked, suddenly suspicious.

"Can't we give you a break without you getting all distrustful?"

Nadia sent her frown from Karissa to Burke, but both of their faces held a forced innocence, a fake geniality.

They weren't saying anything more, so she grabbed the towel off her back and tossed it on the counter.

"Fine. I'll go outside. Check the plants. Make sure everything is ready."

And without another glance back, she strode out of the house.

She paused on the doorstep, unable to stop one more look behind her, wondering what in the world was going on.

Then, with a shrug of resignation, she walked to the tent.

Before she made it to the end of the walk, she heard a vehicle approaching. Curious, she waited to see who it was. When Drew's car swung from around the trees hiding the road, a curious weightlessness surged through her.

And behind that, fear.

If she could have moved her unresponsive feet, she would have run away.

Which would have solved precisely nothing.

She stayed where she was, rooted, her heart hammering in her chest, her hands tingling and a million questions spinning through her mind.

Drew pulled up beside all the other vehicles parked in the yard and got out. He wore sunglasses, so she couldn't see his eyes.

"Hey there," he said, his voice a small sound in the yawning quiet.

All she could do was nod back, the insecurities of the past day and a half crowding in on her.

"Can we walk to the pier?" he asked, pulling his sunglasses off, an uncertain smile teasing his lips.

Lips that had kissed her, she reminded herself, holding the

memory as an anchor, as she wondered why he had come.

"Sure," was all she could manage, sensing the shift in the atmosphere. A waiting.

As they walked in silence to the pier, Nadia felt pieces fall into place. Burke and Karissa must have known he was coming and sent her outside so she could see him.

Their footsteps echoed on the wood, then they stopped at the end. Nadia sat down, once again letting her legs dangle over the edge, a sense of déjà vu washing over her.

"Here we are again," Drew said, his words telling her he felt the same.

Nadia was quiet, her mind flipping through the questions she wanted to ask, trying to find the right one to break this hush between them. A hush that thrummed with expectancy, tantalizing, like a loose thread needing to be pulled.

"First off, I'm sorry for how abrupt I was with you yesterday," Drew said. "I had…things on my mind."

"Your case?" she asked, keeping her gaze on the sun's shimmering on the lake, the small waves catching the pinpricks of light and sending them back.

Drew shook his head. "No, not my case." In her peripheral vision, she saw him turn to her. "You."

The single word snagged her attention, and she faced him squarely.

"Me? How?"

He held her gaze, his expression gentle. "You. It's always been you."

She swallowed at the intensity in his voice, and she knew she couldn't put off what she had to say anymore. Though, the way he'd been acting, the thought of her admission to him terrified her.

What if it made things worse?

"Can I ask you a question?" Drew asked, forestalling anything she wanted to say.

It took her a moment to adjust her mindset. "Sure you

can."

"I have to confess that I overheard you talking to Arlen's friend the other day in the backyard."

Nadia frowned, holding his eyes, the faint sorrow in his voice a surprise to her.

"Okay..." she let the word drag out, not sure what he wanted from her.

"I heard him tell you about the trip he had planned to Vietnam to spread Arlen's ashes. The trip that he said you and Arlen always wanted to take."

This still didn't give her much insight, but she simply nodded. "Yes. It sounds...interesting."

"Just interesting? Not amazing?"

She held his sympathetic gaze, still stumbling around in the dark.

"What are you trying to say?"

"Did you want to go on the trip? Because from what I heard, it sounded like you were enthusiastic about going."

Her mind reeled back over her conversation with Foster.

"I wouldn't say enthusiastic," she hedged, trying to remember what she said. "Interested in the concept, maybe."

"So you're not going?"

She frowned at him, still trying to align his comments with the conversation she'd had with Foster. And then, like gears clicking into place, she realized what assumption he had made. Relief rearranged her emotions, and she sank back, the weight of her worries altering and easing.

"I'm not going. I never intended to. Yes, I think it would be an amazing trip, but not because it would entail spreading Arlen's ashes. I think it would be amazing because it was a trip I had wanted to make for many years. By myself."

He held her gaze, his head shifting to one side as if rearranging her words in his mind.

"You don't want to spread Arlen's ashes?"

"Not at all. Arlen is my past." She wanted to add that

Drew was her future, but she felt things still hovered between them. Things she needed to address.

"Okay. I'm glad to hear that." He reached across the distance between them, taking her hand in his. "Really glad."

"So that's why you were so distant with me? Because you thought I wanted to do this one last thing for Arlen?" She curled her fingers around his, thankful for the warmth of his hand and the spark the simple touch created.

"I did. Like I said, I heard you say it would be amazing. I heard your enthusiasm. I think…much as the macho male in me doesn't want to admit it…I still felt uncertain about any lingering memories you had of him. He was such a large part of your life."

"Operative word being 'was.' You seem to forget that we were got a divorce, after two years of separation."

"I'm not. It's just that some of what my client told me seemed to underline the fact that you might not always forget him."

"I won't. He was a part of my life. Of course, I won't forget him, but I don't want to look back like your mother has been."

"She does love talking about Arlen with you."

Another faint hesitation in his words. "Like I told you, I went along with it for her sake and…and for another reason."

And here it was. The moment she'd been dreading to share with him. Despite what Celeste had told her, she still couldn't stop the faint worry crawling back into her soul, knowing that once she spoke these words to Drew, they weren't just her memories anymore. They were a part of Drew's life, as well. They would be enmeshed in how he saw her.

Thankfully, Drew sensed that this was a tough moment for her, and he simply held her hand, waiting. She looked down at their entwined hands, curling her fingers more tightly around his as if to anchor herself.

"The day Arlen died..." she almost choked on the words, far too aware of what she had to say next. "That day he came to talk to me. He had come to apologize for stealing money from me."

Drew's indrawn breath and hands tightening on hers gave her pause. Should she carry on? Lay everything bare?

But she had told Celeste part of it. Now she needed to tell Drew everything about his brother and their relationship.

"How much?" Drew asked.

"All of what I had saved." She pulled in a sigh and lifted her shoulders in a shrug. "That's why I was broke when I came here."

"Why didn't you tell me before?" Drew asked, then lifted his other hand, stroking her cheek. "Never mind. It doesn't matter."

"I didn't tell you because I wasn't sure of your relationship with Arlen, and I had to deal with my present, not my past." She looked over at him, losing herself in his gentle gaze. "But there's more."

"I'm listening."

Nadia's mind slipped back again, thankful that she'd talked about part of this with Celeste. A trial run, so to speak.

"He said he came to apologize, but he came empty-handed, so the apology seemed empty. I was so angry with him. So frustrated that I hadn't seen that part of him. So angry that he had betrayed me like that. I lost it." She bit her lip, struggling with the old emotions. "I yelled at him. I told him he was useless. That he was nothing but a parasite. A mommy's boy who couldn't measure up to you. I said you would always be a better man than him. That he would always be a struggling and useless artist. Everything I had held back during our marriage, all the grief at how he brushed off the loss of our child, the betrayal I felt despite all I had done...all I had felt with him...poured out of me. I found the worst things I could say, found his deepest insecurities, and I threw them back at him. And then he roared away from my apartment, got into an accident, and died with my horrible words ringing in his ears."

And there it was. The words she'd kept to herself delivered their silent menace, poisonous and potent.

Drew was about to say something, but she held up her hand. She needed to finish this. "If I hadn't been so angry with him, if I hadn't yelled at him, if I hadn't said those horrible things to him, if I hadn't been so cruel, he wouldn't have died. It was all my fault. And now you know what a horrible person I am."

His silence was like a knife, cutting away the precious life-lines she thought she had attached to him.

"I'm so sorry. I should have told you sooner," she said, trying to pull away from him. "But I didn't dare. I didn't want you to see who I really am. I understand if you're angry; if you don't want to be with me – "

"Don't," he said, his voice grim. "Don't say that."

He lifted her chin with the knuckle of his hand, forcing her to look at him.

But instead of condemnation, she saw pity and sorrow wreath his features.

"I want to be with you, and I know exactly who you are," he told her, his voice gentle. "You are a loving person who has been through a gauntlet of grief and betrayal. A sweet and kind woman who was betrayed in so many ways and on so many levels."

She could only stare at him, trying to understand what he was saying. Wonderment and puzzlement were vying for her attention.

"You're not angry?"

"Of course not. Why should I be?"

"I just showed you what a petty and horrible person I am. I told you I caused the death of a brother you love." She pulled in a shaky breath. "And that's why, whenever your mother wanted to talk about Arlen, I did. Not so much because I missed him, but because I felt guilty that I had caused the death of her much-beloved son. I couldn't bear it."

Drew frowned, his gaze shifting to one side as if thinking.

"What time of day did Arlen come to your apartment?"

His question seemed to come from nowhere, but she also knew that Drew was deliberate in his queries.

"Um, I had gotten off work, so about 7:00 in the evening."

Drew nodded, his frown deepening. "Was he drinking?"

Again, she sifted back through the memories. "I don't think so. He seemed lucid. I don't remember smelling alcohol on him, and I always could when he drank."

Another nod and still Drew didn't look at her.

"So he was sober, and he left your apartment after seven?"

"Yeah. It didn't take me long to cut him down."

Then Drew shifted closer to her, taking both her hands in his. "And you found out about his death? When?"

"The next morning. I went to bed after Arlen left. Even though I was wound up, I was exhausted and fell asleep right away." Nadia tried to catch his attention.

"You've been carrying this guilt all this time?"

"For the past year, yes." She frowned at him. "Why are you asking me these questions? Why aren't you more upset? Angry?" It wasn't what she expected would happen.

Drew stroked her hands, giving her a protective smile. "Because you need to know something, Nadia. Arlen crashed his bike at two o'clock after midnight, and he was drunk when it happened."

Nadia blinked a few times, trying to let Drew's words register.

"Are you telling me he didn't get into the accident right after he left me?"

"No. We got the information from the police when they

called, and we were told that you would be told as well. We always thought you knew."

"I didn't. I had...I had no idea." She took in a few quick breaths, dizziness spinning her around, making her lose her footing. "So, he died well after I saw him?"

"Yes. From what we were told, yes. At least seven hours after he left you."

"And he had been drinking."

"Which is what the police assumed contributed to his accident."

Nadia felt like her brain was twisting and pulling, trying to align what she had always believed and what she was now being told.

"You didn't get a call from Foster?" Drew asked.

"The next day. He was with Arlen when he died, but he never gave me the time of Arlen's death. Of course, I probably never gave him a chance. I was in shock and hung up right away. And, of course, I immediately assumed he got into the accident soon afterward."

"So it wasn't your fault," Drew said, his voice gentle. "And you've been carrying this for the past year?"

Nadia was quiet for a moment, her emotions were in turmoil. Slowly, reality set in, and she felt as if a burden she'd been carrying for the past thirteen months sloughed off her.

"Yes. I didn't know any different," she admitted, wonder tingeing her voice. "He was so angry when he left. I watched him out of the window of my apartment and saw him almost lose control of his bike. That's why...I guess...I figured he got into the accident after he left me."

"But he didn't," Drew assured her.

She held his gaze, still trying to sort all the information out. Drew gently caressed her shoulder, as if to ease away the years of guilt she'd been carrying.

"Is that what you wanted to tell me that one day when we were sitting here?" he continued.

She nodded.

"So now we both know," he said.

"Both know what?"

"I know that memories of Arlen don't haunt you the way I thought they did, and you know you don't need to let memories of Arlen haunt you."

Nadia closed her eyes, pressing her lips together, hating the weakness washing over her as she fought the urge to cry.

And then she couldn't, because Drew's lips were on hers, his arms drawing her against him. She slid into his embrace, her arms twining around him, holding him close, returning touch for touch, kiss for kiss, drawing strength from him. Support. Tenderness.

Eventually, they drew back, foreheads resting against each other, breaths mingling, faces a comfortable blur.

"I need to say something else," Drew added. "And it's pretty uncomplicated. I want to tell you I love you. Always have. I love you deeply and truly."

This time, tears found their way down her cheeks as she let the control she'd had over her feelings slip.

"Oh, Drew, I feel so unworthy – "

He stopped her protest with another kiss. "Please, none of us is worthy of love. It's a gift of grace."

She sniffed, backhanding her tears away. "I love you so much. I love you so much. I can't say it enough."

"You don't have to. I'm hoping we'll have the rest of our lives to do it."

Their gazes tangled, love and affection flowing between them, rich, eternal.

"Me too."

He grew quiet, serious. "And Charlotte?"

She sensed a faint vulnerability in his question.

"I love Charlotte. Deeply. I was worried that I would lose both of you."

His smile wound around her wounded heart, healing and

forgiving.

"You won't. I won't let you." Then he grew serious. "I wish we could promise each other that there won't be difficulties. I'm sure there will be, but I want to promise you I'll be at your side every step of the way."

She closed her eyes, as if to hold the moment, impressing it into her memory.

"I promise the same thing."

Then their attention was caught by the cry of a little girl.

They turned to see Charlotte running toward them, her arms wide, her curls bouncing around her flushed face, Roxie trying to keep up with her.

"Mommy! Daddy!" she cried out.

"Sorry. She got away from me," Roxie called out.

Drew jumped to his feet.

"Better catch her before she runs right off this pier and pulls a Nadia," he said.

Nadia couldn't stop her chuckle as she stood to join him.

Drew swung Charlotte up in his arms just as Nadia came alongside them.

Drew pulled Nadia close, and they twined their arms around each other and this little girl.

"Wuv you," Charlotte said, grinning from one to the other.

"Likewise," Nadia said, looking from Drew to Charlotte and then past her to where her family stood at a respectful distance. Watching.

"Guess we better go tell them what's happening," Nadia suggested with a rueful smile.

"I think they have a pretty good idea."

"Maybe we should keep that tent up."

"Nah. I think we'll have our own party our own way."

They shared a smile, then walked together toward her family.

Toward a loving future.

Epilogue

Music flowed over the gathering, a welcome cool breeze sifting off the lake into the open doors of the tent. Guests sat at their assigned seats, looking at the head table, where Aria stood beside Lucas, his arm draped over her shoulder.

She wore a simple white dress, elegant and understated, her hair swept up in a topknot that was effortlessly chic. The gardenia tucked in on one side served as a nod to their tropical wedding. Lucas, in deference to his wife, wore a white shirt, but he had tucked it into blue jeans.

"I want to thank you all for coming," Aria began, looking around the gathering, smiling, her happiness so palpable it flowed over everyone present. "This has been one of the happiest weeks of my life." She gave Lucas a coy look, and he pulled her closer.

"This family, this location, you people…" her voice trembled, clearly overcome.

"We want to thank everyone involved with this. Burke and Karissa for hosting, Roxie and RayAnn for helping where needed, and mostly Nadia and Drew for organizing all of this." He waved his hand over the tables covered with flowers, the mini-lights woven around the tent poles, and the buffet table groaning with food.

He squinted, looking through the crowd, then pointed at Drew and Nadia, who were sitting close to one of the tent walls, by an exit.

"Those two have done a lot of work to get this organized in a short period of time. Thanks, guys. I'm also glad to see you guys together. Another wedding in the family, perhaps?"

Drew held a sleeping Charlotte on his lap, and Nadia sat beside him, her arm curled through his. She had hoped they could avoid detection, knowing Lucas with his lack of filter would say precisely what he just said.

But Drew just grinned, and Nadia kept her features impassive.

Lucas laughed, then turned to the rest of the group, thanking everyone for coming.

"Now, no more speeches. I'm going to dance with my lovely wife, and then we're going to get this party started," he called out, waving toward the DJ.

The lights dimmed, and Lucas led Aria out onto the wooden dance floor that Burke, Drake, and Wade had put together late last night. Slow music was cued up, and to Nadia's surprise, instead of the usual swaying embrace in time to the music, Lucas led Aria in a graceful, flowing waltz.

"Obviously, he's been practicing," Celeste, sitting on the other side of Nadia, murmured.

"I'm impressed."

"Guess there's hope for you yet?" Celeste teased Wade, who just grinned, watching Lucas and Aria.

A few moments later, the music switched, and Roxie and RayAnn, with their friend Isabel Cosgrove, joined Lucas and Aria.

"Nadia, Celeste, Drake, Liam," RayAnn called out to their siblings.

Roxie joined in, carrying a large canvas bag. "Get over here. Jacob, Shelby, you get a pass. Don't want you to have your baby here on the dance floor. Cousin Sandra, you can take her place."

Nadia gave Drew an apologetic look, knowing, thanks to a raft of text messages this morning, what the girls had planned at the last minute.

Roxie dug into her bag and pulled out a stack of cowboy hats of various sizes and wear. Nadia grinned when she realized that her sister had collected all of Lucas' old hats.

"You know what to do?" she asked everyone as she gave them each a hat.

They all nodded, having been told quite clearly in the flow of text messages that had pinged onto their phone the last couple of hours.

RayAnn followed with a piece of paper with a poem written on it as Roxie got a microphone from the DJ.

"All right. We are paying homage to Lucas' cowboy days," Roxie announced. "And that requires everyone to put on these hats and read your part in the poem." She turned back to the DJ. "Some mood music, please?"

He complied, cueing up some old-time Willie Nelson's "You Were Always on My Mind," to play quietly in the background.

Roxie cleared her throat and pointed to Liam. "Oldest first. Read your part."

Liam rolled his eyes but then started in.

"Welcome home, our wayward son,
You've always gone your very own way,
Bustin' broncs and breaking bones
We're hoping now you're here to stay."

Sandra, standing in for Shelby, gave Lucas a grin, then read her verse.

"The wildest one of the family,
Skinning knees and training your horse,
Daring us to come along,

238

But we'd always get hurt, of course."

She gave him a wry look, then handed the microphone to Drake.

"Always running off at the mouth,
We could never get the best of you,
But now you're marrying Aria,
A lawyer who will take you down a notch or two."

Drake gave Aria a grin, "though quite frankly, we're all hoping it's more than a notch."

This netted a laugh as Drake gave the mic to Sandra.

"Now you'll be training and riding broncs.
But only here on the farm.
We hope you manage not to break any bones,
And keep yourself out of harm."

Sandra frowned over at Roxie, then with a shrug, handed the microphone to Nadia.

This was the first she'd seen of the poem, and she hoped she wouldn't mangle it too much. She cleared her throat, looked down at the part Roxie had sent her on her phone and began.

"Lucas, we're thankful you found the love of your life,
And that she's found you too.
We pray that you'll have many a blessed life,
Without a lot of hullabaloo…"

Nadia shot Roxie a frown. "Hullabaloo? Really?"

"I needed a rhyme for 'too' that sounded cowboyish," Roxie returned.

Nadia rolled her eyes and then passed the mic to Burke.

"Hullabaloo aside, we do hope and pray that your lives will be blessed, and that you will find happiness in each other. That we, as a family, may support you and give you guidance. We pray, most of all, that you will trust in our Lord to keep you in his perfect peace through any of the storms you might encounter in your life."

Lucas gave them a gentle smile, and Nadia wondered if it

was just the mini-lights that made his eyes shine, or something else.

"Thanks, all," he called out. "And now, back to the party."

Drew joined Nadia as she handed her cowboy hat back to Roxie, Charlotte still sleeping in his arms.

"What an interesting family," he said, pulling her close.

"Second thoughts?" she teased.

He shook his head, looking around as the music started up again and the twins pulled Jacob onto the dance floor. They were joined by Sandra and Dean Napier's twin girls, their friend Alison Cosgrove, Aubrey, Karissa, Beth, and a few others as they held hands, forming a circle around Aria and Lucas, spinning around the dance floor, bustin' some serious moves.

"I think I might have to take up dancing, though."

Burke caught Karissa in a fancy two-step, joined by Drake and Beth. Spinning, twirling, and laughing as other people joined in.

"Just the two-step and the waltz, and you'll be good," Nadia assured him.

"Good-sized family, though," he said, looking a little dazed.

"So I've been told." Nadia leaned into his embrace, tucking a strand of damp hair away from Charlotte's face. "And getting bigger all the time."

Then Nadia saw some people turn and rush off the dance floor, and she turned to see Shelby sitting on a chair, grimacing in pain.

"Liam, get over here," Dave, her husband, called, panic tingeing his voice. "Where are you?"

"Here," Liam called out, walking calmly over to where Shelby sat, Dave holding her hand, grimacing as she squeezed. Liam knelt down beside Shelby, hand resting on her stomach, then he nodded at Dave. "Start up your truck. I'll meet you at the hospital."

Dave blanched, and Nadia felt a moment's pity for the poor guy. Then he bolted out of the hall, leaving Shelby behind.

Shelby grimaced, as she rode out another contraction, then she laughed.

"You sure he knows what he's doing?" Grady Anderson called out, his arm around his fiancée Brooke.

"I sure hope so," Shelby said, then groaned again.

Liam helped Shelby up just as Dave rushed back into the hall.

"Sorry, sorry," he called out, hurrying to Shelby's side.

The DJ struck up a song Nadia recognized as "We Are the Champions," and despite the drama of the moment, she had to laugh.

"So, do we keep going?" Cole Waldren called out. "Or should we all follow to make sure poor Dave doesn't faint?"

"He's on his own," Burke replied, waving to the crowd. "We've got a wedding to celebrate."

Nadia glanced sidelong at Drew, chuckling at his confusion.

"Hey, she's a Prins. She'll manage. She's got Liam to help."

Aria and Lucas started dancing again, and soon the party was back in full swing.

"This is quite the family I'm becoming a part of," Drew said, pulling Nadia into his arms, nestling Charlotte between them.

"And it's just getting bigger," Nadia returned. "You said at one time that you envied me. I'm sure you'll have a chance to regret that statement. We're a pretty chaotic bunch."

"I don't think so." He swayed in time to the music as Charlotte shifted in his arms, now laying her head on Nadia's shoulder. "I think your family is imperfectly wonderful."

Nadia felt her heart expand as she danced with her fiancée, surrounded by her family.

Surrounded by love.

THANKS FOR READING and finishing A Tender Heart. I hope you enjoyed Nadia and Drew's story.

Want to read more Carolyne Aarsen books?

I'VE GOT YOU COVERED:

I've got a new series coming out the first one is called:

Love Like a Christmas Star

"ONE MAY BE **the loneliest number, but for Simon Steele, it's the safest.**"

PRE-ORDER YOUR COPY today by clicking on the book cover.

Other Series

There are many books and many stories in Aspen Valley. If you want to see them all, click on the links below.

⬜

HEARTS OF ASPEN VALLEY

#1 - A Yearning Heart

#2 - A Seeking Heart

#3 - A Loving Heart

#4 - A Tender Heart

⬜

COWBOYS OF ASPEN VALLEY

#1 Western Hearts

#2 Western Wishes

#3 Western Romance

#4 Western Kisses

#5 Western Vows

#6 Western Blessings

⬜

ASPEN VALLEY HOMECOMING

#1 The Way Back Home

#2 The Way Back to Faith

Untitled

Made in the USA
Monee, IL
17 June 2023

36077947R00146